BETWEEN YOU AND ME

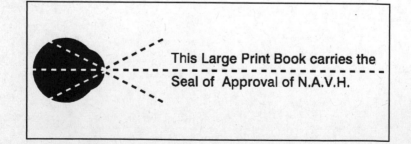

BETWEEN YOU AND ME

EMMA MCLAUGHLIN
AND NICOLA KRAUS

WHEELER PUBLISHING
A part of Gale, Cengage Learning

GALE
CENGAGE Learning·

Detroit • New York • San Francisco • New Haven, Conn • Waterville, Maine • London

GALE
CENGAGE Learning®

LIBRARY OF CONGRESS CATALOGING-IN-PUBLICATION DATA

McLaughlin, Emma.
  Between you and me / by Emma McLaughlin and Nicola Kraus.
    pages ; cm. — (Wheeler Publishing large print hardcover)
  ISBN-13: 978-1-4104-4894-1 (hardcover)
  ISBN-10: 1-4104-4894-0 (hardcover)
  1. Cousins—Fiction. 2. Dysfunctional families—Fiction. 3. Life change events—Fiction. 4. Domestic fiction. 5. Large type books. I. Kraus, Nicola. II. Title.
PS3613.C575B48 2012b
813'.6—dc23   2012009198

Published in 2012 by arrangement with Atria Books, a division of Simon & Schuster, Inc.

Printed in the United States of America
1 2 3 4 5 6 7 16 15 14 13 12

To
Sophie & Theo

A NOTE TO READERS

"When Michael Jackson was six he became a superstar and was perhaps the world's most beloved child. When I was six my mother died. I think he got the shorter end of the stick. I never had a mother, but he never had a childhood."

— Madonna

PART I

CHAPTER ONE

"Okay, we're coming up on our final hill."
Sandra, my instructor, puffs into her microphone, reaching out from her bike to dim
the spin room's lights even further. "I know
it's crazy cold out there, folks." She takes a
jagged breath as she prepares to urge us on.
"I know the sun's not even up yet. But you
are. And you're here. And you're going to
make it — harder. Let's make it harder!
Give me a full turn to the right in . . . five,
four, three, two, one . . . *go, go, go!*"

This was a huge mistake.

Reluctantly, I turn the dial and bear down
with my heels, trying to shift the work to
my hamstrings, trying to pull my focus up
— *up* from the sizzling pain in my legs. But
it goes to my eyebrows, behind which is a
dull throbbing with a pointy wake, like a
wine with full top notes and an acidic finish. Fucking bourbon. Fucking Jeff. I tug
my towel off the handlebars, swiping my

forehead to keep the sweat from stinging my eyes. How many drinks did I even have? One right when I got to the bar. One when he texted he was running late. One when he said he was getting on the subway. And one when I finally decided the subway ate him.

I grab my New York Sports Club water bottle, squeeze another Emergen-C-laced stream into my mouth, my eyes darting to my dark phone tauntingly resting above the resistance dial. Nothing — no word. I thought for sure he'd call around two with some implausible-slash-charming excuse. Or cut straight to leaning on my doorbell.

"And get ready to stand in . . . four, three, two — come on, *up, up, up!*"

I heave myself erect and immediately feel like cayenne pepper's been dropped into my airways. I gasp, trying to focus on exhaling to clear the carbon and acid.

"We're gonna hold it here. Just hold it here. Find the pace, find the rhythm, one, two, one, two." She exhorts us to speed up. Or maybe just me. Maybe everyone else feels like they're getting their hair shampooed. I glance around, taking in the expressions of agony and determination.

"I want you to give your all. Don't hold back!" she shouts at us. "I want you to push yourselves to exhaustion!" As if I'm going home to sleep after this. As if this isn't just the first in a long series of things I have to accomplish before I can crawl into bed tonight. The quarterly report, the teleconference with the Houston office, the projection spreadsheet, the second teleconference to recap the first. And dammit, finding five minutes to fix the smudge on my thumb because I ran to the bar instead of waiting for the polish to dry. Why didn't I just buy the bottle at the salon? Whatever. But not whatever if Jeff's coming tonight. He has to come tonight. Not coming to my party would be — he's coming. I'll just move my one o'clock back and grab a polish fix instead of lunch. My Power Bar backs into my throat. Probably expired. Fucking crazy Charlotte and her crazy fucking stale Power Bars. How my roommate can spend half her time carrying around that ratty Tiffany's catalogue with the corners turned down, plotting her next purchase, and the other half at the dollar store buying translucent toilet paper I will never — I'd much rather use Charmin and eschew shopping in Midtown.

"Okay, guys, almost done. We've just got a last hill and then a one-minute sprint to the finish."

You've got to be kidding me. Seriously, I

am going to puke expired Power Bar right over the handlebars. My legs are burning, my lungs are burning, my arms are going wobbly, I can't, I can't —

"Okay, guys, let's see some joy!" Sandra adjusts the dial on her iPod. Two beats in, I sense everyone perk up. Kelsey Wade detonates out of the speakers, and heads begin to bob, set mouths murmur lyrics, legs speed up. *"I'm unstoppable, unbreakable, unbendable. When you look at me my heart stops — unmendable."* I'm not thinking about my throbbing brow or my screaming shins or even Jeff Stone. Around me, women's wheels whir as their thought bubbles inflate with ex-boyfriends, ex-husbands, ex-bosses . . .

Sandra presses her microphone right to her lips. "What do you have left?" She lets the question hang, looking meaningfully at all of us before screaming, "Don't hold anything back!" Her voice reverberates over Kelsey's, echoing the essence of the song. "Give it all!" And we do. I turn the resistance dial farther, digging deep, letting the adrenaline carry me, the lyrics, the beat. "Can you do it? *Can you?*" We don't know, but we're trying, we're trying, we're trying —

"And . . . done," Sandra says on the last

beat. "Spin out your legs." She scrolls to Kelsey's latest ballad, and we all sit back, smile wearily at one another, and chug our water. My silenced phone lights up. Not Jeff. Los Angeles area code.

I guarantee no one else is listening to *this* song and getting a call from *this* number right now.

"Okay, bring your bike to a complete stop, and let's stretch."

No sooner does that call go to voicemail than my parents' number sets the phone vibrating again. I hit ignore.

We finish cooling down, and I unlock my shoes and dismount, grabbing my bottle and towel. I hit play on the second message. "Happy birthday to you," my mother sings. "Happy birthday, dear Logan . . ." I can picture her, an inveterate early riser, sitting with her finger poking through the coiled cord of the ancient beige phone she refuses to replace. "Twenty-seven," she adds after the song. "I cannot believe it. How did you get so old?" She laughs awkwardly. "I'm going to Babies R Us today — Helen's daughter's having her third," she can't help telling me, and I immediately feel bad. Bad that I'm not currently giving her grandchildren and bad that she can't be more accepting of the life I'm building, one that

17

will get me there eventually. God — and maybe Jeff — willing. "Anyway, call me when you get some free time." She always says this. As if my bon-bon window is coming up in a few hours. "Tonight I'm helping out at the church, but I'll be home by eight if you're home." On my birthday? " 'Bye!"

Sandra notices the contraband phone at my ear and raises an eyebrow before ripping open the Velcro on her shoes. "It's my birthday," I explain. "I was using the wishes to keep me going."

"Happy birthday! How old?"

"I'm heading into my night-cream years."

She smiles as we both make our way to the door. "You looked fierce today."

My eyes widen, and I laugh. "Oh, my God, Sandra, I was dy-ing. Dying. Like carry-me-out-on-a-stretcher dying."

"Well, Wade." She shrugs. "No one could tell."

Skipping lunch continues my totally-wrong-call streak marking this auspicious day. How could I have known that my boss would forget to book a room for the teleconference, leaving our team of financial analysts to meet in the one with the relentless heater, which brings out the carpet's Christmas-parties-of-yore aroma? That getting out of there for everyone would hinge on my having to prematurely share the spreadsheet I'm generating? Which, after tearing my bag down to the lining, I decided had evaporated, forcing everyone to sit there for an hour while I pulled the numbers out of my ass. An hour that I had fantasized would involve a bubble bath, Florence and the Machine, and leisurely applied four-step eyes, an hour in which I could conjure a little sparkle, a little romance.

Instead, I shove my down-clad hip against our front door in a panic, to find Charlotte lounging on the living-room floor of our lower Second Avenue high-rise apartment. She peruses Bluefly while she waits for her arm hair to lighten beneath smears of cream bleach.

"Anything good?" I ask by way of greeting as I drop my straining bag on the little glass-topped dining table and roll my cramping shoulder.

She readjusts her robe to cover a bit more of the boobs her ex gave her. "I can't decide if I want this Marc Jacobs hobo. I don't like the color, but it does have his name on it."

"What about his face?" I hastily unzip my coat and drop it over the Ikea dining chair that's starting to tilt aggressively.

"What do you mean?"

I kick off my boots. "A big jpeg of his face silk-screened on the side. Or his armpit from the cologne ad? What about that giant hairy armpit, and you could paint 'M.J.' over it with nail polish? Did you find the screwdriver? We should fix this chair."

"Why are you home? I was just about to come meet you."

"I can tell." I rush past her half-naked figure to my room, the only space in the apartment that was too small to subdivide. I always pictured myself in a brownstone walk-up in the village, a place with character, not a box whose charmlessness I've overcompensated for with a proliferation of Pier 1 pillows. "Jeff hasn't replied to the Evite yet, *but* he checked it at seven, *which* means he was confirming the location, so I need the red dress." I swipe it from the floor where I dropped it last night in a fit of horny inebriated frustration.

"I don't understand your relationship with that dress," she calls.

"Char, any chance you can vacuum while your bleach bleaches?"

"I'm busy."

I bite my tongue about it being her month to clean, because I don't have time for yet another Dust Bowl dustup. I unzip my pants and toss them into the spot the dress was

20

keeping warm. "That's because you're a blonde." Since the ex. "You'd look good in a suit made of Swiffers. This dress never fails."

"It failed last night."

"No," I correct her, carefully rolling up my stockings. "He never saw it. The rules set forth by the Intergalactic Alliance for Getting Laid say that his eyeballs *must* connect with the color waves." I shimmy into it and then peer into the smudged jewelry-box mirror over my dresser to twist up my brown hair. I wonder if it's age or fatigue that has hollowed my cheekbones, made me look more like my father than I did a year ago, the same wariness to the eyes, although his are the Wade blue. "Never. Fails." I refresh my blush and smudge some liner, a look my mother endearingly terms *night-walker.*

"I'm getting the bag." I hear her pound the laptop definitively. "Oh, Sarah and Lauren texted. They're both running late, but they promise they'll *try* to be there," she says in a way that suggests they really called to lower my expectations. I feel that little twist, that ouch. "Why are we meeting all the way in Midtown again?"

"Because it's elegant, it's Gershwin, it's New York! Charlotte, where are my silk

21

heels?" I call from the bottom of my closet.

"Out here. They'll get ruined in the salt."

"Then what are they doing out there?"

"I was going to borrow them."

I slip-slide on the scuffed parquet to spot them sitting by her room.

"Now what am I going to wear?" she asks petulantly.

"You have a wall of shoeboxes."

"But I don't like any of them."

"I need to drop you on a desert island with the stuff you already own, romantic-comedy-style, so you can go through an adventure with your stuff and come out remembering what you loved about your stuff in the first place." She just looks at me as if she'd mistakenly pressed the SAP button on the remote. "Okay, well, let's do the wall this weekend, for real." I shove my arms into my wool coat that is not in any way warm but won't make me look as if I'm trying to skip a few steps by wearing my mattress to the bar. "The paint and sandpaper are just sitting in the closet. I don't think I'll have to work Saturday. Let's do it." I transfer my keys, lip gloss, condoms, and wallet to my clutch. "We can get some wine, order in . . ."

"Okay." She shrugs, typing her credit-card number. But we both know we won't. Sarah brought me into the apartment share with Rachel, who worked and split the second bedroom with Lauren, who went to school with Charlotte, a chain of friendship strung out like paper dolls. But the links are gone — engaged, enrolled, enticed away. "Oh, answering machine." She points to the blinking light of our land line. This is the one other connection we share, Midwestern parents who hate us living in New York and want to know they can reach us, even in case of blackouts, terrorists, or the Rapture.

"My mom?" I ask.

"No. It was Kelsey's assistant." She taps her fingers together eagerly, as she does on the rare occasions when my life brushes contact with my famous cousin's.

"Delia," I say, referring to Kelsey's and my other cousin, with whom I share a birthday.

Charlotte nods as I realize I never listened to my first voice mail from this morning. "I think she said they're in L.A. I wasn't really listening," she lies. "Maybe *Kelsey* will call you one of these years." Charlotte rolls over, as if getting a tan from the eighties light fixture. "*Then* we could sell the answering machine. You *had* to get left behind." She resmears her flaking bleach.

"Kelsey e-mails me." It's my turn to lie.

When I was little, I always felt my mom and Delia's combining our parties stole my thunder, but now this annual exchange of good wishes is my one remaining link to Kelsey, however superficial. "I'll listen when I get back. How do I look?"

She appraises me from where she lounges. "Annoyingly hot for three minutes of effort."

"Perfect. See you there."

I keep my phone within earshot until the bar gets too packed, then make sure I can catch it lighting up with the eye I don't have set on the door. As my other friends and colleagues arrive to toast me — or put overpriced drinks on my tab — I nurse my sidecar through a straw to keep my gloss perfect until he gets here. I don't slouch, eat a Marcona almond, or excuse myself to pee. Halfway through my second drink, the headache I've been only a mouthful of water ahead of all day breaks.

"Happy birthday!" Lauren tugs Marshall through the suited crowd that new way that she has, hands twisted up by her shoulder, ring facing out. I pull her into a hug, smelling her Pantene and missing those nights pre-Marshall when we'd both get home from work well past midnight and commiserate over a carton of frozen yogurt in the dark galley kitchen.

"Can we buy you a drink?" she offers, and Marshall shoots her the look of a squirrel whose nut's just been hijacked.

"My usual, thanks." I'm tempted to ask for something aged to annoy him further, but I know he'll grab me a well drink anyway.

"These banker bars have you over a chair. I'm getting juice," he announces, and huffs away.

Lauren smiles after him and then reflexively at her ring, which is surprisingly large, but apparently his mother shamed him into it. "You are fabulous," Lauren says, trying to pull a few inches away to look me over. "The red dress. Who's coming?"

"Jeff."

"Logan!" she exclaims as I resume my door vigil. He has to come, he just *has* to. "I thought you were done with him."

"No, I told him to go fuck himself after the Labor Day weekend house-share debacle, but two weeks ago, he sent me flowers at work. Out of the blue. Peonies. In January. Like, thirty of them."

"Which you threw in the trash," she says sternly.

"Which I wore in my hair when I had sex

25

with him a few hours later. Okay, and that's a lot of opinion from —" Future Mrs. Squirrel. "You."

"He's never taken you to meet his parents." She invokes the smugly judgmental tone of the newly engaged, as if we're here to discuss my report card. "You've never even met his sister, and she lives in the city!" She brings up the source of breakup number three of I've-lost-count. "I just don't understand why you keep giving him more chances."

"Because I want to go to brunch with someone. And Jeff and I have this . . . thing. He's gotta grow up sometime." I flex my palms to the ceiling, knowing I'm leaving out that, despite the constant e-mails, texts, and IMs, we haven't seen each other since the peonies. The same ballad from the cooldown at the gym comes on and I imagine Kelsey has a sympathetic hand on my shoulder. *"Standing, reaching, calling, dreaming to get there — to get there."*

"One whiskey soda, a red wine." Marshall slides our drinks in front of us. "And my juice." He reaches into his jacket, extracts a flask with all the stealth of a UN missile inspector, and dumps some vodka into his OJ. I'm tempted to pull out a few bucks and tell the cheap mofo to treat himself, but my bridesmaid dress has already been altered.

"Don't we have a nice guy for Logan?" Lauren inquires, and he squints like she's asked him if they have a parasol.

"Really, I appreciate it." I don't. "But I'm great."

Marshall points to the speaker. "Kelsey's label's stock is down."

"Okay."

"This single didn't hold at the top for as long as her others."

"Well, she has more number ones than Mariah Carey, so I doubt they're going to fire her."

"Tell her to stick with dance tracks. That's money."

"Oh, I'm not in touch with Kelsey," I demur, hating when anyone outside my closest circle knows we're related but having to concede that as my friends pair off, that circle is widening beyond my control. "Oh, look, one of the couches is free."

"Because Kelsey's an asshole?" he follows up. Lauren jabs him with her elbow.

"Because our dads had a falling out, and our families stopped speaking." I reflexively run my finger over the small scar at the base of my hairline, as if reciting the answer from the Braille of raised skin. "But I wish her well." I repeat my stock deflection as I press

27

into the mingling throng.

I glance at my phone. Where *is* he? Two texts from Sarah, who's still waiting for the train and isn't sure she'll make it, but nothing from Jeff. Why did I pick Midtown? Why couldn't I just pick a local dive bar? Why do I need wood paneling and gold-embossed cocktail napkins? I look up at the murals of New York in the twenties. Because I spend my days in a cubicle and my nights in a box. I start to flag. I want to eat. I want to slouch. I excuse myself and make my way, past Charlotte lip-locked with a random, to the tiled hallway outside the bathrooms where I can kick off my heels and rest my forehead against the wall. I unpin my hair, hoping to relieve the tension across my scalp. The cold marble sends seismic ripples up my legs to my brain. Right.

I squeeze behind blazered backs to the couch where Lauren is falling asleep on Marshall's shoulder. "I'm sorry. I have to go," I say, tugging at the wool sleeve protruding from under Marshall's ass. "If Jeff shows up, tell him I left. With a guy. Who likes red." I kiss her cheek and then, with a wave to my drunk colleagues and gym buddies, turn to the door, which I proceed to shove toward like a hurricane correspondent. I press my weight against the glass, stumbling past the smokers — and into Jeff.

"Careful, now, you'll crush your cupcake." Smiling, he holds up the wax-paper bag from my favorite bakery with one hand and slides the other around my waist, his mouth connecting with my neck. Immediately, I'm laughing. I'm laughing in the glittering cold on a perfect New York night with my boyfriend.

He reluctantly breaks our hourlong kiss to drain the last of the Sicilian red into my glass at the quiet wine bar, and my gaze holds on his forearms, the dark hairs, the tan line from the diving watch he wore over the holiday. How is it possible to be hot for someone's forearm? "You still have some catching up to do. I had a lot at my work dinner. Those Germans are tough to keep up with."

"Notoriously so."

He squeezes my thigh under the table and signals for the check, the hidden hand roving to my hem, then moving the hem up while he kisses my neck and earlobe. His fingers pause when he discovers the tops of my stockings, the bare skin beyond, and he grins, his dark hair flopping over his brow. So worth feeling the clasps digging into me all goddamn evening. "Are you wearing panties?"

"Only one way to find out," I say, my lips grazing his cheekbone.

"Oh, no." He shakes his head as he passes his credit card to the bartender, his hand inching higher. "There are so many ways."

I laugh and reach for my crocheted scarf, loopping the cashmere loosely around my neck. He untucks my hair and lets it fall before kissing me again. "I love your hair," he says. "No one has long hair anymore." I nod, drenching myself in the compliment, despite seeing three women in this place alone with pristinely barrel-curled waist-length hair. Mine has not seen the loving attention of an appliance in quite some time.

Jeff signs the check. I hop down, making an effort to keep my movements fluid and contained, despite how everything in my vision swings slightly.

He helps me on with my coat, leading me out onto Madison, where the cold creates halos around embracing couples walking briskly as one. My coat opens so he can still see the dress as I extend my arm for a taxi. He presses his chest against mine and takes my face in his hands. "You look tired."

I nod, wanting to curl inside his concern. "This senior analyst promotion isn't at all as advertised. What happened to 'management' meaning assistants and an actual office with actual walls?"

He kisses my cheekbone. "Something more than a ten-percent increase to offset thirty more hours of labor?"

"When moving up felt *up,* not sideways, you know?"

"Mm," he agrees, nuzzling my neck.

A cab pulls over, and he pops the door. I slide in. And then it shuts after me. Stunned, I twist to the window, my earring catching in the open weave of my scarf. I lower the window while trying to untangle myself with wine-numb fingers. "You're not coming?" I can't stop myself from asking like Charlotte talking to the TV.

He smiles. "I have an early meeting, and it sounds like you need to rest up, birthday girl."

I *need* you to know if I wore panties or not, if we're taking an inventory of what I need. I sit back, and he steps back, and here I am — back.

It's not until I get in the door and am kicking off my salt-stained shoes that I realize I left the cupcake at the bar. Perfect. I go to the kitchen and pull out a box of stale Corn Pops. I drop onto the couch we got in the West Elm sale that was comfortable in the store and stare at the red and green lights Charlotte nailed up last month and will probably never take down. I munch on a handful of Pops and stare at the fresh bleach spot on the carpet that still needs vacuuming. I notice the blinking and reach over to hit play. "Logan, happy birthday!" Our crackly machine can't suppress Delia's exuberance. Delia wouldn't have let me throw the party uptown. A few years older, she was always the practical one, reminding Kelsey and me that it was time to let the frog go, time to do our homework. "Another year, can you believe it?" I can't. "Call me, want to catch up. Let me give you my new cell."

She rattles off her number, and the machine goes quiet. The Christmas lights blink. I look at my doorway, and I can't. I can't take this dress off and go to sleep, admit that this was it, the birthday he put me in a cab, that I'm about to get into bed alone and wake up hungover, that I'm here, *again,* having to make a decision to wait for the next flirty e-mail, the next text, the next late-night phone call, or I have to get over him all over again. "Fuck," I say quietly to the scorch mark on the ceiling. Then I realize Delia's never asked me to call her back before.

One a.m., ten L.A. time. Delia will be at her birthday dinner, and I can leave a message and go eat these Pops properly — in the bathtub. She answers on the first ring. "Happy birthday!"

"Delia, you, too!" I say, trying to moisten my mouthful. "Hope I'm not interrupting your party!"

"No! We did this tasting-menu thing early, an oma-something."

"Omakase?"

"Yes. Oh, my God, they gave me something that tasted like a perm and looked like a used condom." She lets out a whoop like I haven't heard since we last spoke, four or five birthdays ago. "I don't know that everything that gets dragged up from the sea should wind up on a plate, you know what I'm saying?"

"I couldn't agree more." I smile.

"How was your birthday?"

"Terrific." I hedge. "I had a party at this Holden Caulfield-y place, and now I'm just struggling to keep my eyes open." I cross to the bathroom to see if Charlotte still has any Ambien left to quell this building clench under my ribs.

"Well, I won't keep you. I just wanted to ask. Kelsey has a break next week before her tour starts, and she's dying to see you."

My reflection in the medicine cabinet shows my shock. "She is?"

"Totally! She misses you so much. How long has it been since we've all hung out?" She doesn't pause for me to answer. "Uncle Andy and Aunt Michelle would love to see you." Really? "Let me e-mail you a ticket. What do you say?"

I look at the lines, the ones my concealer has settled into around my tired eyes, the ones thick with blackened grout in the wall behind me, the ones on the spreadsheet I apparently left on top of the toilet this morning, and I take a deep breath.

"Sign me up."

CHAPTER TWO

Today I am learning that if you want to pretend things are one thing when they're another, it helps to have millions of dollars at your disposal. For example, it was easy — as I leaped over the three-foot gulch of black slush into the moneyed interior of the town car, as I sank into its leather seat and swiveled open the gratis Evian, as I lay back, letting the driver glide me through Manhattan's rush-hour-congested streets — to tell myself, despite coming off two nights of anticipatory insomnia, that I was on my way to a vacation and not a reunion.

And then, on the plane, even as pictures of my host flashed from the tabloids and smartphones of my fellow passengers, I merely reclined my seat to a true, all-the-way-down flat and said yes to the nuts (warmed), the champagne (chilled), and the fudge sundae (piping). In my extra-wide chair, the coach footprint of which crams half a family, I didn't even get my usual clammy hands when the pilot asked for the doors to be sealed. Two and a half movies of my own choosing while the engine was drowned out by courtesy Bose headphones was better than sex with Jeff Stone. If I had completed this journey only to find myself watching Charlotte shave in our living room, this would have been eight hours of the honeymoon I may never get to take. I now understand how bad movies get made and bad wars get started — it's hard to think through anything when you're *this* comfortable.

But now, as the sun-saturated wind whips my face through the opened limo window, not even the air — fresh, vast, with a hint of brine — not even the view of the Pacific on one side and lush hills sloping up to estates on my right, nothing can calm me. Because every estate might be her estate, and I am now only minutes away from facing the path not chosen. My cell rings, and I dig into the pocket of my handbag.

"Hello?"

"Logan?" my mom says cautiously, despite having called me.

"Yes, hi." I press the lever on the control panel, and the shaded window seals me back inside the dim AC.

36

"I was just calling because — are you okay?" she asks.

"I'm great — why?"

"You didn't call me back."

"Work's been crazy." I shamefully trot out the overworn excuse.

"I'm sure," she replies, not really knowing how to connect with me on this, having never worked outside the home herself. "Your father didn't get in until six-thirty last night."

"Wow. How is he?"

"Oh, good. Well, you know him," she says vaguely, and I don't ask for clarification. "Did you have a fun birthday? You had a date with your boyfriend, didn't you? When are we going to meet him?"

"Yes, it was, well, I ended up having to work, so — thank you for the gift card." I switch tracks, creating a pause.

"I'm glad you liked it. We took a guess."

"No, I'm sure I'll find something great at Penney's." Once I rent a car and drive to New Jersey to find one. The van ahead of us slows abruptly, and my chauffer hits his horn.

"Sounds like you're out and about? I don't understand how you like living somewhere so loud."

"Actually, I'm in . . ." But I can't say —

losing touch with Kelsey is probably the only thing I've ever done that my mother approves of. "Midday traffic. What about you two finally visiting? I could put together a fun time —" I hear a pot clank and change topics again before she can say no. "You're cooking?"

"I'm making a casserole. With a salad and beans."

"Sounds great," I say, picturing them cooked to the palest green and able to fall through a sieve.

"Well, I better get this finished," she says, sensing we're close to exhausting our few tacitly agreed-upon friction-free topics. "You know how he hates to get in the door before dinner's ready."

And all at once, I'm sad for her, but I don't know how to fix it, short of moving home to a place that never felt like one. "I love you, Mom."

"God bless."

I stare at the phone as it dims, giving in to the familiar sink. With a tiny jolt of adrenaline, I form a text to Jeff. "What am I resting up for?" My thumb hovers over the send button as the car slows at the first driveway with a gatehouse. The uniformed guard nods to my chauffeur, and the heavy gate swings open, letting us into what looks like

Central Park.

"Be there in two shakes," the driver says as we move up the winding path through oleander, whose pink blossoms make the foliage appear dotted with confetti, as though we missed the parade. We wind around the tennis courts, plural.

"Are you from Oklahoma?" I ask, identifying the familiar cadence of home that's intensifying my nerves.

"Sure am. Why?"

"You a friend of Andy's?" He looks like one of the guys our dads used to pop a beer with.

"Met on varsity, class of '82, then we both ended up at the insurance company. But I wasn't a paper pusher like him. I worked the lobby. Big demand for security after the bombing. Anyway, hurt my back, ended up on disability. Andy suggested I come out, drive the little lady around. But you really need to have logged time as a fighter pilot for this job." He chuckles. "Always dodging something." The car pulls up at the hilltop mansion, which, like my driver, also feels transplanted, with its red brick façade, cream trim, and columned wrap-around porch. It harks to the houses Kelsey's mom, Michelle, would drive us past on the way to ballet. Little girls in shell-pink leotards and tight buns, we twisted in our duct-tape-patched seats talking in if-onlys and some-days.

I realize my hands are shaking and go ahead and hit send.

The engine hasn't even cut before Delia comes rushing down the veranda's stairs, her rubber flip-flops smacking the brick. "Logan Wade, get out of that car!" she calls. Peering at the house door I climb out and into her embrace, her clipboard momentarily sticking into my spine. "Let me look at you." She steps back, and I take her in, too. Her resemblance to Michelle has strengthened with age. "I was trying to add it up this morning — have I really not seen you since you left for college?"

"No, there was that Christmas we ran into each other at Marshall's."

"You were with Grandma Ruth, so that had to be over ten years ago. You're skinny," she pronounces.

"It's New York." I demur, my eyes scanning the porch only to find it vacant. "Hard living."

"Well, a few days of Uncle Andy's cooking'll give the boys something to look at. You met our driver, Peter."

"Yes." I smile as he sets my suitcase at my feet. "Thank you so much."

"You have a great time." He winks as he returns to the wheel.

"How're your folks?" She takes the handle for me.

"Good, thanks. Dad's still working. Mom's got her church group. Still waiting for my call to say I'm having triplets and moving next door. How are yours?"

"Oh, they're a hoot. Healthy and all that. They miss Oklahoma, but they just couldn't take the winters anymore. Thankfully, my brother moved down there to keep an eye on 'em. I've never known how you and Kelsey do it — being only children is such a responsibility. Come on in." I follow her up the steps, squinting as the sun catches the crystal dragon on her hoodie. Her hair is still that same reddish color, the same long shag she could have gotten at Super Cuts.

We step right into a double-height living room with three sitting areas, the ocean rippling in every window. I spin in search of my host. "This is the main room, or greeeeeeeat room, which Michelle says like the queen of England and I say like Tony the Tiger."

"Wow, Delia, this place is amazing!" *Where is she?*

"This was one of the first houses built here in Malibu, and as soon as Michelle and

Kel saw it, they were in love. Everything else is glass and cement boxes. I know it's big, but I still think it's cozy, don't you?" The room immediately conjures the collages Michelle used to make with us out of back issues of *Good Housekeeping.* Every detail is inviting, from the salmon chenille pillows to the mohair throws on the overstuffed couches. I look to the grand staircase, my ears primed to make out footsteps. "Off there is the kitchen." She points, "Chef Angela should be in there, let her know what you like. The other day, I was having such a crank, PMSing out my ears. I asked her to make me a burger that tastes like Sonic's and she did, just unbelievable. In that wing, you'll find the breakfast room, den, and staff quarters. Seriously, make yourself at home — well, not in the staff area." She chuckles. "They might have a say about that." She points to the other side. "And in that wing is Michelle's sitting room, the game room, screening room, sun room, and the offices. The gym, dance studio, recording studio, and salon are in the basement."

"And where's Kelsey?" I ask, unable to wait a minute longer as I follow her up the stairs.

"Oh, Logan, Kelsey's break has gotten

screwed with its pants on. I'm so sorry." Her shoulders sink.

"Oh?"

"She was supposed to shoot a *Vanity Fair* cover next month, but the photographer had a conflict, so they had to bang it out this week. I just snuck away to get you settled." She pushes open a door at the end of the hallway. "This is yours."

"Wow." My jaw breaks a spring at the canopy bed, the fireplace, and the balcony overlooking the trees. "It takes a week?" I ask.

"Uch." She rolls her eyes. "I can only say this: David LaChapelle and a camel with an attitude problem. They're shooting in the Mojave. Kelsey wanted to do an Arabian thing."

"I understand. Nothing I do at work takes as long as projected. And none of it involves dromedary mood swings."

Looking past me, she laughs a moment later. Her BlackBerry buzzes, and she shakes her head in what seems an attempt to wake up. "So! I have to get back out there. Michelle's in sequin overdrive, Andy's obsessing about overages, even though they don't come out of our pocket."

"How are they?" I ask. "You know, other-wise."

"Otherwise?" She mugs. "Just kidding. Michelle is great — you know her, she thrives on the nuttiness."

"And Andy?" I inquire about my estranged uncle, trying to sound casual, polite.

"Andy's Andy." She smiles.

"I heard he's . . ."

"Sober?" she finishes for me. "Oh, for a while now." She tucks her tongue in the corner of her mouth. "Since Kelsey's first tour." She considers. "I think, you know, Kel and Michelle finally had some leverage. And he had something he wanted to be around for. You have my cell?"

"Yes. So, sorry, but I'm not going to see Kelsey?" I ask as I simultaneously think, could I really have come all this way not to see her? And could I just get to enjoy all this and not have to see her?

"Oh, no, I'm doing everything a girl can so you sit tight." I place my tote on the duvet, and it tips, the tabloid I picked up on the plane sliding out. Delia's smile falters as we stare at Kelsey's first love, Eric Lamont, and his new girlfriend. "I'm so embarrassed — I meant to throw that out at the airport."

"Oh, my gosh, don't be — usually, we don't give a rat's ass, but this — now that Eric's getting serious with this woman." She swipes it up and sticks it in her clipboard. I nod as if I didn't cross the Rockies perusing the pictures rehashing Eric and Kelsey's relationship, from its genesis on *Kids, Inc.*, through the very public breakup last year. "She's going to need — it'll be really good for her to see you." She hugs her board to her chest. "I know it will."

"I'm glad to hear you think so. It's just, you know, I haven't seen her since —"

"Oh, please, you two were attached at the hip!" If Delia knows that the one time we'd spoken, Kelsey offered me the job she ended up taking, she doesn't let on. "Used to drive me crazy when I babysat you guys. No, she's super excited. Everyone is. We just have to get the girl home!"

"And you're sure it's okay for me to be here in the meantime? I could stay at a hotel."

"Don't be silly. I feel terrible. Dragging you across the country and making you wait around. Who *should* feel terrible is that camel." She smiles. "I'll keep you posted."

She gives me another hug and closes the door, shutting me inside the quiet. I pull out my phone to wait for Jeff's text and place it on the night table, where its black face sits like charred toast. Out the bathroom window I see Delia hop into a town car.

Agitated with anticipation that has yet to be relieved, I make my way back along the hallway in search of clues to whom I may or may not get to reconnect with, based on the whim of a camel. I stop to study the photos on the wall. Pictures of our grandmother, her yellow vinyl-sided house, and various extended family members, but my parents are markedly missing — as am I.

I move from frame to frame like a sniffing hound, finally finding a copious display atop the white grand piano. After years of feasting on the bread crumbs of magazine layouts, billboard ads, and tabloid pictures of her with her head tucked, hat and sunglasses obscuring her unreadable face, it's dizzying to see unretouched photos of Kelsey, taken with personal cameras. She finally resembles the blurring image I carry of her in my memory, laughing open-mouthed, the corners of her eyes watering.

Then I'm surprised by the glint of dormant jealousy at images of Kelsey, Delia, and Michelle, draped under towels on a boat, swinging skis from a lift chair, making faces in a dressing-room mirror. Michelle looks beautiful, her blond hair now streaked gray as she embraces Kelsey in that famously daring dress she wore when she won all those Grammys. There are lines around

Michelle's light blue eyes, but they are as sweet as I remember. I run my thumb along the gemstones bordering the picture. No question, I owe the ambition of my Pier 1 pillows to Michelle Wade.

At the piano's curved end I lift a picture of Andy and Michelle huddled in rain ponchos and recognize the observation deck of the Empire State Building. I wonder if Kelsey is on the other side of the lens, wondering if she thought of me as she looked down on my city. I tilt it to the window, studying Andy's smile.

"Can I get you anything?"

I jump, the frame clanking back onto the piano. "Oh, no, thank you. I'm great."

The uniformed woman nods deferentially and departs. But I'm not great. I'm dry-mouthed and a little sweaty and . . . needing more. Up the hall in the opposite direction I pass an open door that reveals a king-size bed with a needlepoint pillow resting in front of two perfectly plumped rows of peach damask. "Bless This Mess." And I remember Michelle needlepointing in the wings while Kelsey warmed up for one of her hundreds of contests. Fringed in lace that has since yellowed, it is the centerpiece of the pristine space.

I continue to the end, placing the master

suite as just on the other side of Andy and Michelle's. I'm reaching for the crystal knob when I think I hear something. I pivot — and spot the red light of a camera where the dentil molding meets the ceiling. I smile to communicate that I was just kidding and concentrate on strolling back to my room. *Oh, me? Just having a good time checking out the doorknobs.* "Lovely!" I say out loud like an idiot.

I close the door behind me and, finding no cameras, face-plant on the bed.

Between the aching temptation to snoop and the images staring from every surface, from which my family and myself are so pointedly absent, I force myself to stay by the pool, even when the temperature every morning hovers in the sixties. I try to read, but one ear is always on the driveway. Jeff, annoyingly, offers no response and, hence, no distraction. Angela, however, distracts me with anything I can dream up, from cheese fries to soufflé, explaining that she gets zero gratification from making oil-free garbanzo-bean salads for the girls in the office.

From the food to the view to the horse-hair-filled chaise cushions, this is an unbelievably great life. There is no question.

The late-afternoon sun has finally lifted the air into the eighties, and as it slips off my toes, I sense it's time for a last dip. I take a peek at my phone, but I haven't heard from Delia since this morning, and her cryptic text — *Blech!* — did not herald a reunion. I can hear the girls calling good night to Angela. When I asked about their roles, three sets of hands started hair twirling as if they were doing a group charade of cotton candy while announcing: "branding," "developing," and "scheduling."

The quiet deepens. I look again at the cornices of the pool bungalow and then the house. No cameras trained directly on the pool. As it seems official — this is my Kelsey Wade–sponsored retreat — I drop into the bathtub-like warmth, thinking, screw it — then untie my bikini and leave it in a small heap on the stone. It feels delicious, conjuring that summer Andy made his quota and Michelle got a membership to the town pool. We swam every day, even when it rained. I smile as I picture Kelsey in her stretched-out Care Bears suit, stomping in the puddles where the cement was cracking, belting "Singing in the Rain." I dive down, taking a lap underwater, relishing the undulating silence.

"Fuck! Security!" I hear the voice before I

can surface. *"Security!"* Bulleting my head into the air, I swipe at my seaweed-like clumps of hair as a speeding golf cart jostles two guards across the lawn. They swerve to a halt at the hedge and leap out, guns drawn. I swivel to see the threat and register that it's me — me! "Oh, God, Andy!" This *cannot* be happening. "It's Logan!" I frantically yell.

A man even bigger than Andy comes racing from the house. "Get back!"

"It's me!" I swim for the wall and press myself into it. "Logan." I splutter, water in my eyes, nose, and throat. "Your niece —"

"Don't fucking move," the huge man instructs as he hauls me out onto the stone. I try to cover myself with my hands, freezing at the sight of two cocked guns.

"I'm — I'm Kelsey's cousin —"

"What the . . . ?" Michelle is suddenly there, swiping my towel off the chaise and pushing past the guards to hold it in front of me. "*Logan?* What on earth?"

"Delia called me, brought me," I rush, as she races across the veranda. "I thought you —"

"Don't shoot!" Delia cries, flapping her arms. "It's a surprise for Kelsey!" *Oh, no. No, no, no.*

"Oh!" Michelle says. "Oh! Well . . .

50

sweetie, well, cover yourself." My eyes on the metal barrel, I slowly wrap the terrycloth around me.

"She's here to keep Kelsey company." Delia puffs, dropping her hands to her knees to catch her breath.

"Wow." Michelle nods from Delia to me. "Well, we just didn't recognize you all grown." I smile feebly while the security guys return their guns to their holsters. I wonder if I have peed myself or the feeling is coming back into my numb legs and that's water. "Andy, isn't this funny?" Michelle prompts him.

"Well . . ." He lifts his hat and lowers it. "Well, now," he says with more conviction. "You gave us a shock, didn't she?"

Michelle smiles and shakes her head emphatically. "Did she!"

He lets out a short laugh. "I was all, 'Logan Wade is in our swimming pool as naked as the day she was born!'" Delia laughs. Michelle laughs. My teeth are chattering. "Well, give your uncle a hug." I have to tell myself to step toward him and then realize I have the excuse of the towel. "Or — uh, later, when you find your suit." He blushes, and while I have many memories of him flushed, I've never seen him blush. "Logan Wade, right here in my pool, crazy."

51

"I'm so sorry."

"Kelsey'll be so excited!" Michelle brings her hands down between her bobbed knees before throwing her palms to the sky. The hulking bodyguard clears his throat. "Thanks, GM." She pats his arm. "False alarm."

"Is Kelsey here?" I ask as the golf cart is driven away.

"Still asleep in the van," Delia says, picking up the Bluetooth that my near death caused to fall from her ear. I didn't realize how much makeup she had on to greet me. The thick lashes are gone, as is the color in her cheeks, replaced by a bruise of exhaustion beneath each eye. "They kept Kel on that camel till almost four o'clock this morning."

Andy bends to sift a leaf from the pool.

"So she doesn't know I'm here?" I try to confirm with Delia, trying not to let my alarm read. Kelsey likes surprises as much as Andy does — at least, she used to.

"Delia knows how to keep things fun. I'm just thinking." Michelle tilts her head. "Let's throw a sheet over you when Kelsey comes in!" Oh, God.

"Awesome." Delia looks to Andy, who gives a sign-off nod. "I'll tell Angela about dinner."

Andy squints at where the water is sucked in under the stone. "That filter's not working like it should."

"So, wow, when did you get in?" Michelle asks.

"The day before yesterday. Delia sent me a ticket. I'm sorry. I misunderstood. I thought —"

"And you're leaving when?" Andy asks.

"The day after tomorrow, if that works for you. That's all my vacation days, so . . ."

"Uh-huh." His lower lip puffs out.

"We're just going to make the best of your time left, aren't we, hon?" Michelle turns to him.

"Sure thing," he confirms as he trails GM back to the house.

"Is it okay that I'm here?" I ask her, officially wishing that I wasn't.

"Oh, don't mind him, he just gets a little lost at dusk," she says matter-of-factly, and I wonder if dusk is code for happy hour. A breeze starts to circle my bare feet. "Wow, Logan . . ." Her hand goes to her chin as she takes me in. "You and Kel could be sisters. You really grew up beautiful."

"Thank you. You, too."

"Oh, pshaw, it's a gallon of Juvéderm keepin' age at bay. Forty-eight next September, God help me." She chuckles. "Now, how long has it been?"

"Since you and Kelsey left for L.A.," I answer.

"Oh, for *Kids, Incorporated,* right," she says, her eyes losing focus as she remembers. "So Kelsey was almost eleven, and you were just —"

"Thirteen." I wonder if she's going to bring up the accident.

"We've all come a long way!" She laughs. I guess not.

"Yes, this house," I say with real awe.

"It's something, huh?" She grins.

"You're the reason I got myself to New York," I say, eager to share the thought that passes through my mind at least once a week. "I always loved your — how you wanted to make things fabulous."

"Aw," she says, putting her hand over her heart as her eyes tear up.

I feel my own dampening. "You know, I think I'm just going to go upstairs and put on something dry."

"Of course, so stupid of me. You must be freezing. I never stick a toe in that pool between October and April. Hank keeps the water warm, but the air gets a real bite. Go take a nice, toasty bath, and we'll catch up at dinner." She takes me by the shoulders and places a firm kiss on my cheek as the early-evening sky shifts to indigo. "It's so great to have you. Kelsey will love it."

I scurry up to the veranda and enter the transformed great room. Around Andy, flat-screen TVs have sprung from every surface, even the gilt mirror above the fireplace has moved aside to reveal one, each tuned to a twenty-four-hour news network. And every recessed light, every lamp, every crystal sconce, is lit. Huddling in my towel, I hurry to the stairs just as Kelsey shuffles in through the open front door, still looking half-asleep and wrapped in a pink blanket. She startles. We stare at each other for the longest moment before her blue eyes widen. *"Logan?"* she asks, sounding almost frightened as Michelle's sandals take the steps behind me and Delia's flip-flops hit the hallway.

"Hi," I say, infusing the solitary syllable with as much apology as I can.

"Surprise!" Delia proclaims. "Logan came to see you!"

"Isn't this great?" Michelle asks, louder than is required to be heard over the pundits' buzz.

Her face still slack, eyes apprehensive, she stares at me as if questioning the veracity of my appearance.

"Kel?" I say tentatively. Andy turns from

the couch.

"Kelsey?" Delia prompts. "Logan missed you." Kelsey looks from Delia to an inscrutable Andy.

"We're burritos!" she suddenly exclaims. I look down at myself in my towel, realizing that we mirror each other with our gripping fingers tucked under our chins. She throws her blanket off like a cape, revealing a T-shirt and cut-offs, and jogs over to engulf me in a hug.

I feel a warm shock at her reception but am unable to return it without pulling her against my naked body. "Sorry, I'm — I was skinny-dipping, actually. I didn't know when you were going to — whatever. Hi!" I lean into her and tilt my elbows forward as a gesture of embrace. She stiffens almost imperceptibly. "It's so good to see you!" I say through her sprayed-crunchy chestnut waves.

"Yeah!" She matches my enthusiasm before pulling back and turning to Delia, her face reslackening. "I'm gonna try to keep napping. Come get me when it's time for dinner." She ascends the stairs, and I'm left to watch the soles of her bare feet as she disappears.

Two hours later, I'm dressed, blown out,

56

and fully made up as I perch awkwardly on the patio wall while Andy intently mans the steaks. The minute I see Kelsey, I'm going in for a do-over hug. I'm just going to step up, arms wide, face beaming —

"Logan."

He stands over me in his canvas apron, the shadows obscuring his face. "Hi!" I rise, pulling my wrap sweater tight with crossing arms. "How's the grilling?"

"Oh, fine. Look, I, uh, just before everyone comes down . . ." He tilts back as if wishing only his loafers needed to be present. "I wanted to tell you that I'm sorry for the suffering that my addiction may have caused you. Okay?"

Despite the rote delivery, my stomach twists in on itself. "Yes, I . . . I didn't even —" I start to lie, but he cuts me off.

"Great." He drops his arms heavily around me, and I tell myself to hug back. "You seem just fine." He pats me and retreats to his smoking meat.

"Honey, that smells fantastic!" Michelle emerges from the glass doors in a pair of capris, and I shakily follow her to the wrought-iron table. "Angela has perfected Coleman's potato salad, Logan, honey. You'll think you're back home at the diner. We even have Frito chili pie. You're in for a real treat."

"I've been worshiping at the altar of Angela since I arrived." Desperately wishing that wine was being offered, I drag out one of the heavy dining chairs.

"Hit the fairy lights, would you, babe?" Michelle calls to Andy. Carrying a platter, he bumps a column with his elbow, illuminating the pergola. "Now it's a party," Michelle pronounces as she tugs her napkin from its crystal ring.

"You all set out there?" Delia steps onto the patio, her clipboard in hand as she sips a soda.

"Is that girl still sleeping?" Andy shakes his head.

I see past him to the glowing great room, where Kelsey is dropping weightily down each step of the staircase, her gaze cast to the hem of her sweatpants. "I think she's —" I hesitate when she pauses before raising her face and breaking open a smile. "Coming now," I finish, psyching myself to take this from the top.

"That smells *so* good, Daddy. I could eat a horse, seriously." Kelsey gooses Delia, who jumps before swatting her on the butt with her clipboard. "Logan, how good is this food? We even have queso."

"So good." I go to stand, but my metal

chair barely budges. "Let me give you a proper —"

"Oh, my God, sit, eat!" She waves me down. I hover over my plate, knowing that any later attempts are going to be flat-out weird. Deciding for me, Kelsey grabs a piece of corn bread and folds herself into a seat.

I focus on replacing my napkin. That went great.

"Dig in!" Michelle sinks a spoon into the potato salad. Kelsey takes a long gulp of her iced tea, eyeing me over the tumbler.

"How was your nap?" I ask. And the last decade and a half?

"Oh, I couldn't really. Just went over the choreography in my mind."

Kelsey and I both reach for the coleslaw spoon. "Sorry." I drop it.

"You're the guest," she says, stretching to flip a heaping scoop onto my plate. "I was thinking." She turns to Andy. "I don't know about another LaChapelle shoot. Next time, we should go with Leibovitz, and then —"

"Kel." Andy shakes his head once, while continuing to chew.

"You want to work with that freak show again?"

"No," he agrees.

"Right —" But she stops as he swivels his eyes in my direction, then back at his plate.

59

Kelsey picks up her fork.

"This is so fun!" Michelle fills the silence. "Logan, right here at our table." I struggle for appropriate conversation, but every polite inquiry sounds like a blog post. "Oh, Delia, how's your momma doing after that root canal? Those things are hell."

"Talking funny, but good. Thanks for asking."

"I spent a week with a mouth full of cotton. Looked like a fat chipmunk, didn't I, Kel?"

Kelsey nods as she takes another mouthful. We all eat for a few cricket-filled moments. Kelsey drops her head to Delia's shoulder.

Andy pushes his chair back. "I'm gonna watch the game."

"But we haven't had a proper meal at an honest-to-goodness table in weeks," Michelle says. "Kelsey, how funny was that camel?"

Kelsey straightens up. "*So* funny. Logan, you will not believe this." As Andy resumes eating she launches into the story at full throttle, complete with voicing the thoughts of the camel, until I'm holding my sides from laughing. And yet, despite the empirical intimacy, I can't shake the feeling that I'm still watching her on a screen.

CHAPTER THREE

A few hours later, I startle awake to Delia nudging me. I lurch to sit, squinting at her in the darkness. "What's wrong?"

"I was thinking, since you're leaving tomorrow, maybe you'd want to bring breakfast in to Kelsey so you two can hang out."

"Um." I inhale. "Sure. Just . . . get me in the morning."

"Or how about now?"

"Now?" I fumble to turn the clock. "What time is it?"

"Five-forty-something. Angela's got the tray ready to go. Want to come get it?" She steps leadingly backward.

"Sure. Sure." I pull on my jeans as she hovers at the bedroom door. On the staircase I hear *Good Morning America*'s Robin Roberts welcoming viewers back from commercial. Michelle stands behind Andy, who sits with his elbows on his knees, head dropped as if his team just fumbled on fourth and goal.

"So, have you picked a location, or is that a secret?" Robin Roberts smiles warmly at Eric Lamont and his girlfriend, who has just parlayed being a VJ into a judgeship on *American Idol*.

"We hope to keep it that way." He grins, setting off his famous dimples. "Our wedding's just for family."

"Oh!" I say, my hand going to my mouth. Michelle wipes her eyes.

Delia tugs me to the kitchen, where Angela silently hands off a tray replete with crystal-vased rose.

Andy turns off the TV and tosses the remote with disgust. "What's that?" He points at my tray but directs the question to Delia.

"Just a little something to get Kel going."

"That's sweet, Dee," Michelle says, blowing her nose.

Andy circles the couch to us in two long steps. "She has wall-to-wall press — the tickets for Asia go on sale this weekend, this is our only promo, and now every question's gonna be Eric, Eric, Eric. We can't let this suck her under."

"Oh, I know," Delia says lightly, nonetheless steering me to the stairs. "I just thought she could use a little extra TLC before she gets in front of those cameras."

The four of us start up.

"Telling her right now is ridiculous," Andy says.

"It's almost nine in New York," Delia counters. "It'll be online in a matter of minutes. I still think we should've kept her schedule clear."

"Oh, for Christ's sake," Andy spits. "She's tough as nails. We can't bench her every time you hear a rumor. What, was she not going to work this whole week?"

"My friend at MTV isn't a rumor." Step by step, all four of us, and one enormous tray, are jockeying up the stairs like a carnival stall horse race. "I told you this was coming —"

"But Eric hasn't even known that VJ girl a year," Michelle cuts Delia off in a tone that implies that this is not the first round of this conversation. "She's so uppity — I thought he was just getting her out of his system. I'll do it." Michelle takes the tray from me as I put together the timing of my invitation.

"Logan," Andy whispers as we approach Kelsey's door, "You should just go right on back to bed —"

"Mornin', sunshine," Delia calls as she

pushes inside. For a moment, no one moves. I peer around Andy to see Kelsey on the pink carpet in her T-shirt, her forehead dropped to the floor. *Good Morning America* drones on the screen over her fireplace. "Kelsey." Delia darts past Michelle. Kelsey pushes her contorted face into Delia's waist, her frame shuddering. Andy turns off the TV.

Michelle flips on the chandelier. "Do you need a cold washcloth? Logan, get her a washcloth."

I hustle into the bathroom where I take in the wall-size case displaying Kelsey's ribbons and trophies, first ice skating and then the talent contests, from Little Miss Cornstalk to Miss Honeybee, and on to the big leagues, the statewides, the regionals, the nationals, the ones that led to real opportunities, to this.

Kelsey cries soundlessly into Delia's lap. I put the washcloth to her inflamed cheek. She lets it drop to the floor.

"Kelsey." Michelle swipes it up, looking miserable. "You have to let it go, sweetie. I mean, if we're all honest, you're the one who cheated —"

"Ep," Andy cuts her off. "Logan, this here is a private matter," he says sharply.

"Sorry, I'll um . . ." I cross toward the

door, having just gotten the confirmation of Kelsey's infidelity that's eluded the tabloids.

"Kelsey." She doesn't respond. "Rambo." Andy invokes the nickname he coined for her because she was so strong on the ice for her size. "You need to be in downtown Los Angeles. In exactly two hours. Looking like you could give a flying shit."

She pushes herself to sit.

"Delia, I want five minutes when y'all get home." He walks out.

Michelle wriggles a piece of toast from the sterling rack and butters it. "And I've got to beat those costumes into shape. They didn't come back like how I wanted. Don't tell him," she says quietly as we hear him clomp downstairs. She takes a bite. "Just get him all riled up again. Logan, Andy's right. We didn't need to get you up at this obscene hour on the last day of your vacation."

Delia doesn't meet my eyes.

"Really, go on, now," Michelle repeats emphatically, and, not knowing how else to help as Kelsey stares into the carpet, I do.

A short time later, I peer through the roll— ing mist from my bathroom window as Kelsey and the team climb into cars. I spend the rest of the morning sidestepping the growing cast of staffers, who circle the house talking to one another and their phones about the pending tour. I take a sandwich to my room and curl up on my balcony to field calls from Lauren, Charlotte, Rachel, and Sarah, in which I find myself saying, "Oh, really, he is? *Engaged*? No, no talk of it here. She must not care." Then I divert their attention by revealing nothing details that feel like something tidbits. Kelsey Wade's carpet is . . . pink! In her bathroom, she has . . . washcloths!

But no call from Jeff. For the first time, I find myself wishing I'd told him I was related to her. Because indulging in dead-end banter would be better than ruminating on this. Delia obviously thought my being here would help — but how?

Later, I hear the car return and stand, waiting to see if I might be summoned. Instead, I see Kelsey appear on the lawn below. She hurries to its wooded periphery and, glancing over her shoulder, slips out of sight.

As this may be my last chance, I quickly make my way downstairs and across the grass where I discover a worn path into the shaded overgrowth. I arrive at a clearing of moss-covered rocks. Kelsey sits on one, smoking, her grief making art of her face as black rivulets from her eyes catch the coral of her cheeks and seep with her sprayed tan into her white tank. She has a leather-bound notebook in her lap, its spine cracked through from use.

I turn to leave, snapping a twig underfoot. "Shit!"

I spin back. Kelsey has dropped the cigarette.

"Sorry," I say, yet again.

"You scared me."

"Do you want to be alone? I mean, obviously, you do. I just thought —"

"Just working out some lyrics." She holds it up so I can see a scribbled poem riddled with cross-outs and ringed with musical notes in the margins. She slaps it shut and drops it between her ankles. "Whatever." She produces a pack of American Spirits and taps one out for me.

"I'm good."

"Really?" she asks skeptically, lighting another for herself.

"I quit."

"Impressive." She takes a deep inhale, leaving a metallic pink ring on the filter.

"My last was the September after graduation at three-fourteen AM after a nothing call from a nothing guy. I was ashing in a toilet, and it just hit me that every time I smoked, it was because I was pissed at a guy. I'm so jealous of the people who can just do it socially, but I craved one every time I got frustrated, which was, I discovered, a lot. So I had to go cold turkey. But I still dream about it, think about it, am inhaling vicariously as we speak."

She cocks her head before exhaling a stream of smoke to the skylight made by the thinning canopy. "Thanks. I don't feel like an asshole at all now."

"Oh, no! That's not what I meant. Sorry. After this morning, you deserve to smoke American Spirit headquarters. Was the event okay?" I ask the safest question.

"Oh, sure. I love nothing more than spending my quote *break* driving two hours round trip to spend three hours standing in some high-rise business brunch while people talk Japanese around me but never to me, like I'm an ice sculpture."

"That sounds awful."

"Well, the sushi was good." She smiles then drops the stub in a pyramid of similarly disposed. She hops up. "Come on."

"It's okay if I join you?"

"You already have." She doesn't mask her resignation as she resumes pushing through the trees, the sun dappled across her back. At one point, she looks over her shoulder to check that I'm following, and it's like her perfume spot. Which I saw at a Days Inn in Akron while snarfing down an Egg McMuffin before some conference and remembered our summers spent weaving between corn stalks in search of a spot to play.

"Ginger! Ginger bear," she starts calling, speeding up. I duck under a low branch. "Ginger!" she sing-songs. I step over a decaying tree stump and then out from behind a kennel. Clapping, Kelsey jogs around the building, while, off in the distance, I can see a series of gardens bordering a hulking mansion that makes Kelsey's look like the guest house. "Holy sh—"

A howling interrupts me, announcing the arrival of a large caramel-brown dog. Kelsey lets herself inside the fence, and it wags excitedly. "What breed?" I ask.

"Rhodesian ridgeback." Kelsey crouches to embrace Ginger, her false blue lashes grazing the short hairs of the dog's neck. "Yes, hello! Hello! Where're your babies, Ginger? Show me those sweet babies." Kelsey rubs the flat of the dog's head and opens the door into the kennel. She drops her knees to the newspaper-strewn linoleum, attracting the tussling tan puppies like metal shards to a magnet. "Hey, guys, hi!" The glow in her cheeks puts whatever top-of-the-line product was airbrushed there to shame.

"They're adorable." I crouch to ruffle the nearest puppy.

"The owners are never around. It's so sad. Ginger's my girl. Ginger and her snaps here." She flops a puppy onto its back and rubs its tummy. "It's her third litter." She gazes over the brood in consternation. "It looks like she's already had two taken." Ginger leans her nose down to Kelsey's. "I'm sorry, Momma," Kelsey murmurs, stroking Ginger's ears. "I know what you need."

She leads the dog out to the lush grass of the bordering garden.

"So they let you just come and play with her?"

"What?" she asks as she weaves in front of Ginger.

"Sorry, nothing."

"No, what?"

"Your neighbors?"

"Never met him." She claps at the dog. "I just talked to the breeder a few times. Ginger!" Kelsey takes off, and Ginger bolts after her. Kelsey laughs with delight as she darts around the garden statues, conjuring the old videos of her dad bolting for the touchdown. Ginger faithfully follows her

70

every move, forgetting her swaying belly, racing as she was bred to.

"Is that a . . . ?" I venture.

"Yup," Kelsey says a while later as she slows to a stop in front of the bench where I've parked myself, a panting Ginger at her heels.

"Ah," I say, having been staring at the topiaries and mentally trying to match their shapes to various long-nosed animals without success. She pivots and points down the line of hedges closest to us. "Dick. Big vag. Boobs. Balls. Balls with a dick."

"This guy sounds charming."

"Come on."

"There's more?" I stand.

"Yeah, super fun. This way."

Ginger and I follow as we pass a trampoline, an infinity pool, a trapeze, a skeet-shooting hut, a life-size chess set, a garden with a strippers' pole at its center, and finally stop at — "Shuffleboard?" I take in the two triangles of numbers facing each other on a stretch of flower-bordered pavement.

"You say that, but I'm gonna kick your ass."

"I haven't played this in forever." I take the pole she offers me while Ginger plops down under a looming cypress. We all learned together, at Grandma Ruth's retirement home. "You're going to have to give me a refresher."

"Delia always goes second." She lines up a set of disks. "You try to score and shove each other out. You remember." She glances at me.

"Vaguely."

"Hottest place you ever hooked up." Kelsey pushes into the pole like a janitor with a broom, and it takes me a second to realize she's asking a question.

I watch the disk slow over the 8, doing a mental slide show of my bar life. "Okay, this is so profoundly wrong. Know that I know how wrong this is before I tell you. But I met up with this guy I'd been seeing or, really, got him to meet up with me. Anyway. We'd been drinking and making out, and it's the moment, but, like, he wasn't going to invite me back to his place, and my place was a million miles in the wrong direction, and I remembered I had a friend who lived only a block away. So we get into her lobby, and I say to the doorman, all chipper, 'Oh, hey, I'm just here to see Victoria.' At three in the morning or whatever. Anyway, we ducked into the fire stairs and had sex against the wall and then got in two cabs.

As I'm saying this, I realize I should have sent Victoria some flowers."

"Or her doorman."

Having shifted from awkward, stilted reverence to TMI — "What about you?" I push myself to ask, as she chose the topic.

"I want to have sex in a stairwell."

"Oh, my God, if you could have sex in any square inch of your house, you do not want to downgrade to a stairwell."

"Oh, yeah, where? In my room — with the adjoining wall to my parents?" She pushes into her next disk and then waits for me to line up my shot.

"I can see that would be . . ."

"Right?"

She knocks my disk out. "I want to get a place somewhere, or a maybe a whole island or something, and just spend a weekend wandering around with my guy in our underwear."

"You've done that in, like, four of your videos."

"Cuz that experience is totally how it looks," she cracks. "It's freezing cold, there's forty crew guys standing around in down coats and ski masks, and the dude I'm frolicking with is gay." She pushes the next disk, and it makes a soft sliding *whoosh* as it departs from her pole. "It's hard to

73

imagine there's someone you could spend that much time with, desert-island time, and still want to spend more. Someone where you don't even have to talk, but you feel he's just so there for you."

"I'd settle for someone sharing a cab ride to my apartment."

She lines up her last disk. "I haven't even kissed a guy in . . . forever."

"Really? Not even that football dude?" It flies out of my mouth.

She spins to me. "Are you seriously asking me that right now?"

"Sorry —"

"He smells like jock-itch spray. Just a little bit, you keep sniffing around him because you're, like, is that? It can't be . . . sniff, it is! Gross. Have some confidence in me, Logan."

"I do." I laugh, relieved.

"Your turn."

I line up my pole.

"It takes a light touch," she advises as she wedges hers under her arm like a crutch. "So, you have a boyfriend? Mr. Stairwell Guy?"

"Yes, I have a" — how to put this — "guy." I look to the palm fronds. "Who texts me" — I pull my sleeves down over the heels of my hands — "with his penis."

74

She cracks up. "That's good. Delia's not really one to talk the girl talk from experience. One more match?"

"Sure!"

She beats me three more times before announcing that we have to get back. As we cut into the thicket between the properties, her shoulders have come down a discernible inch. Mine are starting to. She retrieves her notebook from the rock pile. "Oh, Logan, I feel like Eric was it. He was the one I got."

"I can't believe life works like that." I follow her gaze to the patch of clouds. "Do you mind if I ask what happened to you two?"

She drops her head. "Like, every possible thing that could. We were both on the road. We'd been together forever. We were both getting restless — I mean, really, I was getting restless. You'd have to be pretty antsy to look twice at John Mayer." She shrugs. "I want to be in love again," she says as she lights a final cigarette.

"Me, too," I agree, running my hand over the moss. "I thought I would be. In Oklahoma, we'd be on our third kid by now."

"But you can just meet someone." She squints as she inhales.

"And you can meet an-y-one."

75

"But it's impossible to tell if anyone's for real. Impossible. Even girls. Even just a friend — someone who isn't either on my payroll or some editor's."

"I've really missed you," I say, because five days ago, I was in a cubicle, and two hours ago, she wasn't talking to me, and now we're here in this cove of trees. "And I hope you know that's for real."

She abruptly stubs out her smoke, pursing her lips as she unfolds her mirrored aviators. She slides them on despite the dimming light. "You hung up on me." She cuts to where I've been afraid to go.

"I — I'm sorry," I stammer. "It's just I hadn't heard from you in years."

"I'd been a little busy." She crosses her arms like one of her video personas.

"I know," I say, forcing my voice not to abrade in response, because how could I not? When I got that call in college, *her* voice was not only coming through my phone, but also both dorm-room walls.

"I was offering you Delia's job."

"I appreciated that, believe me, but —"

"But what?"

"You were acting like we'd talked five minutes ago." I feel myself getting hot, unable to temper this plume of anger I thought extinguished. "Not five years."

" 'Make Me Yours' had just gone platinum. I was excited," she says, sounding small again. "My life was finally changing. Everything. I wanted you there."

"But *my* life had changed. I fought my parents so hard to go to NYU, they refused to pay. I was working a million jobs to cover tuition. My grades were barely hanging on. How could I just drop everything to go on some tour?"

"You didn't think I was going to make it," she says simply.

"Kelsey, I always have. Everyone always has." I look away from my distorted reflection in her lenses. "I hope you can forgive —"

"I don't do that." She walks away.

It takes me a second to follow.

I'm at a total loss. So I tried. I got a tan, I got some sleep, I ate Michelin-starred interpretations of my hometown food, and now I'm ready to go back to my miserable, crap-box apartment and say I tried.

"Kelsey, where've you been?" Michelle stands from the couch. "I need to check fits, and I was looking everywhere. Delia said you went running, but you weren't in the gym —"

" 'Cause we were down at the beach. I'm hungrier than a wakin' bear, Momma. Let me grab something. What time's your plane tomorrow, Logan?" Kelsey calls as she continues to the kitchen with Michelle in tow.

"Eleven AM?"

"Well, I don't want to keep you from your packing and all that," she says with undeniable finality before disappearing around the corner. My face stinging, I turn toward the staircase, but see, down the hall to the offices, the blondes all leaning toward Delia's door like frightened children.

"Andy, I didn't see the harm." Delia's voice rises.

"That girl's a stranger!"

"Logan's family!"

I freeze.

"Which is exactly why you should've run it by me — just stick to your job!"

"Taking care of Kelsey is my job!"

"She's gonna be fine!"

"How?"

"You have no idea what you're talking about!"

Then she says something that I can't make out.

Glass smashes — my breath catches. I walk directly up to my room and turn the lock.

I'm just packing the last of my things and

Googling airport hotels when what sounds like the howl of a wounded animal reverberates through the house. I run out to see Delia walking quickly up the steps, her expression inscrutable.

"I don't understand!" Kelsey shouts from below. "Delia, apologize!" she cries desperately, twisting in Michelle's arms. "Daddy, she'll apologize." But Delia just climbs, her hand gripping the railing. "Apologize!" she screams.

"I can't," Delia says, her voice low as she inhales her tears, continuing past me without turning back.

"Daddy?" Kelsey entreats, but he just lifts his hands in defense, like an overwhelmed parent facing a remorseful dog and a bitten child.

Michelle tries to shield Kelsey, pulling her close, but she breaks away and runs up the staircase, flying past me to slam her door on all of us.

An hour later, I watch from my bathroom window as Delia, laden with suitcases, gets into the limo with Peter's assistance. A wet-faced Michelle hugs her good-bye, but Kelsey doesn't come out. I make myself dinner from a can of mixed nuts scavenged from the armoire. Any lingering instincts I had to rebroach the past with Kelsey have been snuffed, and now I'm just trying to make myself very small in this very large room and hold my breath until Peter can assist me out of here, too.

"Logan?" My door cracks, and I jump from the bed.

"Hi! Oh, my God, how are you?" It opens all the way to reveal Kelsey wearing a glittering minidress and carrying peep-toe stilettos, her only accessory a tiny gold pendant inlaid with a diamond K.

She shuts the door soundlessly behind her. "I'm showing you L.A."

"The designer?" Confused but going with it. "It's a gorgeous dress."

She unzips my suitcase. "The city. I'm showing you. Tonight." She roots through my clothes, her eyes puffy beneath deftly applied concealer.

"But —"

She's still for a moment. "Please." Her voice is faint, and I have to lean in to hear her. "Don't make me ask."

I quickly get dressed as she paces outside the bathroom door, tapping the heels of her shoes together. "You ready?" She peers in as I dot on blush. "Wow, you look really pretty."

"Thank you. Are you sure you feel up —"

"You have to take your shoes off, okay?"

I step out of them, and she flicks off the bathroom light. I pick up my clutch and go to the door.

"No," she whispers. "This way." She steps on the toilet lid and throws her leg over the windowsill to the trellis below. "Just don't knock the camera on the right when you come down," she whispers before descending the greenery as if it were a ladder here solely for this purpose. Peering over the sill as her feet find the dirt, I get a glimpse of the adolescence we missed sharing. An adolescence in which she seems suspended.

I've barely reached the flower bed before Kelsey takes off sprinting down the winding drive, and I race to keep up, our bare feet slapping the pavement. "Kelsey," I whisper breathlessly. "Are we running to L.A.?"

"There." She points to waiting headlights.

Kelsey spends most of the cab ride on her phone, calling her dancers, who make no effort to cover their shock that she's choosing to go out and be in public on the heels of Eric's announcement. But her cheerful voice does not betray either heartbreak bracketing her day. "We're passing the giant doughnut — we'll be there in ten." She flips open her clutch, pulls out a small package of wipes, and begins to dab the dirt from her feet. She rubs until her skin is reddening.

"Kel."

She looks to me, brow tight, whitened teeth digging into her glossed lower lip, and I'm incongruously reminded of a day in ballet class. She couldn't have been more than eight and was already *the* most organized of any of us, keeping all of her rubber bands, bobby pins, and hairnets in separate containers, old metal Band-Aid boxes she covered in glitter. But that day, she couldn't find her tights. She emptied out her tote over and over, knowing that Miss Natalia, so not her real name, wouldn't let her in bare-legged but would charge Michelle for the class anyway. Kelsey just looked at me and started to shake. I don't remember what happened next, just the expression on her face, begging me to fix it.

"You should clean your feet," she says. "I don't want you to mess up your shoes."

"I'm . . . I could give a shit about these shoes."

She smiles, and then tears overtake her.

"Oh, Kelsey, I'm so sorry my coming here has made such a mess. I think Delia —"

"No. Nope!" She dabs under her each of her kohled eyes. "I don't want to talk about her. At all. Don't talk about her, okay?"

"Okay," I agree.

"I just." She exhales. "I don't know how we're going to get in. Usually, it's all set up for me. I'm not even sure how to —"

"I obviously don't know the first thing about any of this, but what if we just roll up to the front door and kind of zoom in?"

"Zoom?"

"Zoom. Maybe we could zoom."

The car pulls up outside a shuttered 1940s movie theater in a stretch of dilapidated, abandoned storefronts. Half the light bulbs are missing, and the glass of the marquee is shattered. But then, I see that the carpet to the door is fresh and there's a line of teens waiting to get in. "They're all so *young*," I say.

"Studio execs' kids," she surmises from the LVs and double Cs emblazoned on their accessories.

"Who look like they're going to a costume party — come as your jaded twenty-something self."

"Far cry from Coleman's," she says, referring to the only place that would let high-schoolers loiter on a Saturday night.

"Ready?" She grips my hand and I time to pull us onto the sidewalk right behind the girls from another car. They go to join the line, but we walk straight for the bouncer. He's about to redirect us when Kelsey tilts her face up. The papparazi cameras flash. He unclips the rope, and we slide in just as the teens' phones are raised en masse, thumbs clicking away.

"Isn't it a school night?" I ask over the thump radiating from the end of the long corridor.

"I think they all have tutors who do their homework for them," she says as she follows me down the hall, which has been left untouched. Or demolished and rebuilt yesterday to look like this. The walls are covered in peeling, dust-encrusted silk. The carpet is worn to lace. The snack counter is open, and two ladies dressed like *Rocky Horror* extras are slinging truffled popcorn. Above their heads, where prices should be, someone has written in chalk, *Concessions! 1. Your political party will never accomplish what you need it to. 2. Your taxes will always be higher than you want them to be. 3. You will fall out of love.*

I pull her along into the theater, hugging the wall as I get our bearings. The room is vast, with a carved wood ceiling like the Ziegfeld. But the seats have all been torn out, and people are dancing on the sloping floor. On the stage, a translucent partition has been erected to put the VIPs tantalizingly just out of reach but not out of view. There doesn't seem to be any way to get up there, so I just make for the exit sign nearest and pray that someone who works here can escort us. Suddenly, I feel Kelsey tug me back and turn to realize an Ed Hardy-bedecked dude has grabbed her hand.

"No," I say forcefully to him, as if I'm correcting a Doberman. Tugging on her other arm, I can't ballast myself in these shoes.

"Are you hot for me?" he says, quoting her lyrics as his posse laughs and presses themselves into us. "Want me to make you moan?" I whip out my phone to dial the police, because that's all I can think of, when a man reaches over their shoulders and takes Kelsey's.

"Miss Wade, your table is waiting," the blond guy says firmly as he pulls out his walkie-talkie. "Miss Wade is on her way to her table." Our aggressors spring apart, and she looks up at him, relieved. "Follow me." With his height and broad shoulders, he cuts a path for us to the stage, where he expertly spins Kelsey, grabs her hips, and tosses her up over the barrier into the safety of the VIP area. She gracefully lands on a low velvet couch and twists back to stare at him through the Plexiglas.

He gestures for me, and I beckon him down to my mouth. "I'll break something!" I shout in his ear, waving my hands to ward off the attempt. "And no one cares about me! Point me to the long way around!"

He smiles a crazily handsome smile and directs me to the doorway I'd been focused on before the douche brigade. I blow through it to find a stairwell lined with couples having vertical mostly dressed sex. After Kelsey vouches for me to the skeptical bouncer I step awkwardly over the cast of everything currently playing at the Angelika to make it to her. She pointedly ignores the ripple of intrigue around us.

"That was so nice of that guy — is he the manager?" I ask, as we both watch her savior make his way back onto the dance floor.

"Aaron? He doesn't work here, isn't that so funny? He was just talking into his turned-off phone!"

"Do you know him?"

"We've met a couple of times. He sang backup on Eric's last tour," she says as she rises to watch Aaron ease into the groove. "Oh, look, here're my guys!" A group of very pretty Latino boys bound over to us. Beaming, she kisses everyone hello. "How are you?"

"Oh, sweet Jesus, this is the first day I can walk." One of them turns to me. "Because she works us so hard, not because of my sex life. I'm Duane."

"Duane is my choreographer." I'm surprised when Kelsey puts her arm around my waist. "Guys, this is my cousin, Logan."

"I'm Pita," another dancer says, taking off his white Elton John sunglasses. "Stands for Pain in the Ass."

I shake hands.

"Apologies for the calluses," Duane says as we reseat ourselves. "But there's a lot of acrobatics on this tour."

"I like a man with strong hands." Kelsey mugs, nudging him.

"So, Eric and his ho-bride aside, how has your break been, honey?" Pita asks her, and she snorts, pulling up her hem to show the bruises from the shoot.

"Are you trying to tell us you've been working hard — or you've finally found yourself a real man?"

"I finally found myself a real camel." She regales them with the saga while I sip my drink and look surreptitiously around at those surreptitiously looking at Kelsey. I learn that Zoe Deschanel is as beautiful in person, Robert Pattinson has lost his keys, and January Jones has no sense of rhythm.

I'm enjoying being behind the ropes for this one night. As we pass midnight and the population hits critical mass, the music segues from generic beats to recognizable songs.

I stand. "I'm gonna go to the ladies' room. Want anything?"

"A tampon?" she asks jokingly.

"I meant *from the bar.*"

She inhales sharply, throwing her shoulders back and pressing her hands into her midriff. "Better not, my tummy's on the countdown to being reviewed."

Appreciating that mine is not, I follow Zoe to the VIP ladies' room, which turns out to be one unisex space carved out of the old backstage from before this was even a movie theater. We shuffle past the makeup tables with their dusty wig stands, mustaches, and ancient bottles of spirit gum left as if still waiting for the next matinee.

"They must save a fortune on cleaning supplies," the guy in front of me says.

"I can't figure out if it's that," I respond, "or they clean it and then reapply false dust."

He turns his cute face to me. "Art direction?"

"Sorry?" I ask.

"You work in art direction?"

"That is one of those mysterious Oscar categories no one gets. I'm a camel wrangler."

"Of course." He smiles as I note that even in my skyscraping heels, he's a little taller. "Is there a lot of call for that anymore? Since Valentino died — and *Ishtar* bombed."

"I did a shoot for *Vanity Fair* just this week. Watch for it — May issue. When you see the pictures, how glossy his coat is, think of me and the hours I spend making sure he gets his beta carotene."

His blue eyes take me in, and I know we're both thinking the same thing: tonight just got unexpectedly interesting. "So, do you live here?" he asks.

"Are you asking because Zoe and I are the only two pale brunettes on this line, if not the whole club, if not the city?"

He considers me for a moment as we move another step forward. "You do have an exotic quality about you, and by that I mean Botox-free."

"I'm just passing through on my way back to the desert. You?"

"I think everyone is just passing through."

"Not the Kardashians," I remind him.

"I've got it, you're a network comedy writer for some hit show, fresh from New York, and the honchos brought you here tonight to keep you from quitting now that you know what the hours are."

"Oh, I like that vision of me." Shoulders raised, eyes wide with delight, I bring my hands together, thumbs under my chin. "This is so exciting. Yes, it's *Medium* meets *Dancing with the Stars*. It's *House* meets *Bones* on Animal Planet. It's *Law & Order SVU* but funny."

"Okay, okay, I'll stop trying to figure you out."

"Please don't," I volley back.

He reaches the front of the line as we realize both toilets have been vacated simultaneously. He looks to the adjacent doors swinging open on their creaky hinges and back at me. "So, we have to pause our witty banter to pee in adjacent stalls now, which I think means we're skipping dates one through five."

I nod to acknowledge this awful truth.

He lightly touches my elbow. "Meet you back here by the gunk-crusted sinks, and you'll let me buy you a drink, or twelve, whatever it'll take to obliterate the memory?"

"You're on."

We boldly step forward, and he holds my stall door open. I freeze.

"What?" he asks as I start to laugh.

"What if you looked down after all that and our feet were facing the same way?"

A few hours later, Finn has done a masterfully thorough job of obliterating all memories of Jeff with his mouth. "Let's get out of here," he says.

"Where?"

"I have a suite at the Chichester."

My brain simultaneously plays through the absolute best and worst that could mean. I pull back to look into his eyes. "While I'm not sure if this is true for the other girls here, I think you should know that nowhere on my bucket list does it say be found dead in a five-star hotel."

"I don't think it's five stars; it might only be four."

"In that case, kill away."

He takes my hand, but I pull him back. "I just need to let my cousin know I'm leaving."

"Your cousin from the bedbug convention?"

"That's the one. Just give me two minutes — I'll meet you by the popcorn stand."

"Keep an eye out — I heard Kelsey Wade's here tonight, showing the world she doesn't need a ring on it." He gives me a hard kiss. "And if you try to sneak out the back, I'll have my paparazzi friends personally deliver you to my car."

"Aw, you even make creepy sound endearing." I push him toward the exit, then snake over to our couch, which has been abandoned, and dig my clutch from under the guys' jackets. I don't see Kelsey. Maybe she's on the powder-room line. Two minutes might have been ambitious. I turn around, colliding with Duane.

"Hey!" I say. "I've been —"

"Making out with the hottie — we know!"

"You don't think he's too cute?"

He puts the backs of his hands on his hips. "I'm not sure what that means."

"I usually date guys who have a — I don't know — a broken nose or a crooked tooth, something a little off-center about their hotness. But he's just mouthwash-commercial symmetrically cute. He's cute. Like, hand him a ball of yarn."

"I want your problems."

"He asked me to go to the Chichester with him."

"Again, why am I sensing you're asking?"

"Is it okay? I mean, in New York, if a guy asks you back to his hotel, it means he wants to post pictures of your corpse on the Web."

"This is L.A. If a guy asks you back to his hotel, it means he wants to blow your mind.

Go have your mind blown."

"I have to tell Kelsey. She can't think I abandoned her."

"A, we'll get her out the back door, and B, no offense, I'm sure she cares about your well-being and all." Duane points to the main dance floor. "But right now, she doesn't even know her name." I crane and finally spot them, her sweaty body entwined with Aaron's like two egg beaters blurred into one by the jolt of electricity passing between their hungry lips.

I don't think this is just any suite. We've taken the elevator to the top floor, and there's only one door. Without releasing his warm grip, Finn submerges the key, revealing a very disjointed vision. I pull away as I take in what it could mean. It's exquisite, what I would've described, had I never seen Kelsey's house, as the most beautiful place I'd ever been. Floor-to-ceiling windows look out on a vast balcony with private pool. The dining table is marble, the curtains grey velvet, the staircase seems to twist out of spun sugar.

And it is trashed.

The dining chairs lie on their sides, the table has been shoved to the wall, and littered with fetid takeout containers and diet

Red Bull cans. The pool area is sodden with discarded towels left in chlorinated moguls.

"Well, you had quite a night," I say, crossing my arms, realizing that I've deserted my cousin for some trust-fund asshole with a coke problem.

He looks around, seemingly suddenly seeing what I'm seeing. "Oh, no, I had no night — wait." He catches himself. "Ever since I decided to excuse myself from a bunch of Italian advertising executives to use the bathroom, I have had a spectacular evening. But before that, I got up at four AM to get here, where we spent the day shooting a cologne campaign with the fervor of neonatal oncologists, then out to an excruciating dinner with a bunch of guys from Milan and their honest-to-God escorts." He holds out his hand. "But I have this place until noon, and we never made it upstairs. Upstairs is pristine. The bed is pristine."

I smile, letting him lure me up the floating steps. "How can I resist a guy who says pristine after four whiskeys?"

Before the sun has risen, I awaken in a downy mound of bedding, feeling utterly limp and delicious. I push to sit but don't see or sense Finn. I twist on the lamp to find he's left a piece of the hotel's linen notepaper atop my cell. It reads, "Thank you for a wonderful night, Miss Logan. I'm sorry to rush off, but my boss texted. Stay. Enjoy yourself. Order the caviar eggs, have the concierge call you a town car, it all gets charged back to the Italians. I've programmed my number into your phone. XX Finn."

I throw myself back onto the bed, not sure if I, or my phone, can take it.

When the town car pulls past Kelsey's guard booth the sky is streaked orange. Peter steps from the apartment over the garage while tying his tie. He waves. I wave back, wondering if he knows my mother and if he'll tell her that I'm rolling home with the sun.

Kelsey comes around the side of the house, one hand clutching a lavender blanket around her, the other interlaced with Aaron's.

"Hi."

She smiles a warm, drowsy smile as he leads her toward me, holding his shirt. "This is my cousin, Logan. Logan, this is Aaron. I think y'all met last night." She rests her head against his bicep.

"Pleasure," he replies.

One of the garage doors rise. "Nice to meet you, formally. Thanks again for saving

95

our butts last night."

He tips his fingers to his forehead in a loose mime of a salute. "At your service."

Kelsey turns her nose into his skin and closes her eyes. "Well, I'll let you two say your good-byes."

Andy seems to have found his way to bed, and the living-room TVs are black. But on the circular entry table sits a Cartier box with a flat notecard. *"Was waiting to give you these for opening night but thought you could use the cheer now. Love, Daddy."* The box sits here expectantly for when she returns through the front door. I did more than my fair share of sneaking out, but my returns were met with fury, not Cartier. However, I wasn't paying the mortgage.

I'm drawn to the wall of glass that looks out to the green-gray ocean. I lift the neckline of my dress and inhale the citrusy remnants of Finn's cologne. That was . . . that was like nothing I have waiting for me in New York.

I turn to see Kelsey pick up the red box. "Uch," she says with disgust as she reads the card, dropping it back onto the marble like an overdue electric bill. She raises her face to me, slipping back into post-coital reverie. "Holy crap." She shuffles across the rug.

"Me, too." I sigh. "Were you in the pool house?"

She smiles slyly. "On the big pile of floaties."

"Okay, remind me to stay off your floaties." Even though we both know that I'll probably never be here again.

"I was improvising," she says impishly. "I've never brought anyone back before." She comes to stand beside me, the grate in the floor between us blowing warm air up our legs. She rests her forehead against the glass and twists her face to mine. "Let's go down to the beach."

"Lead the way."

She sort of half-skips down the lawn, through the bracing dew, and then under an arch in the hedge down to the lower lawn, across and down again, over and over, descending toward the ocean while I take long strides behind her, savoring this last bit of sea-salty air. Finally, we reach a gate to a private tunnel that leads under the PCH. One more door, and we're there.

The volume of the surf is at once turned up. I blink at the shimmering crests as they roar into the sand. We run down to where the icy water swells. Standing there with the lavender hem of her blanket swirling, the warming sun on my back, the sky stretching

97

out seamlessly — it is almost the delivery on the invitation Delia made to me.

Before I know it, Kelsey has handed off her blanket and sliced headfirst into an oncoming wave. With an exhilarated shriek, she comes racing back out, wriggling her fingers for the cashmere. I wrap it around her, and she drops onto the beach with a sigh. "Fucking awesome." She shakes her hair. "Aaron, I mean."

I laugh, sitting beside her. "You were officially due."

"Payment in full." She pulls her hair to the side, untangling it from her K necklace, and squeezes it out, the water running down her arm. "I didn't expect him to be so . . . he was . . . tender." She nudges me. "And you?"

"He had skills."

We nod and sit there, smiling at the sea. A pair of joggers kick sand as they pass, driven forward by their iPods. "So," I ask brazenly, "a bunny?"

She laughs, sitting up on one cheek and twisting her head as if she could see her own butt. "Not just a bunny. It's the Velveteen Rabbit."

"I am blown away that Andy let you get a tattoo."

"I did it with Eric. They trusted him to

keep an eye on me." She picks up a cracked shell and makes an arc in the sand. "Don't tell anyone. Some blogger guessed it's a teddy bear, but that's as close as people have gotten."

"No, sure. Why the Velveteen Rabbit?"

"You'll just have to read it to your child someday to find out."

"That's far off."

"I hope not." She adjusts the blanket. "I want a family so badly. That thing, you know." Blissed-out, she stares at the encroaching tide. "That guy, that love. It's all I think about."

"For the record" — I dare to revisit yesterday's conversation — "I believe you're going to find that."

"Back at ya." She rests her head on her knee. "I think I could actually sleep."

"I'm not sure I have time to."

She turns her face to the surf, and we watch the seagulls dive for their breakfast. "I want to share this with you."

"We could stay in touch now, Kel."

"No." She shakes her head. "You're the person."

"Person?"

"Do this with me, Logan. Take her job. I know you'd be amazing." She looks at me searchingly. "It's time."

I run a quick inventory of what I've acquired since she last made this offer: a job more demanding than fulfilling, an apartment more habitat than home, a guy more sex than substance, and a group of friends who've somehow found all of those dream things and are intently moving on. Somehow the life I've spent the last decade building is losing relevance, the veneer I've spun frantic circles to secure showing its cracks.

I feel myself nodding yes. A jogger puffs box office numbers into his cell as he approaches, oblivious.

I wrap my arm around her cool shoulders, unsurprised at the ease with which we fit, and realize how weird it's been to be with her these days and barely touch. She drops her head into my lap, turning on her side as I pull the wet strands from her cheek. And then she closes her eyes. I lean back, wriggling my fingers beneath the warming sand as Kelsey's breath slows until she's asleep.

PART II

CHAPTER FOUR

Once again, I wake in my berth as soon as the tour bus's engine cuts. I stop the Berlitz app, and check the time — three-fifteen AM, not bad. If I was in New York right now, it'd be after nine, and I'd still be in the office, eating cold takeout. Instead, we just made it from Budapest to Vienna in less than four hours. When I first saw the crammed schedule, I thought — well, I thought a lot of things, one of them being that there was logistically no way we'd be able to hop from country to country like this, a show every day or every other, each for a different nationality. But with three weeks and sixteen cities notched in my belt, I've learned that Europe is actually very small, and connected by a network of superhighways that we only traverse after midnight.

Hearing Andy heaving Kelsey's wheelie to the aisle with a grunt, I fling back the curtain, knowing we can't afford a repeat of

Athens. "Hi!" I say brightly, swinging my flats to the metal treads. "Welcome to Vienna! *Willkommen!*" I call to everyone in the surrounding berths. I hop down the bus steps into the hotel's underground parking lot and sprint to the elevator bank. In the silent lobby, a dour-looking matron mans the desk, her pin curls locked in place. I arm myself with an Austro-Hungarian-size smile, bigger than German but way smaller than Oklahoman. *"Guten morgen!"* I say chipperly. *"Wir sind mit der Gruppe Namens Wade. Viden dank."*

"Wade?" she asks, pronouncing it "Vade" with obvious displeasure, even though I called, at Andy's urging, to confirm our pending arrival somewhere outside Bratislava.

"Ja." I nod, nearly at the end of my Berlitz.

"One moment." She leaves the console to rouse her colleagues, as, with three people going top speed, it will still take more than an hour to check in all two-hundred-something of us. Now well versed in the odd economics of tour accommodations, I've learned that only a handful of hotels have drive-in parking with tour-bus clearance, which security mandates. Of those, maybe two have the class of rooms that Michelle demands on Kelsey's behalf, which no one begrudges. I'm not dancing for a hundred and twenty straight minutes a night, and I'd like a soaking tub.

I would have thought that these establishments would be falling all over themselves to secure such massive group bookings. But our travel coordinator explained that hotels also host conventions. And whom would you prefer, insurance salesmen who'll leave your establishment cleaner than they found it, and with hefty in-room porn billings to boot, or assorted dancers, singers, gymnasts, and crew who'll scuff, snag, and stain not just the rooms but the hallways, no matter how much I beg, and whose keynote equivalent will choke the entrance with paparazzi? Which is why when Andy went red-faced and pounded the desk with his varsity ring in Athens, the clerks obstinately refused to bring on more staff to speed check-in, dancers fell asleep in the lobby, were late to rehearsal, and the run-through was a disaster.

This clerk quickly returns, and I can hear her colleagues stirring through the office doorway. "Thank you so much," I say, "I greatly appreciate it. Could you be so kind as to process the suite for Miss Wade and her parents first, and then we can do the rest in this order?" I hand her the stack of passports.

Andy steps off the elevator in his rumpled tracksuit and aggressive stubble, pulling Kelsey's bag. "All set?" he asks gruffly. "Can I tell GM to wake her?"

I give him a thumbs-up, and he leaves her case by the ashtray. I tell Fraulein I'll be back, and head to the top floor to complete my daily ritual. It's challenging, each time the elevator whisks me past the plebeian floors, not to flash to my initiation into the world of penthouse suites, and pull out my phone. But each day I don't call Finn is a day I can look forward to calling Finn. As Jeff Stone taught me, savor the anticipation because reality has a way of depositing you in a cab.

In the presidential suite I kick off my sneakers, because Michelle hates tread marks on freshly vacuumed wall-to-wall. First I order Michelle's chamomile tea while I open the balcony doors, letting in fresh air to vanquish the predecessor's or the predecessor's conquest's perfume. Michelle has a very sensitive nose from her days as a mall spritzer. Then I turn on Kelsey's tub, set out her toiletry case, and run across the suite to make sure the hotel completed the turn-down service in Michelle and Andy's room. By the time Kelsey's bath is run, she's usually listing bleary-eyed in the doorway. Andy throws the TV on full blast and settles in on the couch while Michelle follows Kelsey to the bathroom, seating herself on the toilet lid with her tea to discuss the performance, the day, the next day, while Kelsey, her eyelids drooping, musters murmured responses, her mouth managing to stay just above the bubbles. While simultaneously supervising the check-in of two hundred plus other people, I periodically swing back to make sure that Michelle doesn't need anything. And finally, when they hear the TV mute, Kelsey gets out, Michelle goes to bed, and I am dismissed for the night.

Today we're doing pretaped segments, which means I don't need to wake Kelsey until eight. I'm about to knock on the Presidential Suite when I feel my hand buzz with a voice mail. I don't even bother to check the time stamp. My messages are slowly finding me, hours, days, sometimes weeks later, like birds thrown off their migratory pattern by electric wires.

"Logan, it's your mother. I just spoke with some man named Greg who answered the phone in your apartment. He has never heard of you and was quite emphatic that you don't live there. *What* is going on? Have you moved? Call me back."

Fuck.

I tap the door with my forehead, and Michelle answers, already in her TV outfit, a royal-blue cashmere sweater over black slacks, her blond hair rinsed gray-free for the tour. Andy's in his sweats in a wing chair, mopping up his runny egg yolks. "Mornin', honey," she says, pouring me my second coffee. "Sleep well?"

"Thank you, yes. You?"

"The sheets here aren't as soft as — where were we Tuesday? With the gold wallpaper?"

"Prague."

"Yes, those sheets were heaven, but the water pressure here is better. Make a note of it in the file for next time, could you?"

Andy is flipping channels. "I never can get it." He lifts his toast at the screen. "Is something news or isn't it, did it happen or didn't it? BBC is leading with this toxic spill in Hungary, but CNN hasn't even covered it. Does that means it's bullshit, or CNN isn't doin' their job properly?"

I slide the cup onto a nearby chest. "They're probably gearing the coverage to their audience. You could Tweet Wolf Blitzer."

He points to the map on BBC World.

"Well, if it goes across that valley there, we're gonna have to change our route next week. Come on, Wolf, help a dad out." He looks at me, and I take my cue to sit next to him, my phone full of vital e-mails at the ready. "VIP list been given to stadium security?" he asks, because, as he has repeatedly shared, one time it wasn't, and from what I can ascertain, some people were stuck momentarily in a hallway feeling unimportant.

"Check," I affirm, scrolling my screen.

"Souvenirs arrived at the stadium?" he asks, because one time, they didn't, which represented thousands in lost revenue, of the million or more that Kelsey, Inc., takes in nightly.

"Check."

"Costumes gone on ahead?" And so on, through every anxiety dream that's ever come to life over the last eight years, a daily litany of responsibilities that should be outside our purview but which were once bungled and now compete to inspire my first gray hair.

"And the radio stations have their gift baskets?"

"I —" Inhale. And then sit there, chest taut, jaw open. "Will get right on that."

"These things have got to be dealt with

first thing. First. Thing."

"I know. I'm sorry."

"It may not be some fancy Wall Street job, but you still have to take this seriously —"

"I do!" I'm quick to reassure him. I quit that job — over the phone — and let Charlotte put my stuff in storage, which probably means she's wearing all of it while she has sex with this Greg, so, "I could not take this more seriously."

"Oh, Andy just wishes he could be driving the bus himself." Michelle places a thin piece of ham on brown bread. "I love how they give you sandwich fixings for breakfast here. So fun. I'm gonna make one to put in my purse for later."

I look at my binder, determined not to screw up another thing today, as the door to Kelsey's room opens and she stumbles out in her pink pajamas.

"Mornin', Drowsy," Andy greets her.

"Mornin', Daddy." She gives her mom a kiss and fixes herself a plate from what's left while I turn my still beating face to the side table. These suites have so much furniture, as if people live full lives here, requiring sideboards and breakfronts and oversized vases.

"Logan," Michelle says. "Want to walk us through the day?"

Taking a steadying breath, I clap my hands. "Okay, so this morning's pretaped interviews are at the Vienna Opera House, and it's a huge honor they're letting us film there." Michelle pumps her fists like a toy boxer while Kelsey eats. "You'll do your usual bits."

"Who are the local guys?" Michelle asks.

I've memorized the answer. "Someone named Franz Schekele. He's the Austrian Anderson Cooper."

"That's so sad," Kelsey says, leaning forward to take a piece of bacon off Andy's abandoned plate.

"What?" I ask her without looking at him.

"You work your whole life," Kelsey says, catching a crumb from rolling down her shirt. "Going from covering the local pig fair to city politics to national news, and you don't get to be Hans Goatherder, the star, you're the Austrian somebody else, the Japanese Ellen, the Korean Paula Abdul." She turns to her mom. "Remember that white woman we were told was the German Oprah? How?"

"You should bring that up in interviews, break the ice," I say.

"Really?"

"No. And *then,* as a special treat, we're going across the street to the Hotel Sacher

111

for a late lunch, and we will have whipped cream on everything."

"Woo-hoo!" Michelle gets even more excited. "Honey," she prompts Andy, who has pulled the binder from my lap. "We're gonna take the girls for strudel."

He grunts.

There's a knock at the door, and Michelle lets in Dax, the hair guru, and Binky, the makeup artist who always reminds me of a Swedish ornament. "What're you wearing?" she asks, her daily greeting.

"Let's pick," Michelle says, leading them to Kelsey's room. Delighted to shift out of Andy's crosshairs, I follow.

Michelle pulls out the ripped jeans and custom-made besparkled, beglittered tops while Binky peruses the options politely.

"This one feels Austrian," Michelle says, fingering a hot-pink tank with a parrot across one boob.

Kelsey stands on the other side of the bed, arms crossed, her ability to muster enthusiasm for these shirts, one or another of which she's been wearing for weeks, fatiguing. Michelle looks down from her daughter's less-than-thrilled expression. "Kel, just pick one," she says with a glimmer of impatience.

"I love what Logan has on," she ventures with a determined casualness, referring to my blue knit with a twisted ribbon neckline.

"Take it," I say.

"I *love* that idea." Binky rushes in as Dax nods furiously, mouth full of clips.

Michelle bites her left pointer finger. "That won't feel boring?"

My jaw opens prematurely while my mind speeds toward a statement. "No! Oh, no, it'll really allow the costumes you designed to be the focus." I pull off the shirt and pass it over, shrugging on the discarded hotel bathrobe.

Michelle purses her lips. "But it clashes with my sweater."

"Then let's go pick something fun for you!" Kelsey says, as if the trip across the living room is a girls' day out.

Michelle blinks.

"Michelle?" I ask, putting my hand on her arm. "If you don't feel like —"

Andy knocks on the door. "I'm not hearing any blow-dryers. We got thirty minutes on the clock."

"Let's just keep moving." Michelle sighs. "We'll do what Kelsey wants."

By the time we get to the Opera House, I have a second voice mail from my mother. "Logan, I just spoke to your office. They said you quit. If you don't call me back, I'm

113

calling the police." Trying not to panic as I imagine Greg being thrown onto the bleached carpet and hauled off for questioning, I survey where the publicity rep's set up Kelsey's costumes. In this grand space, where Mozart is staged and Mahler conducted, they kind of look like a stripper's trousseau. While allowing myself to wonder which is preferable, letting my parents think I'm dead or telling them I'm with Kelsey, I switch the garments around so there's a visual flow by color. I try to keep the mannequins at arm's length as I work. These are the B-set. The A-set is at the arena right now, being steamed and hung on the quick-change bar. The B-set should be at a dry cleaner's in Stuttgart. But it's not. It's wafting under my nose. There's a reason people don't work out in velvet.

In the wings, Binky is giving Michelle a last dusting of powder. Kelsey has started picking at a cuticle. "We good?" I ask as a ping of blood appears.

"I would give my left tit for a cigarette," she whispers to me.

"Are you sure this sweater is all right?" Michelle asks. "I really felt cuter in the navy one." Kelsey works her cuticle.

"No," Binky answers warmly. "I'm loving that color with your eyes."

"Okay." I step out from the wings. "Miss and Mrs. Wade," I announce. Franz Schekele approaches, tapping his microphone.

"Guten morgen," he says briskly, as if he's here to review their foreclosure application.

"Good morning," Michelle replies with American oomph, while Kelsey just looks to the camera, waiting for the red light.

"Drei, zwei, eins . . ." The light glows. *"Wir sind heih mit Kelsey Wade!"* He is suddenly freakishly animated.

"Hi, Austria!" Kelsey matches him, fluttering her fingers coquettishly, and I see that she must have popped the acrylic loose.

"Michelle, you make ze cohstumes?" he asks. "How did zis come to be?"

"Well, first she skated, and I made all those little dresses," Michelle answers in her foreign-interview cadence, extra bubbly, a little slow. "I didn't know what I was doing at first, but I got pretty good with a sewing machine, I can tell you!" She does her laugh.

"Zo the theme, theh is a theme?" he asks. "To the show?" he clarifies.

"Oh, yes! Well, Kelsey has always loved dollhouses —"

"Pupen?" he asks, and Michelle's face stops.

"Poopin'?" she repeats uncertainly.

"Pupen," he repeats. "Dolls!"

"Oh, yes, poopin. Yes. So she thought, why not make the set like a dollhouse? With all these different rooms, and I could dress her like a different doll for every number."

A dollhouse. I haven't seen the show yet, but the set looks more like a, well, like a sex hotel. Dollhouse, fine, sure.

"Und, Kelsey, you und your muter are very close?"

Not hearing Kelsey's usual response I look up from my binder. "She's my best friend!" Michelle rushes to fill in Kelsey's sound bite. "Since she was little, I could tell her *anything.*"

"Kelsey?" he prompts her.

She snaps to. "We had a huge sycamore tree in the yard, and we'd sit under it, and I'd tell my momma about my day and my dreams, and we'd make plans for the future. That's why I sang 'Dream a Little Dream' on *Star Search.*"

"Yes, ve have a clip of that. *Vunderbar.* Ve are very excited to have you in Wien and to see the show tonight. Thank you!"

"Thank *you!*" Michelle beams.

"Now, just kiss me on the cheek und say, I love Franz Schekele!"

Kelsey inhales briefly before doing as instructed.

"Great." He winds the cord around his

116

forearm and walks away like a john who can't get out of the room fast enough.

"What was *that?*" Kelsey asks.

"His promo," the rep explains.

"You'll be spliced in between Johnny Depp and Cee Lo kissing him, if that makes it feel any less ooky," I add.

"It does, actually."

Michelle tugs at her sweater. "I think I'm getting itchy."

"Let's refresh your sexy eyes." Binky leads her away.

"Are you okay?" I whisper to Kelsey as she worries the raw stub of her pointer.

"I just went blank for a sec."

"Yeah. I gotta ask, sycamore tree? The only tree in your yard looked like it was waiting to star in *A Charlie Brown Christmas.*"

"It's a bit our first publicist gave me cuz of *Star Search,* and I've been saying it so long I can see it. Dammit, what am I gonna say now?"

"That you and your mom swapped dreams and gum on line at the DQ?"

"Gross." She looks down for a moment, dropping her platform heel to the side. "This is so not sex on a pile of floaties."

"Still no text?" I ask.

"Would you text me?"

"Yes!"

"If you were Aaron?"

"Of course," I reassure her. But she's right. Now he's the backup singer who had sex with Kelsey Wade — which is far preferable to being the guy whose text she blew off. "He's probably busy."

"Like you're too busy to text Finn?"

"Exactly — just like that."

Binky leads Michelle back.

"Okay, next up is Rai Uno," the rep announces as a sixty-something woman, in a skirt almost displaying her La Perla, climbs over the orchestra pit in stratospherically high heels.

"Ciao!" She then spews a barrage of rapid-fire Italian while Kelsey and Michelle stand by awkwardly, waiting to be addressed.

"Thanks for your support with the shirt," I whisper to Binky.

"I'm surprised they're even here. Kelsey made it sound like they weren't coming." She pulls a brush out of her hip holster, ready for the next touch-up. "Can you imagine doing this with *your* mother?"

I think of the conversation I have coming. I think of the hours Kelsey and I spent as girls under that sad excuse for a tree. How we used to imagine we were secretly really not just cousins but sisters, never actually saying which parents we'd erase from the equation if we could. "Yes," I whisper back. "My mother would just smile and say, 'Hi, I'm Judy Wade, and I'm saved. This is my daughter, Logan Anne, and she, sadly, is going to hell.' "

Even though the interviews ran long, Michelle insisted we make it to our late lunch. The three of us watch Andy bite into what's essentially a hot dog and then squint as his eyes tear from the horseradish. Enjoying the challenge and the audience, he makes his final bite the biggest.

"Oh, for God's sake, Andy," Michelle says, lifting his water glass to him. He pushes it away as he cracks up, dabbing his eyes with his starched napkin.

"Damn good." He coughs. "Clears the sinuses right out."

Having lost her window to rest, Kelsey pours another packet of sweetener into her iced tea and stifles a yawn with Olympian finesse. The management has graciously cleared the Belle Époque dining room, and while the first time we ate at an emptied restaurant felt thrillingly insider-y, it is starting to conjure staff dinners circa my undergrad waitress days. I never realized how much of the pleasure of dining out is watching people. Otherwise it feels like ordering in with better utensils.

"Terrance!" Kelsey practically topples her red velvet chair as she jumps to her feet. Michelle and Andy follow, and I leap up to see Terrance DuGrey — hours ahead of his scheduled postshow visit — moving across the landmark room with an unimpressed air. A multiplatinum hip-hop star in his own right, Terrance retired to oversee the label that made him famous. His iconic hard stare breaks into a grin, and I'm oddly proud of her ability to elicit such a reaction from such a man.

Michelle sucks the chocolate from her teeth. "We weren't expecting you until tonight!"

"I couldn't wait to check in on my favorite family." His arm draped around her, he walks Kelsey back to our table, his two GM equivalents taking unobtrusive station by the drapes. "Mr. Wade." He and Andy do a shake-slash-bro-hug, and he gives Michelle a kiss on the cheek. "Sit, sit." He waves us all down and, before a waiter can get there, flips around a chair from a neighboring table and drops into it.

"How's business?" Andy asks.

Terrance shakes his head, his smile turning rueful. "I am having a week, Andy.

Susan fucking Boyle. Susan *fucking* Boyle. I can't sell shit right now." He rubs his eyebrows.

Andy nods, taking this in, and I wonder if Terrance is implying that shit extends to the album this tour is promoting.

"This cake is just amazing, Terrance," Michelle says, flagging a waiter. "You have to have a piece. Can you please get a piece for our guest? Would you like a Viennese coffee? They serve it with whipped cream, it's so delicious. Or maybe an espresso?"

"Oh, no." The tension in his face evaporates like the steam from my cup as he waves off the server and then pats his chunky cable knit. "Got to watch the calories. Thank you, though. You all enjoy." We immediately resume eating, but I'm guessing none of us tastes anything. "Someone want to introduce me?" Terrance asks in my direction, tempting me to blurt that every guy I ever hooked up with would give a testicle to be me right now. Suck it, Jeff.

"Where are my manners?" Kelsey jumps in. "This is my cousin, Logan. She's taken over from — as my assistant. She's doing an amazing job. Just amazing. Isn't she, Daddy?"

Andy sits forward. "You were in the studio, so I ran it by your team."

121

Terrance lifts his palm. "What do you think of our show, Cousin Logan?" His stare back in place, he turns it on me. Frug.

"I actually haven't seen it," I admit.

Andy intercedes, "What she means is —"

"I mean that nine PM here is noon in L.A., and that's when I get most of my calls. So I thought it more prudent to devote the time to back end —"

"All business. Okay, then. So, Kel, how's the grind?"

"I'm having a blast." Kelsey draws out the last word for emphasis as our waiter places the leather bill in front of her with a half bow, and she, as she does everywhere, slides it to Andy, who tugs out his wallet and offers up a credit card, even though it goes to her accountant. "It's such a treat to see you. You sure you don't want even a bite of this cake? It's insane."

"My head of European sales caught the Bucharest performance. He said in the second-to-last number —"

" 'Chemistry Lesson'?" Andy clarifies.

"Yeah. He said you're flagging."

"Oh." Kelsey grips either side of her seat. "Well, I'm switching into the harness in the middle, so —"

"The guy who's popping a mortgage payment to take his three daughters to see

Kelsey Wade doesn't know about the harness. He just knows Kelsey Wade isn't bringing it."

"No, right —"

"That shoot with LaChapelle was tight, though. Real tight. You did good."

"Kelsey, tell him about the camel," Andy prods.

"Oh, I don't know if Terrance would —" she demurs.

"Oh, yes, it's too good!" Michelle affirms. We are all, I realize, nodding. As if Kelsey's a well and our movement will pump the story out of her.

"You're gonna love this, T." Andy beckons his cupped hand and in a second flat, Kelsey breaks into her reenactment, hopping up to straddle the chair and make it wobble on the marble for effect. And, despite having heard it to the point that I can recite it, even I'm laughing when she flops back down.

Terrence drops his head and cracks up into his turtleneck. "You should save that for Letterman," he says as he stands, his spiced cologne lingering. He holds Kelsey by her shoulders, appraising her. "The shirt —"

"Thank you!" Michelle throws her hands out. "I've been saying it all day!"

"She's working it. That flashy shit is turning. It's starting to put age on her, you know what I mean?"

"Yes, oh, yes, absolutely, Terrance." Michelle recovers.

He pulls Kelsey in for another hug.

"Logan lent it to me," she shares quickly over his shoulder.

"Nice," he offers me as he releases her. "Take it tonight." He points at Kelsey.

"Can't wait."

"That's what I like to hear."

Kelsey is soon stationed in the preshow reception, and I am push-weaving toward her through the packed room of dignitaries and their adolescent children and/or dates. Michelle sits these out after being asked one too many demeaning times if she was a fan and takes a cat nap on the bus while Andy positions himself in the hall to gauge the "satisfaction" of everyone as they depart.

I'm not at Kelsey's side, because Terrance had been erroneously seated in the stage-right VIP box, which tonight has a slight obstruction from the smoke jets, which had to be brought forward three feet to — I don't have space to care. He's now seated in the stage-left VIP box with a scotch, which also dates back to — I don't have space to care. "Sorry, excuse me, excuse me, excuse me . . ."

"I have loved to sing since as far back as I can remember. I would just beg Momma to take me to the contests," Kelsey answers for the — she sees me and flashes her hands twice by her thigh and then flicks one finger as if she's brushing off an aggressive piece of lint — twenty-first time in the last hour.

"You vill teach my daughter." A gentleman pushes forward what looks to be a painfully shy middle-schooler.

"That's sweet," Kelsey says, but I can tell she's unclear.

"You teach her to sing. Go ahead, Gertrude, sing for Kelsey Vade."

The girl stares down at her boots as if she's willing the rug to swallow her.

"Oh, that's okay, she doesn't have to. You don't have to." Kelsey puts her hand on the girl's.

"But you teach her." The man says something fast and instructional in German to Gertrude but to no avail. She waits on that hungry rug.

"So, do y'all get much snow?" Kelsey asks the room.

"Ahhhh." The girl ekes out a note, and her father puffs up.

"You make better." He tosses his hands at Kelsey as if we are now getting somewhere.

125

"I'm so sorry." I step in. "Miss Wade has to get ready now." To a chorus of "awws" I steer her out of the room.

After a nod from Andy, we march the cinder-block hallway as Kelsey exchanges her untouched cocktail for a Red Bull. "How was that supposed to work?" she asks. "What did he see happening, do you think?"

"You handled it really well."

She belches loudly and hands off the emptied can for a cold-cream-smeared towel. "Can you please get me my iPod with 'Chemistry Lesson' queued up?" she asks as we descend the stairwell to her dressing room.

"On it."

"Frauleins." Kelsey mugs from the doorway before plopping down and lifting her face to Binky's air-brusher. "I want details from za tourist front."

Michelle holds up earrings to replace one that went flying last night. "Do you approve of these?" she asks.

"Perfect!" Kelsey cheers.

"I wouldn't want to put age on you," she mutters, and Binky and I lock eyes in the mirror. There's a knock. I toss Kelsey her iPod and crack the door to a middle-aged woman carrying a valise.

"I am Berta. The hotel sent me to do nails?"

"Fantastic. I'm Logan. I hope you're up for doing this pit-crew style." I pull it open to reveal Kelsey mid-makeover. Berta reddens as she tentatively steps inside to cover for our manicurist, Jen, who's sweating off bad street sausage on the bus. "Guys, this is Berta. Berta, this is Binky, Dax, Michelle, and Kelsey." They gesture hello with their tools.

"Hey, Berta!" Kelsey says to the ceiling as Binky lines her eyes. "Welcome to the chaos."

Michelle pulls me aside while Berta fumbles open her case. "She signed the NDA, right?" Michelle whispers. "I don't want Andy going through the roof again."

"Yep." All twelve pages. Same as me. The only thing more thorough is a lobotomy. Kelsey watches as Berta wipes her shaking palms on her lap.

Kelsey interrupts Dax's description of schnitzel. "Did Logan tell you guys about this Italian chick this morning? Oh, my God, I have to show you. Berta, I did all these silly interviews today with these crazy reporters." Michelle turns to leave. "Momma, I can't tell this story without you!" Kelsey squeezes Berta's hands as if

127

she was waiting all day to share this story just with her. She hops up and, with a bud feeding her "Chemistry Lesson" in one ear, does a perfect pantomime of the journalist, swinging the ensnarled round brush from her hair to use as a microphone and pulling Michelle disarmingly into the act, an arm around her waist, a kiss on her cheek at the punchline. Kelsey eases her hand back into Berta's now steady one. Michelle stays put, and Kelsey resumes volleying jokes back and forth, determinedly turning the dull grind into a good time for all present.

Soon we're traversing the tunnels as Kelsey runs scales against the overhead roar generated by tens of thousands of people finding their seats. Michelle hurries behind with the freshly steamed tutu. Kelsey interrupts her vocal warm-up to chirp "Hey" to each passing crew member, all while tilting her head and swishing her hands as she mentally reruns the "Chemistry" choreography.

To my daily relief, we arrive not in some sub-basement steam room but under the stage, where the dancers are doing their final stretches. As she approaches them, Franz Schekele gets out of the pink Barbie Corvette she'll drive on for the finale. His cameraman turns on the lights. Kelsey instinctively recoils.

"Yeah, Kel," Andy says, coming from behind them. "These guys are gonna shoot backstage tonight, quick changes, that kinda thing."

"Why?" she asks quietly, her back to the lights.

"You heard Terrance today. More's more. I'm thinking he could syndicate the footage across all our markets. Just do your normal stuff — pretend they're not there."

She nods with a stiff smile, Pita reaches out a hand and Michelle, Andy, and I join the prayer circle.

We look to Kelsey as adrenaline makes a complete circuit through our joined palms. "Dear God." She drops her head to speak to the empty space given shape by our toes. "We thank you for this opportunity to use the gifts you have blessed us with. Please give us your grace to do an awesome show and to perform safely. And, most of all, to bring it to the kind folks of Vienna. Amen!"

"Amen!" Everyone claps and breaks apart, expressions set with precurtain focus.

"So, Logan." I'm surprised to hear Franz address me as I trail Kelsey to the rigging, her Swarovski fishnets teasing the light spilling down from the stage. "Zis mohning I did not realize you ah Kelsey's cousin."

"Yep," I reply.

Kelsey takes off her K necklace for Michelle to hold. "Best friends since they were babies," Michelle prompts me, but I'm uncomfortable with trying to package memories into soundbites. "Logan helped Kel learn to walk — it was the cutest thing," Michelle adds before giving her daughter's reflexively proffered forehead a kiss. Kelsey lifts her foot onto the first rung.

Franz checks his notecard. "But zis is yoh first touah." He addresses me again. "You didn't vant to come befoah?"

Michelle's hand tugs Kelsey's heel just as it lifts above our heads. Kelsey scampers back down. "Honey, show them that nutty Italian lady."

Kelsey looks up at the three-story ladder she has to climb.

"She only has a few minutes before lights," I remind them. I hear Andy clear his throat.

Everyone looks to me, and with a sharp exhale I face the camera. "She's always been more like a sister to me, really. Like Michelle said, we were pretty inseparable, first cousins, just a few blocks apart."

"Vat vas Kelsey like when she was little?"

I look over his shoulder to Andy. I have no idea what to say, what this part of her story is other than her love of ice-skating

130

and nonexistent trees. I decide the safest option is just to tell the truth. "Small, shy. I always had to keep an eye out for her at school."

"That's sweet," Michelle says.

And home, I want to add.

"Vat vas it like when you first heard Kelsey on ze radio? Veh weh you?"

On my way to NYU Freshman English.

"Um, let me think. We were in L.A., and we were shopping." Avoiding Kelsey's eyes, I try to verbalize a moment I've frequently imagined. "We were in the Gap, and 'Make Me Yours' came on . . . and we screamed." I can see it so clearly. "No one in the store knew who Kelsey was, and we pointed and said, *that's her!* Michelle took us straight for hot fudge sundaes. It all started to change pretty fast after that."

A techie extends his arm to draw our attention to the lowering lights. The preshow music starts to fall away, leaving a low, throbbing base.

"Zat's goot." The camera darkens and drops.

"Well, go on. Get up there!" Michelle exhorts.

I start to walk away, but Andy steps in my path. "You coulda said you'd started college — never lie."

My phone buzzes.

"Logan Wade," I answer, eager to get away.

"Logan! I found Logan!" my mother calls to my father as I chastise myself for not checking the caller ID.

"Mom, hi. I'm so sorry I worried you." I watch Andy hustle down the hall with Michelle.

"Worried sick."

"I was just waiting to tell you — I'm in Europe."

"Europe?" she says.

"I have a new job. There's a lot of traveling involved."

"Doing what?"

Andy's words spin me. "I'm Kelsey's assistant."

There's a pause. "Kelsey, *your cousin?*"

"Yes."

Silence.

"Mom?"

"Why? Why would you do that?"

"It's a great opportunity."

"I don't understand —"

"I'm helping run the tour, and it's amazing — can't you just be happy for me?" I ask. "Please?"

"No, I can't."

"I could have just lied to you, Mom — is that what you want?"

"You're a test." Her voice shakes, "God sent you to test me." She slams the phone down as the floor starts to vibrate.

I murmur apologies as I inch along the aisle of the VIP box and take the chair Andy insisted I have beside Terrance, who sits with his fingers tented in front of his face, waiting to be wowed. "Andy and Michelle coming, Cousin Logan?" he asks.

"Momentarily."

"They're good people. They're on it."

"Yes, they're great managers."

"They're not her managers."

"Oh, I thought, they're so —"

"Not formally, no percentage. But they run the show."

"Right, yes, no, that's what I meant, they run the show."

The usher retracts his flashlight just as the bass slows to a booming pulse and the stadium goes black. My stomach makes that familiar, slithery U-turn as my mother's cutting words reverberate. People in the seats below start to clap and then to scream as — pulse — the lights come on in the living room of the three-story dollhouse set. Duane, dressed like a Ken, stiffly reads a paper, while one of the other dancers woodenly moves a vacuum. Pulse. The kitchen lights up, and Pita mimes carving a turkey while his Barbie sets the table. Pulse. A kids' room on the floor above them lights up, and a dancer reads a large storybook to two others in their twin beds. Pulse. The master bedroom beside it lights up, and a Ken and Barbie exchange a prim good-night kiss and reach for their bedside lamps. Pulse. All of the dancers look up. The audience is standing, screaming, stomping. Pulse. The house is backlit, and a bare bulb turns on in the attic. Kelsey, the rebel doll, stands defiantly at its center. The crowd around me erupts to full throttle. She hits her first note, somehow staring penetratingly out into the eyes of every one of us. Holding our gaze, she struts down the stairs through each floor, gathering the other "dolls," who tear off their ties and aprons to dance behind her. Charisma electrifies her face, blown up on the Jumbotrons. Her eyes demand the singular attention of the twenty-eight thousand people singing right along with her.

Reaching the stage floor, she kicks off into the first gymnastic sequence. Michelle squeals, and my attention is momentarily pulled from the stage as Andy gives her neck a quick kiss. I realize that she's changed back into the navy sweater she wore this morning. "I feel so much better!"

134

she says to me.

"Oh, good."

"I left my nude bra in the bathroom in Bratislava, and I'm sure the lights were going right through that knit to my white one, uch." She shakes her head.

"Is that why you didn't want to wear it?" I ask. "I wish you'd just told us —"

"Oh, no." She squeezes my shoulder. "I didn't want to bother y'all." She turns back to enjoy the show. I stare at her for a moment, seeing my mother, allowing myself in the dark, surrounded by thousands of people stomping in euphoria, to feel the wound, but mostly the confusion.

Kelsey's rendition of "Chemistry Lesson" brings Terrance to his feet, pumping his arm in the air. "That." He leans in. "*That* is the real deal." Kelsey swivels her hips as the lift carries her out over the floor seats and her posse gyrates on its poles for the final number. "She took it," he says forcefully. "Two hours — straight. She took it."

I unspool the years, realizing, as Andy watches Terrance clap for her third drenched bow, that we have both had to take it for a really, really long time.

CHAPTER FIVE

We've plowed through three more cities in as many days when just past sunup, I stand by the entrance of the Royal Amsterdam Inn, waiting for GM and Andy to help Kelsey stumble off the bus. Bumped, because of a gas leak, from our garage-equipped hotel of choice, Kelsey must now traverse the flashbulb-filled cobblestone holding up her travel pillow to block the shots.

Our new lodging is made up of a series of adjoined seventeenth-century riverhouses, which require us to navigate two claustrophobically narrow staircases before we get to the tiny elevator leading to her suite. Surveying the tight fit, Andy steps back to wait for the next one. "The pillow might have to wait, too," I mutter as the door slides shut and an ancient pulley creaks into motion.

"Huh?" she asks, dropping her head

against the wall of the car.

"Nothing, sorry. Stay asleep." I scroll my e-mail, seeing one from Rachel about Lauren's bachelorette party, all of the bridesmaids cc'd. "We were thinking suites for all of us wherever Kelsey's staying, then a spa day (can Kelsey join?), then dinner wherever she likes (private dining room???), VIP clubbing (she likes to dance, right?), and in-room massages the next day with brunch. So excited! XO, R."

She forgot to specify if she expects Kelsey to perform the in-room massages. I'm sure she does.

I dump my phone back into my pocket, thinking of switching to Gmail and not telling anyone.

"You feeling okay?" I ask, studying Kelsey's greenish pallor under the crystal pendant.

"Achy." She lifts her pajama-sleeve-covered hand over her mouth as she yawns.

"Let's get you into a bath."

"I don't want a bath." She closes her eyes and grimaces. "I can't listen to her right now."

On the landing we wait beneath mildewed wallpaper for the elevator to bring Andy.

"And it was the Limited," she says.

"Sorry?"

137

"Not the Gap. When I first heard myself on the radio." Kelsey smiles. "The rest you got right."

The Presidential Suite feels a little less Obama than Roosevelt — Teddy. Michelle is already in the bathroom, removing her makeup as the tub fills.

"I'm sorry, this place was listed as a boutique option —" Dust fills my nose, and I sneeze.

"Whatever. It's fine," Kelsey says as she goes to tug the shutters closed.

"She's not feeling great." I update Michelle. "Maybe we should skip the bath?" I offer. "I could keep you company, and Kelsey can go to sleep?" Kelsey shoots me a grateful look.

"Oh, she just needs a nap and a Mc-Flurry." Andy clicks on the TV as he drops onto the nearby couch.

Michelle opens the complimentary toiletries and sniffs each one. "It'll help you unwind, Kel, after all those photographers."

Andy raises his arm in my direction. "Oh, and Cheryl's e-mailing you talking points."

"Thank you." I tug my phone out of my pocket and see that she's already sent me the document, subject line *Logan and Kelsey's History.*

"Night, Logan. Happy face in the morn-

138

ing." Michelle waves me off, and I hear her ask Kelsey, "Now what was that woman saying in your dressing room?"

"Which woman?"

"In the red dress and the funny hat, you remember? What was she saying?"

I let the door shut behind me and traverse another warren of hallways to a dust-mite-caked bed, where I face-plant, clothes still on, and remain motionless for a whopping four hours.

Then it's time to tug open the drapes and flip the shutters to an icy rain splattering the canal that sends Michelle hurrying out to track down a camera-friendly raincoat. Andy brings Kelsey a bottle of Coke Light to nurse as Binky blushes her cheeks back to a semblance of health. She chatters about the weather while tearing her toast into bites that don't make it into her mouth.

"She'll rally." Andy waves me off with a strip of bacon when I inquire if we should reconfigure the schedule. Which is a guilty relief, as I wouldn't begin to know how, given there's more free space in that tiny elevator than there is in my binder.

And rally she somehow does. While one journalist after another asks her droning questions between puffs of unfiltered Marlboros in the hotel's windowless library. They weirdly don't raise their voices at the ends of queries. "You wrote an album." "You like to sing." "You are traveling through Europe." As if they're listing her offenses.

"Only one more print." I update her as I click the door closed, leaving us briefly alone. "Thank God."

"Come on, three hours of smoke is just what the doctor ordered," she says, allowing herself to indulge in the phlegmy cough she's been suppressing. She falls forward in her wing chair like a collapsed marionette.

"It's my privilege to inform you that fresh air is next on the docket." I grab the coffee and refill her cup. "The costume piece is in a park. I assume it's tented given the downpour — and the local network wants to show you strolling the streets."

"That explains why the last guy asked if I was a streetwalker." She kicks off her heels.

"Yeah." I drop into the chair across from her. "Something was getting lost there."

"Or not." She sits back up, bracing her temples as she pulls her legs in. I flip through today's FedEx to confirm the tent. Otherwise, Michelle will need to find a golf umbrella to match the trench she's currently shaking down Gucci for. The beamed ceiling creaks. Kelsey sneezes and then lets out an involuntary moan. I pass her the tissues.

"Oh, my gosh," she says. "I keep thinking of what I can fill you in on, but I guess you've been with me since I woke up."

"Mmm," I say, marking my place in the schedule with my finger. She pulls out an interview smile, and then her face contorts into another sneeze.

"Kel?"

"Yeah?"

"You really don't have to."

"Don't have to what?" she asks, wiping her reddening nose.

"Endear me, entertain me, engage me. If it starts with an 'e,' you don't have to do it. I'm here. I'm in. It's not your responsibility to make this a good time for me. Consider my presence an off switch." I was hoping I would remember the producer's name once I saw it, but the call sheet is in Dutch, and all of these words look the same. "I swear, at some point, Poland and Holland had a language grab, and Poland ran off with all the consonants, and Holland got stuck with the vowels." There's a knock on the door. I realize that Kelsey has been staring at me with a strange expression. "You okay?" I put my hand on her knee. She nods slowly.

I open the door to a disappointed man. "You are not Kelsey."

"And you must be here for the interview! Come on in."

Then we are out in that air, which isn't fresh so much as damp, like being licked with a cold cloth. The canals weave under the streets, between the buildings, releasing an icy vapor that penetrates everything. No wonder people like to take refuge in steamy cafés and imbibe hot smoke. As Kelsey and the interviewer walk, I teeter along beside them, reaching onto my toes to keep the umbrella out of frame. Icy water makes rivulets down my neck and sleeves. Kelsey fights stumbling as the producer keeps gesturing for her to look at the interviewer and not the uneven cobblestones threatening to upend the thin heels of her boots. Michelle waits beneath the tent with the costumed mannequins. Kelsey waves at the crowd, and I see a sheen of sweat on her upper lip.

"Hey." I touch the elbow of Andy's bomber jacket, and he tucks down. "She's really not feeling well, and the five takes of that hike didn't help. What's the protocol when she gets sick?"

He chews the inside of his cheek as Kelsey invokes the mythical sycamore. "Call the office. They'll have the number for someone who can meet us backstage. A B12 shot in the ass'll fix her right up."

"Great, and I'll cancel lunch with the radio contest winners so she can nap —"

"No, don't. She'll never get back up if she stops. She'll be fine — Rambo, remember?" He pats me on the back as the drizzle increases around us.

I don't know how she got through the show. Between songs, we sprayed her throat with numbing solution while she gave in to flu shudders, before bracing herself to go back out and dance her shot-up ass off for forty-two thousand people.

Afterward, on the bus to Belgium, Kelsey sits next to me up front, coughing and staring out the window as I try to doze. Once we cross the border, I realize which of the three thousand niggling thoughts is keeping me from sleeping and send an e-mail. "Hi, Rachel & Co — so excited for the bachelorette! Working on the hotel thing — you guys might have to share." On my Discover points. "Let me know where you want me to try to get a dinner reservation — of course can't use K's name. Clubbing totally. And K was so excited to hear about L's wedding she wants to treat you guys to the spa day. XO, L." That *has* to be good enough, right?

For the first time Kelsey is the first one off the bus.

"It'll take a moment for them to get us checked in," I inform her, resting my back against the front desk as the stunned clerk fumbles to program our key cards. "I don't usually wake you for this part."

"No, that's good, because I was thinking . . ." Her scratchy voice momentarily trails off as she sees her parents' luggage wheeled in.

"Uh-huh?" I yawn as Michelle follows Andy off the elevator. He lifts his cap to give his scalp a thorough agitating.

"Wait!" Kelsey croaks after the bellboy, and he stops. "Mom." Kelsey waves her over. "Why don't you take Logan's room, and Logan'll be in the suite with me?" Her voice gives out completely, and she swallows. "This way, my cough won't keep you up. Don't you think, Logan?"

I am too tired to form an answer that, from the expressions on Andy's and Michelle's faces, could possibly satisfy all parties. "Whatever's good for you guys. Seriously, toss me that throw pillow," I say, pointing to the nearby settee. "And I'd be happy to curl up right here."

"Well, Kelsey . . ." Michelle looks to Andy.

"Delia never —"

"Right." Kelsey's eyes harden for the briefest second. "Not a second thought." She wheezes. "You'll come for breakfast. So!" Without waiting for a response, she directs the bellboy at her baffled parents' luggage. "These to the room next door. Now, give me a kiss, Momma, or you know I'll never be able to sleep." She goes to lower her forehead but is wracked by a hard cough. "Happy face in the morning," she spits out in breathy bursts.

The next morning, I order up everyone's usual breakfast, text Andy to let him know the food is waiting, and then sit with the day's FedEx packet to get organized.

After thirty minutes, I text him again, and then Michelle, wondering if he forgot to charge his phone.

After opting to let Kelsey sleep in I'm just making her a sandwich for the road when her door opens. "Sorry. It's so quiet, I overslept." She blows her chapped nose and looks around the room with watery eyes. "Where are they?"

I shrug.

"What, are they pouting?" She goes out to the hallway, and starts tapping on the door kitty-corner. "Momma, Daddy, come on, now. Do you really want my germs? My germs," she repeats in a German accent.

There's no answer.

She raises her fist to pound, but the door falls open at the first strike. I look at her motionless back.

"What is it?" I dart out to see.

The room's empty. The bed has been slept in, but Andy and Michelle are gone. She immediately starts to shake. "Oh, my God. It's okay, it's going to be okay, Kel."

I cancel the day's interviews, the photo ops, the VIP reception, pleading flu, pleading exhaustion. But silently to Andy and Michelle, merely pleading.

The next day, I wake in Munich on the chaise across from Kelsey's bed. Her nightmares reached me through the suite's walls at around five while I was staring at the ceiling. Belgium's front desk informed me that in the time I was watching their breakfasts cool, Andy and Michelle ordered a car to the airport and were seen rolling their wheelies through the lobby of their own volition. So the worst was ruled out, leaving a range of hurtful possibilities.

I roll over on the uncomfortably tufted silk, pushing my hair off my face. Kelsey is passed out on her stomach, reminding me of endless sleepovers. Michelle loved having us stay up, letting us play with her makeup — as long as I removed it before my dad picked me up. That house was such a craved change from the stillness of my own. Now I look at the vestiges of the manicure I chewed off yesterday, to say nothing of Kelsey's raw cuticles, and I can't reconcile that they could just leave us.

Amex won't tell me where their cards are being used, because Andy's changed the password. The office is at a total loss. The girls promised to call me the *second* Andy checks in. The only person left to reach out to is Terrance — and I can't bring myself to tell him I lost the Wades. How many days of mother-daughter interviews sans mother can go unnoticed?

Shit.

I blow a steady stream of air to the ceiling. *Shitshitshit. What* is going on?

A few hours later, I rub my exhausted face fast and hard, past even the powers of European coffee, and refocus on my checklist. Without Andy to pace in my periphery, I just have his voice haranguing me with questions, trying to figure out what I've forgotten before I've forgotten it.

Sitting on the edge of the materializing stage, I lift the inside of my sweatshirt to take a deep whiff. It's not me. "What is that smell?" I ask.

"The wind shifted," one of the crew says as he passes lugging a pipe. Insurance mandates that every two weeks the set be inspected, a tedious process that doubles the crew's day, yet something Andy oversaw with visible relish. I hit refresh on my phone and then Kelsey's. Nothing.

"What do you mean, the wind shifted?" I ask, readjusting my perch on the two folding chairs I've shoved together.

More guys pass carrying a cage. "All the hops factories are just next door. When the wind shifts —"

"It smells like I'm trapped in a foot," I say.

They pause to balance it on their thighs while one of them adjusts his grip. "Just wait till we drive through Parma. It's like a yeast infection in the ass of a pig."

"How are none of you guys married?"

"Woo-hoo!"

Kelsey is locked into her harness on the upper catwalk. She's answered every inquiry into her parents' whereabouts with "Taking a breather," delivered through a locked smile. Knowing that the riggers need a little extra cajoling on inspection days, she pretends to trip, and I cover my eyes as the guys laugh. I don't know how she can be terrified to fly but love being flung through the air on a piece of floss. I turn away as she back-dives off the ledge and cram the end of my pen between my teeth.

"Okay, dismount," a guy calls over the loudspeaker, and she rockets to the stage floor, as flames shoot in quick bursts from the sides. She turns to the back and gives a thumbs-up, then pivots to me. "Any word?"

I shake my head.

"Call them."

"Me?" I ask.

She nods, her expression one of raw need.

"Okay."

"Okay!" The smile rises. "Gotta go test the floor trap." Hopped up on local cold medicine that would have serious street value stateside, she runs to center stage. What do I even say? Hi, your daughter wanted a breath of space to have a lozenge, not even have a lozenge, have the sore throat that required the lozenge, which somehow inspired a full-blown exodus, and can you please come back now because your child woke screaming in the night?

I dial Michelle's number, chewing the pen until I feel the plastic crack under my incisors. It goes to voice mail. "Michelle, hi, it's Logan. I'm just calling because — because we're not totally sure where you are — which is probably just a communication glitch. Anyway, we'd love to hear from you — and we miss you!" I hang up before I ramble into something unhelpful, such as, actually, this equipment check has gone twice as fast without Andy yelling at everybody until they drop things.

I know what I should do next if I was worthy of my paycheck — I scroll to Andy's number — but I can't — I can't. Again, I think of Delia. Kelsey flips across the stage, sweat flying off the ends of her hair. *Fuck.*

The phone goes dark, and I find myself needing to quell this sickeningly familiar feeling, a paradoxical cellular conviction that only I can fix this *and* it is unfixable. I take a ragged breath before texting Finn the message I've had almost a month to perfect: "Trashed any good hotel rooms lately?"

But in the time it takes for the icon to cross the screen, I want to tug it back, recapture a moment ago, when I was still hoarding the prospect of reaching out, like a half-eaten caramel wrapped in my pocket. Because that's it. Now I've sent the only text I can send, and I will never hear back, and he's probably pulling off someone else's panties with his teeth right now.

My phone vibrates. "Hello, Logan speaking."

"I thought you'd taken your camel and hit the road."

Stunned, I bolt upright and start flapping my hands for the entire arena to be quiet. "We did. We're in glorious Munich."

"Ah, Munich," Finn says longingly. "I bet you can't tell what's the camel —"

"And what's the hops? Yep. I have just been informed by everyone in my — meeting — that the wind has shifted."

"Oh, man, sorry."

"Yeah, who knew?"

"So, what're you doing in Munich?"

I mentally pull up half-developed slides of half-baked funnies. "Working," I finally say, deciding to go for not-funny-not-trying-to-be over trying-and-failing.

He gallantly waits for a punchline that's not coming. "Look," he says, "I know we skipped a few steps —"

"With the peeing?" I ask.

"I was thinking with the sex. But would you like to have dinner?"

"In Munich?" I balk. "No — I mean, not just with you," I rush to clarify. "I think with anyone. Eating's pretty much out at this point."

He laughs. "How about not in Munich?"

"How not in Munich are we talking? I won't be back in L.A. for another few months." Assuming I'm not fired, in which case I'm never back in L.A.

"I'm in Paris," he says.

"Wow. For how long?" I ask, trying not to sound like I'm booking a ticket with my feet. "I'll be there in two weeks."

"Shit. I'll be in L.A. by then."

"Oh," I say, wanting to pour myself through the phone and all over him.

"I'm going to Italy Friday," he throws out. "Maybe I could get a few hours off, meet up in Munich?"

I sit so far forward that I slip off the edge of the seat and catch myself with my elbow. "By Friday, I'll be in Milan. Close?"

"I can stop off on my way to Rome."

"I'll be in Rome Saturday!" I scream. Get. A. Grip.

"Well, then, it's a date, Miss Logan." The dress is getting burned. That is officially now my good luck underwear. "We can compare hotels —"

"Smells," I toss off.

"International smells," he counters.

"I'll text you my details."

"Five-seven-ish, natural brunette, a 34C if I had to take a guess."

"I was thinking more like Hotel de Russie,

152

three AM arrival."

"Wow, that's some S&M outfit you work for," he marvels.

"What do you mean?"

"Well, they're putting you up at the best hotel, but your hours suck."

I sigh at his observation. "Oh, Finn." I let myself say his name. "Buy a girl a gelato, and you'll hear all about it. *Ciao*." Then I force myself to hang up while I'm on alluring ground. I throw the phone down and, squealing, kick the floor with my heels. Kelsey lets go of the pole she's been dancing with. "The guy?" she calls.

I nod.

She releases her metal partner and runs to fling herself into my lap. "Logan has a boyfriend!" she shouts loud enough that the guys sweeping the stadium entrance will be able to tell their wives tonight.

"A date," I correct her.

"Logan has a date!"

Then my phone vibrates. A text. From Michelle.

"NOT a communication glitch."

I blink at the frescoed ceiling, the Frette sheets of Finn's hotel room pulled up to my armpits as the sun slips between the drapes. Finn finishes emptying the water bottle on

153

his nightstand and rolls back to me, flopping his right arm over my waist and tucking his face into my neck.

Is this a date?

For seventy-two hours, Kelsey threw herself into planning this encounter with the anxious fervor her parents bring to — everything. Between interviews she's now fielding solo, she offered outfit and activity suggestions, pausing every so often to ask, only half-jokingly, if I'll leave her if I get married. Meanwhile, I've been too busy to put more effort into this than simply getting Finn and me in the same location.

I finally went, at Kelsey's impassioned insistence, with her pink Chanel dress and matching bouclé coat. Dax and Binky, hardly oblivious to the magnitude of the Wades' absence and eager to participate in any activity that cheers Kelsey, gave up sleep to participate in my transformation.

So, two hours ago, when we met in the lobby for an early breakfast, because that was the only mutual window we could find, I thought it was a date. We even got as far as ordering eggs. Then he tossed his menu down on the little black marble table, said, "They have room service," took my hand, and led me to the elevator with what I would describe as a *Brokeback* level of

154

urgency. Some of Kelsey's Chanel may actually still be in the hall.

"*Now* let's order food," he says, kissing my collarbone.

He gets up and walks his insanely cute — I am turning the corner on cute; I am making peace with symmetrical and twinkly — nakedness across the room to get the menu. He brings it with a bottle of water for me and starts perusing the offerings.

"What time do you have to report?" he asks as I sit up and bring my knees to my chest.

"Eleven." Kelsey and I have decided, in addition to refocusing interviews from the costumes to her vocal capabilities, to cancel group breakfasts to improve her sleep-to-talk ratio.

He glances at the bedside clock. "We have time. They're very fast here. You still want the truffled eggs?" he asks, perusing the engraved menu.

Well, yes. But . . . I glance at the ravaged sheets.

"Logan?" He looks up.

"I wore a dress," I say, fully inhabiting the vagueness that is my birthright.

"A great dress."

"And I sort of saw myself, you know, a little more Audrey Hepburn, a little less

Cicciolina. Maybe wearing it —"

"In public," he says, slapping the menu shut. "Let's go have a date."

"Is that okay?"

"We're in Rome!"

"Right?"

Inside of twenty minutes, we're huddled on the Spanish Steps eating panini and drinking steaming espresso. I have lost Binky's makeup job and Dax's ponytail, but I've gained a memory to savor in my rocking-chair days.

"I want to see you again," he says as my iPhone chimes the cue for my departure. But then I remind myself: Peonies. In January. Thirty of them.

"Maybe in a few months —"

"Are you sure you can't get out of your client thing?" he asks, and I reluctantly shake my head, knowing that Kelsey needs me close as each hour goes by, each text unanswered. "Okay, here's the thing. I have an extra ticket tonight to Kelsey Wade." He hedges as if he's having a philanthropical crisis.

"Oh?" I stall, debating if this is the moment, if this is the guy I tell.

"Yeah, she's here on tour. We're doing the

backstage thing before the show, the whole bit."

" 'We,' as in the perfume execs, the hooker buyers?"

"No, my direct boss, actually." He fusses with the toggle of his down jacket. "You should come."

"Oh, I wish I could. I bet it'll be *awesome*." I stand, brushing off the pink coat. "Thank you for a great date."

He steps down one stair so we're nose to nose and smiles, wrapping his arms around my waist. "I've never had anyone decline an offer for seriously cool, seriously free stuff before."

I take his face in my hands and give him one last deep kiss. "Finn, if you haven't figured out that I'm not just anyone yet, I'm going to have to work harder." And with that, I turn and scamper down the steps, like Cinderella, like Kelsey in her perfume ad, like a girl being watched, longingly, from above.

"This is not a dress," I inform Kelsey with consternation. "This is a top." I take in my reflection, where the gold knit grazes my upper thighs. She insisted that we bring her suitcase to the stadium so that she can "dress me like a freakin' girl" for my pend-

157

ing surprise reveal, but this tunic needs —
"Pants. I'm sorry, Kelsey, but in the real world, this requires pants."

"Then throw on some fishnets!" she says with exasperation, almost upending Jen as she grips Kelsey's drying acrylics. "Sorry, Jen." Kelsey frowns at her. "We're just so damn close to a masterpiece of hotness here."

"Okay, I'm just going to come out and say it, Kel. Fishnets —" I bow my head with solemnity. "Are not a neutral."

"Sacrilege." Dax gasps as Binky throws her hand to her mouth in horror. "Someone call the pope!"

"Okay, now you're just being mean." Kelsey pouts. "You have such long legs — you should show them. You look hot."

I pull the fabric up from where it slouches suggestively off my shoulders. "How can I *possibly* make it seem like I just threw *this* on to run you through the bowels of the stadium and gesticulate with a million Italian dignitaries? This says, in addition to 'slip some money in my thong,' you know, 'trying.' "

"This says Hollywood, bitch!" Kelsey snaps in front of her chest. Her phone lights up, and she lunges for it. We are all suddenly silent, stomachs held. Seeing it's neither of her parents, her shoulders slump, the corner of her eye waters.

"Kel?" I say.

Her face pops up to us. "And you're not supposed to wear it with panties."

"No panties, no lines," the room recites in unison, quickly moving us on.

I look questioningly to Kelsey, and she minutely shakes her head, her eyes asking me just to keep us all focused on my make-over. "I can't believe I came down here in yoga pants." I look up at the clock to see if there's time to make it across the miles-long parking lot to the bus before the VIP meet-and-greet.

"Do it with K's black jeggings," Binky suggests. "And Dax can give you beachy waves."

"Love," Dax confirms, tapping the air in my direction with his hair tongs like Glinda.

"With the patent platforms!" Kelsey claps, keeping her fingers spread as they dry.

"Still too much." My eyes zero in on Jen's gray suede bootie heels. "What size are you?"

"Eight and a half, and with that outfit, to quote Rachel Zoe, major." Jen sticks her foot out to me without pausing in her buffing of Kelsey's pinkie toe. There is a moment of silence while we collectively picture.

"Fine," Kelsey concedes. "But I'm doing your makeup."

Thus it is through the Kelsified reddest of lips that I inhale a steadying breath and, with my binder clenched by team-dried red nails, turn into the VIP room of the Stadio Olimpico. I nervously make my way through the clusters of leather-clad Italian celebrities with their unperturbed air of "yeah, you're looking at me." Scanning the crowd, I'm unable to spot Finn but am surprised to catch sight of Kelsey's genuine listening face. I arrive at the broad back of the blond guy engaging her, a Prada parka tied around his waist as if she's a campfire from which he had to cool off.

"Logan!" Kelsey pulls me to her. "This is Travis. Travis, this is my cousin, and she's a born and bred Okie, too." Travis Moynihan turns with his trademark toothy grin, his blue eyes twinkling, a leather necklace taut around his chiseled neck.

"I'm her assistant — also," I stammer.

"No way!" He high-fives me, and I slap what looks like a catcher's mitt. He's so . . . meaty and . . . manly that I immediately understand why every A-list actress of the last decade has been paired with him for ninety pratfall-filled minutes, realizing he's the love of their lives. The color in Kelsey's cheeks indicates she's trying on a similar time frame.

"Way." She giggles.

"Bet y'all are missing some barbecue right about now." He winks at Kelsey, and she drops her head back.

"Ugh, yes!"

"Well, we have to get you a fix! I know a killer place."

"Except." Kelsey pouts sweetly. "I kind of have a show to do."

"What a co-in-ky-dink. I kinda got one to watch." I look from one tan to the other in this charisma-off and then scan the rest of the room. What the hell, was he lying? "Finn! Dude! Come on over!" I jerk my face around just as Finn turns from the bar, parting a path toward us with two glasses aloft. Kelsey mouths an "O.M.G." at me before two tween girls accost her. Awash in adrenaline, I duck while Travis reaches over me to take his glass. "Finn, meet some hometown girls! This is my assistant, Finn Harris." Touché. "This is Kelsey Wade's assistant, Logan from Oklahoma."

"Hi." I smile as Travis guzzles his drink. "Glad you could make it." Travis's ice clinks into his teeth, and he wipes his upper lip before patting a dumbstruck Finn.

"We've uh . . . yeah, we've met."

I check the time. "I have to take her backstage. Kel?" I loop my hand through her arm, and she apologizes to the girls.

"Where were we?" she asks Travis.

"Steak! We're getting you a real steak before you waste away."

"Awesome. We'll meet you after the show. Just give Logan the details."

"Except after the show, we are . . ." I try to communicate telepathically *getting on a bus for Barcelona.*

"Catching a plane to Barcelona, but that's not for a few hours, right, Lo?"

"Then we are co-pa-se-tic." Travis mambos his torso along with the syllables. "Finn, give her the address for Paolo's."

"Um." Finn, catches up. "We can take you, actually," he says. "After the show, if that, uh, works for you."

"Sure." I shrug. "We just need a second car for our security detail. Now, can I get Marco to refresh your drinks?"

"Oh, I'm just water. High on life." Travis rocks on the heels of his boots.

"We're all set." Finn says to me.

"Good," I return.

"Good."

"Great!" Travis rubs his hands, and I pivot Kelsey to the exit.

■ ■ ■ ■

"That was Finn!" Kelsey says for the eight-millionth time or, rather, sings it in a scale, as she gallops behind me holding her tutu.

"That was Finn," I echo as we arrive backstage.

"So cute!" She glides up to her waiting dancers, and we all take hands and drop heads. "Dear God, we thank you for this opportunity to use the gifts you have bestowed on us. Please bless us with your grace to do an awesome show and to perform safely. To bring it to the kind folks of Rome and, most of all, to get Logan, here, laid. Amen!"

"Kel," I moan.

"Amen!" Everyone gives me a thumbs-up and heads to the starting position.

"Not cool," I admonish with beating cheeks as we walk to the rigging.

"What? If we want our babies to be playing together on our back porches while Travis and Finn man the barbecues, there's no harm in asking for a little extra attention from the Almighty. Come on, this is too perfect. Get excited, that's an order." She hands off her necklace, then I hold out my palm, and she spits her lozenge into it, before grabbing her tutu and lifting a heel to the rail. She drops her head back, and I place a symbolic peck on her forehead.

"That was the most amazing five minutes of my dating life, and I don't want to push my luck. Besides, I notice you neglected to ask for His blessing on *your* getting laid tonight."

"Do you remember the movie where Travis was all sweaty, the serious one where he was the lawyer and everyone was all sweaty?" She dangles by one arm.

"The Grisham one?"

"I intend to catch a few droplets of my own tonight."

"Oh, Kelkel!" I intone Michelle. "That's just why all the girls look up to you."

"Bite me." She laughs, and the crew guy extends his arm at the dimming lights.

"I'll leave that to Travis." I smack her fishnetted tush as it passes.

It turns out that Paolo is *the* Paolo of the Michelin-starred Paolo's, and the address Finn gives me is for Paolo's apartment, where Paolo will be personally cooking for the four of us. I send the buses on ahead and arrange for a crack-of-dawn eight-seater charter flight to Spain for Kelsey and me. Which means she *really* wants this date. The

164

last note is still hovering in the air when she strips off her costume, baby-wipes herself down, and pulls on a micro-tube dress, sans jeggings, of course.

When Travis swaggers into the dressing room to spin Kelsey to him, she visibly swoons — until her eyes pop as her face makes contact with his infamous chest or, rather, his black shirt which has a darkened V beneath his neck, because, "Man! I danced my ass off, I tell you what!"

"What do I do?" she asks as she tugs me into the bathroom to finish lacing up her heels on the toilet seat.

"About?" I reapply the red lipstick and check my teeth in prep to see Finn, who's getting the car.

"About how bad he smells. Logan, oh, my God." She grabs me by the shoulders to stress the severity. "You have to tell Finn that Travis's deodorant timed out."

"How can I say that?"

"Finn's his assistant. It's his job. If I smelled like that — if I smelled like a one on the scale of a million that is that smell, I would want you to tell me. Strike that, I would want you to shoot me."

I promise I will try, and once we're all packed into the limo, it's impossible to imagine that Finn — hell, it's impossible to

165

imagine the northern coast of Africa — could not be eye-wateringly aware of it. But the thing is, Finn is enraptured.

I know it's hyperbole, but he is. And it's a shame that the experience of someone so ridiculously cute being enraptured with me had to come with one of my senses under such assault, but after so many years of trying so valiantly to hold the attention of idiots, only to lose it when they had something vital to do, like sneeze, this is heady stuff.

As we all hang around the refectory table that makes up the center of Paolo's kitchen, Kelsey runs her finger around her untouched wine glass, while Travis "loves hard" on the tender steak, the bowl of cheesy pasta, the delicately fried zucchini, and finally, the ricotta cake that is being plated up. Finn's fingers have found my thigh and made me increasingly regret straying from Kelsey's original vision for this dress.

"Sorry, which way to the ladies'?" I ask when an opening presents itself in Travis's love as he audibly masticates the cake.

"Oh, I'll show you." Finn hops up before the question is fully out and points down the adjoining hall.

"Thanks," I say lightly, walking ahead.

Within a second, he is at my side, pulling me into a darkened bedroom and swinging me around against the door as it shuts. "Finn —"

He firmly shifts my head to the side, and I gasp as his warm lips descend on my neck, his other hand gripping my ass to lift my leg around his waist. "Finn."

"Logan," he murmurs.

"Logan?" I hear Kelsey on the other side of the door.

"One sec!" I call, pushing him back against every instinct. He runs his hand over his hair and blows out a steadying stream of air to the floor.

"Holy shit, you surprise me," he says.

"Good." I smile.

"That's one hell of a camel," he whispers at the door.

"Speaking of which, yours needs a new Speed Stick." I adjust my tunic. "Badly."

"Oh, that, yeah. He doesn't believe in deodorant."

"I wasn't aware it required faith."

"Logan," Kelsey says plaintively, and I can picture her crossing her arms.

"Sorry, coming." I open the door.

"Travis wants to show us some fountain." Kelsey's eyebrow lifts as Finn appears behind me.

"Oh, Trevi, he loves that thing." Finn clears his throat.

"Yeah, he loves a lot of things," Kelsey mutters as she walks around us and closes the bathroom door.

But Cupid might be making a last-minute comeback when one of Travis's enthusiastic gestures leads him to upend his double espresso on his shirt and Finn reaches into his messenger bag for a fresh one. I look forward to comparing bags with Finn. Where mine is filled with lingerie tape, clear polish, spare fishnets, and a large Versace scarf that can pinch-hit as a shirt or skirt, Finn seems to dig through half a Home Depot circular before pulling out the Mylar-wrapped package.

As we speed though the quiet streets, Travis's attention now has nowhere to go but Kelsey, who is perking up from his refreshed presence. Obviously generating his own heat, Travis leaves his parka in the car, as does Kelsey in favor of modeling a standing view of her dress. Finn and I, however, zip up to our chins.

Walking across the darkened plaza, she turns back to smile at me as we both take in the winged stone horses scrambling up Neptune's feet. "Oh, Lo," she murmurs, and I realize that it's the first chance on tour that we've been able to see something of a city that's not obstructed by a camera. Travis runs past Finn and me strolling hand-in-hand to swoop up Kelsey in his arms. She kicks with delight as he carries her down to the fountain's glowing edge, and Finn pulls me back for a kiss.

"So, how did you end up here?" he asks, letting our hands drop.

"How did you?" I volley back reflexively.

"I landed a grunt-level job at Warner Brothers out of film school and got assigned to be Travis's on-set guy. We hit it off, and he asked me to run his development company."

"Oh, sorry," I say, embarrassed. "I thought you were just an assistant like me." I try to put it together. The girls in Kelsey's office aren't here carrying her spare hose.

"Nah, I'm reading scripts. He's really hungry to branch out. So, did you guys go to high school together?"

I raise an eyebrow. "Did Travis go to high school?"

"Point taken."

"Finn."

"What?"

I study him, not sure if he's teasing me. "Our dads are brothers." He looks totally blown away for the second time this evening, but not in a good way. "You didn't notice the last name?" I ask. "The dare-I-say-it resemblance? You know, if I had a team?"

He shakes his head. "My mom's from Minnesota, same tiny town as Jessica Lange. Everyone looks like Jessica Lange. I thought maybe you were, like, the hot Wades from Wadesville." He steps back, taking me in afresh.

"What?" I ask.

"I thought you were just an assistant like me," he parrots, his voice tinged with a slight edge. "But you're not 'just.' "

"I am —"

"I can be fired tomorrow, and he won't remember me in two days, but you, you're family. You've got security. You'll always —" We both turn at the sound of a splash.

We run as Kelsy flails in the fountain where Travis dropped her. He gleefully vaults the low stone ledge, then dolphins under the water. He whoops up to the inky sky, his voice echoing off the square. Kelsey struggles in her heels to get hold of the ledge. Then an engine guns and a flash goes off from a side street. Travis throws open his arms and grins as a string of paparazzi scooters figure-eight around the fountain.

Kelsey scrambles out while I hold my hand up against the blinding strobe.

"Finn!" Travis yells, and my date leaves us in the fray without a second glance. "To the Colosseum! We need to howl at the moon!"

GM is suddenly at our side, running interference with the charging bikes while getting us to the car. He throws Kelsey inside.

"The airport," he instructs the driver, who screeches through the labyrinth of narrow streets, a dogged scooter still behind us. "Get her seatbelt on." GM calls ahead to security. "Next time, I'm strolling with you. I don't care how much of America's Sweetheart the guy is."

"Kelsey, oh, my God, I'm so sorry." The car swerves and we strap ourselves in with shaking hands. "Can you please turn up the heat, sir?" I ask the driver. "And GM, could we borrow your sweatshirt?"

He tugs off his coat and lifts it back. "Give her this, it's warmer."

I wrap the heavy leather around her shivering shoulders, hugging her tight. Her face collapses in tears. "I'm so sorry. What a freak," I say. She shakes her head, her wet hair cold on my neck. "As soon as we get to the plane, we're going to wrap you like a mummy in blankets and order you a hot chocolate. You have so earned a hot chocolate."

"Finn seems really nice." Her teeth chattering, she wipes her hand under her nose as she pulls away.

"He wasn't exactly a prince just now, so I'm not sure what that means."

She stares out the window at the lit ruins, tears rolling down her cheeks. "You guys seemed pretty into each other."

"Kel."

"I just miss it, that feeling of being matched. I put so much out, and I just get . . . nothing." She drops her head back. "I mean, I know I get everything, I know. I'm not complaining, I'm not. But really, really, it's nothing, you know?"

"Yes."

"Where are my parents, Logan?" She turns to me.

"I don't know."

We ride in silence for another mile. "He wanted me to feel how amazing it is."

"What?"

"The life he's so high on, I guess." She sighs. "It's just been so boring, and then he wandered into the room, and my parents weren't there to freak out that we weren't getting on the bus, and —"

"This is ridiculous."

"What?"

"You are one of the most sexy, accomplished women in the world." We swerve and she knocks into me as the scooters gain on us.

"So —"

"So you don't need to be waiting for some guy to wander into a room. We're acting like you're me sitting in my crap apartment in my crap life waiting for a crap text. This is like the president complaining he wants something to eat. What do you want to eat, Kelsey?"

"What the hell are you talking about?"

"If any woman can make a booty call, Kelsey Wade" — I slap her clutch into her lap — "it's you."

CHAPTER SIX

"Bienvenido a Barcelona." This time two days ago, I was full of panini and trying on a gold dress/shirt. Now I'm in yet another country, navigating yet another language, back to the airport to ferry Kelsey's transatlantic booty call directly to the stage door. Because, after exhaustive supposition, it was decided not to depend on her driver, Diego, for the full report of "exactly" what Aaron seems like when he arrives or, more precisely, "really, really how he seems, like, if he's happy or put out or psyched or what."

The luggage carousel spins in hypnotic loops as I shift my weight, adjusting my stance in the middle of waiting family, friends, and drivers. Being none of the above, I stare attentively at the steady trickle of arriving passengers. Information filters through the airport speakers and then through some reactivated seventh-grade section of my brain that is annoyingly compelled to translate but ill equipped to identify. *Please . . . take* — no. *Take back* — no. *Give* — no. *El carrito? De equipaje.* Baggage? Baggage. *Salidas* — stop. I have to stop. This does not matter. I'm not getting on or off a plane.

I focus on the bubble-gum-and-banana-colored cover of a magazine protruding from the bag of a woman in front of me until it registers that I'm looking at a photo of my own gold arm clenched around Kelsey's dripping shoulder. *Oh, my God.*

"Sorry, um, *por favor,* may I look?" I tap the woman, and she spins around. I point to the magazine. Her hand protectively clenches her bag. "No! Oh, no, not your bag. Just the magazine." I put my hands together and peel them open, pantomiming a book. "Just to see for a second?" I point to my sunglasses, then back at the magazine, then at my watch. She hands it off and then beetles away to wait unaccosted.

Tucking Aaron's sign under my arm, I hastily unbend the cover to see Kelsey, her wet dress flash-bulbed transparent, and the headline says something about Eric, about her being made . . . *wild* . . . with something . . . *celos.* Sorry? *Celos . . . jealousy?* Jealousy of Eric.

And no mention of Travis. So she just

175

leaped in of her own accord like a crazy person?

I frantically flip the glossy pictures of celebrities mid-stride on beaches, parking lots, and the occasional red carpet. And there's Travis with his hair slicked back, his wet shirt clinging. The shot is cropped so he's laughing, with the fountain in the background, not up to his knees. His chiseled pecs make the looming Neptune's look girly. It's one photo of many capturing Travis's European jaunt, which features an inordinate amount of shirtless jogging, you know, for March. The collective impression is of a carefree bachelor enjoying the sites. *How?* How is the story not, smelly nutball let loose on unsuspecting pop star and four-hundred-year-old monument?

I call Finn.

"Logan Wade," he answers.

"Hi."

"Sorry, let me just find a quiet spot . . . Okay. So, hi! You made it to Spain."

"Barely," I say.

"Travis loves that fountain."

"You knew he was going to do that?"

"If I'd've known, I'd've brought along a towel and a flu shot," he offers as if that's that. "I'm glad you called."

"But you're going to have his publicist tell

people he dumped Kelsey in there, right? That she wasn't crazed or something."

"What?"

"You're going to fix this. I mean, you kind of have to, Finn."

"You're serious," he says uncertainly. "That's . . . not really how it's done. The news cycle turns on the hour, Logan. I'm sorry, but —"

"Great." I allow my annoyance to surge through the phone as I catch sight of Aaron parting the waiting clusters with his out-stretched duffle. "Whatever. I have to go."

"Logan —"

"No. I get it, Finn. Thanks for your words of industry wisdom." I hang up, and Aaron's eyebrows rise in recognition as I lift my sign. "Aaron, hi, I'm —"

"Kelsey's cousin from the club. I remember. What's up?" he greets me as he tugs his hood off. He's shaved his head since we met in L.A., but his allure is undiminished by having flown so far so fast. "No need for a sign." He tugs his ear buds out.

"Oh! Well, it was a while ago that we — we weren't sure if — Okay!" I quickly fold it. "Welcome to Barcelona!"

"Thanks." He grins. "You didn't have to . . ." He nods at Diego, who insistently takes his Adidas duffle. "Thanks, man."

177

"I don't have a car here. Of course, I don't. But this was the only way to pick you up." He purses his lips, the fact that I've been assigned to tail him that obvious.

"I appreciate it, but I could've taken a cab or the Metro." He slips his hands into the pockets of his coat as we walk. "I mean, that would've been fine. I wasn't expecting —"

"I was running around anyway, so it's not a big deal," I say, as if I was picking up one of the crew. Who would have taken a cab or the Metro.

"Well, thanks," he says. "It's cool of you. You guys having a good time?" Diego hurriedly beats us to the car and opens the trunk. Aaron continues his steady gait, with its touch of Terrance-like performance swagger.

"Yes, thanks. It's cold here, right?" I say, opening the front passenger door of the Mercedes for myself. "You hear 'Barcelona,' and you think espadrilles and linen, but it's so not that." I huddle in my down puffer.

Aaron folds himself in behind me.

"Oh, I should come back there. Keep you company." I twist in my seat.

"Nah, I'm good." He clicks his seatbelt and pulls at his jeans. I shift my chair forward off his knees. "Ah, thanks."

"Sure!" We smile stupidly at each other.

"So, you're managing?" he asks.

"I am." I let out a breath. "I mean, the schedule is like some sixties psych experiment to induce mania, but yeah, I'm hanging in there, thanks."

He cracks up, his blue eyes twinkling. "I meant the tour, but good to know."

"Oh." I smile sheepishly. "That."

"This shit can be tiring." He gives my shoulder a good-natured pat.

"Thanks," I say, disarmed.

"I'm guessing you don't mind if I?" He lifts his ear buds.

"Not at all."

He drops his head back on the seat as Diego starts the car and I peek in my side-view mirror to gather adjectives for my report. Aaron's eyes meet mine, and then he stares out his window, his gaze at a studious half-mast. I watch the Gaudi buildings pass as I gird myself to be fired.

"You put him in the best section?" Kelsey gleefully inquires as she all but pirouettes to the base of the rigging.

"Check." I hand her the tutu.

"And he seems psyched?"

"Like I said, he's kind of a cool customer, but yes, I think he is."

"Okay, Michelle." She rolls her eyes.

179

"Cool customer."

"I'm saying, for someone who was flown in overnight to, what did you call it?"

"Catch up." She giggles.

"Right. I'm just saying he's infinitely more under control than I would be if I was waiting in a VIP seat to 'catch up' with Bono."

"Ew, Logan, gross. He's old enough to be our dad."

"But did you see how excited he was to play the inauguration?" I pat my sternum. "It touched me deep."

"Nerd." The house lights dim.

"Kel, real quick, I just wanted you to know I called Finn and told him Travis needs to fix this."

"No, he doesn't," she protests.

"Everyone thinks you jumped in!"

She snorts. "It doesn't matter — they make shit up every week. Nobody cares." She tilts her forehead back for me to kiss before ascending to commence the world's most overattended foreplay.

Feeling burgeoning pangs of mortification, I retreat to the dressing room to set up camp in Kelsey's makeup chair.

My mailbox has filled since I tucked my phone away an hour ago. I roll my neck and dig in, reminding myself that in one month as Kelsey's assistant, with my sole overhead being a single box of tampons and five packs of gum, I've almost paid off my MBA student loans. Okay, here goes . . . three messages from her deliriously excited publicist, two from Kelsey's over-the-moon manager, one from her licensing agent, one from the senior VP of marketing at Maybelline wanting me to convey her adoration directly. One from the senior VP of marketing at L'Oréal wanting me to convey *her* adoration directly. One from pretty much every company that makes a waterproof mascara in search of celebrity endorsement for which they are "already seeing a fountain spread, it's going to be killer/fantastic/ gorgeous!"

Okay, upside: the worst fuckup on my watch may result in an endorsement. And downside: replying to any of these messages requires authorization from the two people who are still MIA. Oh, and I made a total fool of myself.

A roar above signifies a stadium of fans pointlessly trying to entice a third curtain call. None choreographed, none coming.

A man and a woman dressed identically in fitted hot-pink Kelsey T-shirts walk in.

"Hello?" I say, unsure why they're here.

181

"Can I help you?"

They raise the badges. "We're Garcia and Garcia!" they announce. "We make building designs. We love Kelsey!"

I stick my head out to GM. "What's going on?" I ask as the line of people proceeds inside, instead of being escorted by security one at a time.

"Kelsey's orders," he says. "She wanted a crowd."

The local notables mingle around the makeup table, waiting to congratulate her. Aaron arrives, scanning the room. He forgoes the couch and armchairs to take an unassuming metal folding seat against the back wall.

After a good twenty minutes people are getting restless to the point of annoyed. But as I turn, there she is in the doorway in the lace-up leather pants and bra from the finale, freshened so she looks as if she's ready to start the show. Everyone claps, and she smiles graciously, but her gaze, that of the rebel doll, is locked on Aaron. For once, the sensuous dominance that infuses her onstage persona has not melted as she steps off.

"Hey." She tugs off her earrings as she struts through the parting crowd to her chair. "Glad you could make it," she says to him.

"Great show." He lifts his arms over the back of his seat and settles into an open slouch.

"Thanks." She langorously stretches to unzip her boots.

"Kel," I interrupt before he lunges to unlace her pants. "If I could just introduce you to some of your guests?"

She rolls up, flipping her hair over her bare back before turning a melting grin to her fans. "Where are my manners?" She hops down, switching energies with an alacrity that recalls our basement dress-up days, where the doffing of Michelle's black scarf would transform Kelsey from the Queen to Snow White in a breath. "Thank you all so much for coming! Did you have fun?" she leans in to ask Pedro Almódovar.

Aaron's eyes follow as she charms them all, his hand resting on the plastic Aquarel bottle between his jittery legs. I pack up my bag, feeling an acute pang of jealousy at the palpable anticipation between them. I pray that the seemingly endless learning curve of this job hasn't cost me my chance at that.

The next few days feel different from the usual blur of load-ins, load-outs, interviews, and appearances. While I phrase and re-phrase and translate into Spanish an apology to Finn, Kelsey has stopped asking if I've heard from her parents. And I find her grinning to herself. I would be too, if I were having mad, hot, passionate everything, everywhere. Cheeks flushed, pupils dilated, she all but gives off a shock if you shuffle past her. Needless to say, Binky and Dax are on permanent standby to freshen gloss and flatten hair. I, meanwhile, am having mad, hot, passionate with my binder, and it's frankly not bringing it the way I need it to be brung.

In the freed time that Kelsey's distraction has rewarded me, I indulgingly replay the beats of my Rome date with Finn as if it will reveal the secret to a wrinkle-free life. This loop becomes particularly unsparing at about three AM, after I've gotten everyone settled for the night. With Aaron taking over drawing Kelsey's bath so he can join her in it, I'm in bed minutes sooner. Where, acutely conscious of the pressure to use these few hours to recharge, I twist in the ironed linens.

Somewhere along the Riviera my phone buzzes on the night table with an 800 number.

"Hello?"

"There she is."

"Andy?" I sit up.

"Alrighty, that's all of us," he says.

"Sorry?" I turn on the lamp. "We've been hoping you'd —"

"Logan's on the line." Michelle cuts me off. "Now all three of us are here, so yes, please go right on ahead."

"Isn't Kelsey joining?" I recognize the gruff voice of Kelsey's agent.

"Oh, no. We're letting her sleep," Michelle says. "Logan'll fill Kel in, won't you, Lo."

"Sure?" *What?*

"Y'all go ahead," Andy says. "Logan'll take notes for us."

A woman starts to talk with a thick French accent, telling a *fantastique* story about a *fantastique* mascara commercial and its *fantastique* filming. I jump to the desk in search of a pen to scribble notes about booking time for sit-downs in Paris with the brand's executives, and, most important, how Kelsey cannot be seen in public using any brand other than this one or someone will be shot. Seriously. And this is why I am on this call.

"Great!" I hear Andy clap his all-done clap.

"Oh, this is just going to be wonderful, right, Logan?" Michelle gushes. "We're going to grab a good night's sleep on it, and we'll get back to you," she says as if I'm beside her on a couch.

"Sure, yes, of course." Where? Where's the couch?!

"Y'all have a good night, then," Michelle says.

"Night," Andy adds, along with an overlapping round of the same sentiment in a couple of other languages, and the line goes dead.

I sit heavily in the desk chair. What. The hell. I stay like this for a while, waiting for them to call back. Waiting for explanation, direction, context, contact. But nothing.

Hoping Dax and Duane are dragging out their postshow nightcap, I pull on my jeans and let myself into the darkened suite and then out to the hall, where the illumination of a hotel's public spaces in the early AM hours always gives me the oddly infantilizing sense that the parents are still awake.

In the grand lobby the massive circular Aubusson is being team-vacuumed by maids. But the bar has closed. Ugh. I don't really want to be out. I don't want to be alone.

Not that I begrudge Kelsey one second of what she's having with Aaron, but I do miss the nights before he came, when I'd hear her rattling around too post-show wired to sleep, and we'd curl up to co-narrate what-ever crappy movie was on demand, just like we once did with Michelle's soaps.

I press the heavy brass lever of the French doors to the veranda. The sea air feels as if I've stepped into a sheet of refrigerated aluminum foil. I weave the teetering bases of cinched umbrellas to the railing overlook-ing the surf — as if Finn might be waiting there among the pebbles. The icy wind permeates my jeans. I turn back, gripping my hair off my face as I take in the Belle Époque hotel.

I see the light to our top-floor suite go on and realize I forgot to draw the drapes. Kelsey walks into the living room in a T-shirt of Aaron's, coming up behind him with a bottle of Evian. Wearing only a towel, he takes a swig as she leans her face into his chest and he wraps his arms around her.

I slide my phone out of my back pocket and, not wanting to be tempered by the san-ity of the heated lobby, tuck next to the shuttered bar to block the wind.

"Yaaloo."

"Finn?"

"No, ma'am."

"Travis?"

"Yes."

"Is Finn there? This is, uh, Logan."

187

"Finn is here, but he is procuring me dos primo tacos s'il vous plait."

"Then I should hold?"

"The sun is so choice today. My man is standing in line at the best taqueria cart this side of the border. They cook the meat up in this trash can. Stew it for days. Ooo-eee! It's gonna be good. Tell me about where you are. Is this sun gracing your life?"

Oy. "Is it a long line?"

"It's all in how you look at it, señorita."

"Could you maybe give him a message for me?"

"Shoot."

Sensing that I can't risk the translation, I keep it succinct. "Tell him I said I'm an ass-hole."

"Got it."

"Do you maybe want to say it back to me?"

"You got to love yourself, Logan."

"Okay."

"You got to eat dos supremo tacos."

"Okay. Thanks. Enjoy the sun."

Photos of Kelsey embraced by Aaron in his towel hit TMZ before we've had our coffee. Shredding her cuticle, Kelsey stands over my shoulder at the suite's desk, looking at the shots of her hotel window, *our* hotel

188

window, on my laptop.

"It's so creepy," I say, angling the screen to cut down the glare. "I mean, I know I'm a neophyte, but it is, right?"

"It could've been some bellboy out for a smoke," Aaron says.

"These weren't taken with a smartphone. That's a serious telephoto lens." Kelsey shudders. "I don't know why I felt covered facing the ocean."

"Because it's off-season." I back her up. "And the town is closed up."

"Maybe we're dealing with the world's first paparazzi seagull?" Aaron suggests as Kelsey scrolls from TMZ to Perez to Pop-Sugar.

"I guess I have a boyfriend," she says tentatively.

"Yeah, you do!" Aaron tickles her, and she squeals. They fall over the back of the couch.

"Get a room," I say. "With a drawn curtain. Dax and Binky'll be up at three — we leave for Monaco at four."

"What *is* it?" Aaron puts away his book and takes the crystal award from Kelsey as she and I get back in the limo after the ceremony.

"It's the Monaco something." I hold up what looks like a fetus in a paperweight.

"The Princess Grace something. It's very prestigious." I hedge. "Jack Nicholson got one."

"We have no fucking idea." Kelsey cuts to it. "But I had to listen *and react to* speeches in French, and watch people dressed up like lamé cats dance to zen-flute covers of my songs." She drops against him as I check my phone, hoping my message didn't take the same route out of Travis as those truck tacos.

Aaron snuggles her close. "Sounds like you could use a chance to let loose."

An hour later, surrounded by dancers on the hallway floor, Aaron has dislodged the alien globe from its marble base and lined up empty bottles as pins for strip bowling. Kelsey's lost both earrings, both shoes, and is about to take her next turn in her bra.

"It's Perez Hilton's soul!" Duane calls out his latest guess as Kelsey stops laughing long enough to put down her beer and wind up. Everyone whoops as the bottles scatter, and when the elevator door opens, I'm glad we've fully booked the floors above and below.

"What the fuck?" I know Andy's voice without turning around.

Kelsey scrambles to throw on her shirt.

"We drove down from Paris as soon as we

saw those pictures of you and that boy. Do you have any idea what time it is?"

"Kelsey Anne, in the elevator!"

"Thanks, guys, for the awesome game," Kelsey says with a slight tremor. "I'm gonna turn in. Don't have too much fun without me." She swipes her shoes from the floor and walks past everyone, who instinctively stand with dropped heads, as if for inspection.

"Logan, you, too," Andy barks.

"Nice to meet you, sir." Aaron extends his hand to Andy as the door shuts.

"Daddy, Momma, this is Aaron Watts," Kelsey says.

Andy does not return the gesture.

Kelsey surreptitiously reaches out her pinkie finger and loops it with Aaron's. The same way she used to loop mine when we'd hear Andy's Chevy pull into the darkened driveway.

"First things first, we need to find you a room," Michelle says to Aaron as we get off at the top floor.

"Sure, ma'am," Aaron says. "I can leave now if that's —"

"No!" Kelsey rushes. "No, you don't have to leave — unless you want to?"

"I didn't mean — no." Aaron looks helplessly from Kelsey's stricken expression to

191

Andy's radiating ire.

"We have to take account for appearances," Michelle says to Andy. "She and Eric never shared a room."

Kelsey's stiffens. "Baby, would you go run my bath?"

"Nice to meet y'all."

"*What* are you doing?" Michelle hisses as their door shuts.

"He flew all the way out here to keep me company."

Andy snorts.

"What?" Kelsey says.

"Well, you're a very rich little girl."

"He *loves* me."

Andy rolls his eyes as if he can't even believe they're having this conversation. "Go to bed, we'll discuss this in the morning."

Her chest rises with a breath she can't release, and she slams the door behind her. Andy opens the one opposite, and Michelle gestures. "Logan?"

I reluctantly follow inside, where the small overnight bags sit, still unpacked. "Okay, give it to us straight," Michelle asks simply, sitting down on the bed.

"How did you let this happen?"

"They met back home," I answer him. "She flew him out. And he hasn't taken a

192

thing. Hasn't let her buy him a thing."

Andy snorts again.

"This is big, Logan," Michelle says. "Unless someone huge dies this week — and I hate to admit I've caught myself praying — those pics are the cover of every magazine stateside come Monday."

"We're just going on sale for our American dates," Andy adds emphatically, sitting.

"This'll seem like a rebound —"

"Create drama." Andy drops his elbows to his knees.

"It seems slutty."

"She sings about love every day," I say. "Her fans will be happy she's —"

"Love?" Michelle does a double take. "That girl doesn't know — Logan. She's not like you. She's never been out on her own. She's a creative spirit, that's her fortune, but you have to treat her . . . Kelsey has lived a *really* sheltered life. She doesn't know what things really cost. Or what her limits are. She wanted to eat pizza before her first dance recital. 'I can do it, Momma!' And there she was in the wings, puking it all up. She doesn't think like you or me. Look how these pictures got taken —"

"Because I didn't close the drapes."

"Because *she* didn't close the drapes. I know you know what I'm talking about."

I don't nod or shake my head.

"You've only been here for a few months — out of how many years. Are you an expert, can you say that?" She abruptly switches tacks.

I cringe . . . I'm not. "Okay, but you two left. And honestly, I don't really know why."

Michelle blinks. "The road is so hectic. We needed to catch our breath. We've had to be vigilant every single second since the breakup —"

"Since she stopped wearing her purity ring."

"To make sure she doesn't end up seeming — available." From the woman who beads her thongs. "So much more than you can wrap your head around, Logan — is riding on this. Every person on those buses depends on us to make good decisions for their livelihood to feed their families."

"I'm sorry," I say, because I sense that's required, but truly not sure for what. "What do you want me to do?" They search the other's face, and it seems the experts don't know, either. "I mean, he's here. She's working hard, hasn't missed a single commitment."

"We're gonna call Terrance," Michelle says, standing and swiping at the back of her slacks. "We're stuck with this for a bit anyhow — to make it seem legitimate. She can end it when we get back to the States. What time are we departing?"

"Six AM," I hear myself say. "Rolling straight to Paris for Kelsey's first interview at nine."

"With who?" Andy asks.

"Karl Lagerfeld in front of the tents for Fashion Week."

"Oh, that'll be a hoot — I've always wanted to meet him." Michelle brightens as she walks me out. "Okay, well, then let's get some sleep."

"If you left because of the room thing — I really don't care where I sleep. I was just trying to help Kelsey."

"Oh, honey." She touches the gumball-size emerald pendant Kelsey gave her for her fortieth. "Don't try to help so hard." The door swings shut.

The night of the mascara shoot, Kelsey, after keeping Wembley Stadium on the brink of hysteria for two hours, has asked for the first-ever five-minute deviation from the schedule so she can entertain Gwen Stefani in her dressing room.

Michelle paces the hall just outside. "Andy's waiting," she says to me again, her wool coat already buttoned. "London traffic is a nightmare."

"Her call time's not for another hour."

"A cosmetics endorsement makes her a classic."

"I know."

She pauses her gait. "Logan, please just go in and get her. She won't listen to me."

Taking a breath, I knock.

"How?" Kelsey is asking.

"What do you mean, how?" Gwen counters, pulling her tartan camisole away from her sweaty torso.

"I have press all day every day — every city."

"You're shitting me." Her red mouth hangs open. Kelsey shakes her head. "That's *crazy.* I do four days of press for the whole tour. What does your manager say?"

"He answers to my dad."

"Baby, you need more days off between shows."

"How do you do it?"

"Being Mommy comes first, and everyone else just has to deal."

Just then GM passes his cell phone over my head. "Kel, it's Andy. He sounds pissed."

And so kicked off our night — from pissed-off Andy to the lighting guy who is doing, in the director's estimation, a piss-poor job,

196

to the account executive running the shoot who is, since lunch, piss-drunk, to the rain, the pissing, pissing rain. Yet I remind myself, as I run from the all-night drug store in my sodden sneakers back to St. Paul's Cathedral, I am experiencing all of this from the privileged position of the ground. While overhead, a crane currently suspends Kelsey hundreds of heart-stopping feet above an ever-growing crowd.

The security guard nods me through to the nave, which has been transformed into a maze of can lights and wire spools. Passing Aaron, camped on one of the benches, hat down, iPod on, I dodge between the smoke machines to hand off the first-aid cotton to a crew guy. "On its way," I type.

"Dont want blood 2 show," Michelle texts back.

"Break!" the director's voice booms. On the monitors the crane moves Kelsey off-screen, presumably in to the hands of Michelle, who's been waiting to cushion the straps of the harness.

Andy walks alongside the unshaven director, who has propositioned me no fewer than four times. Um, what about my dirty hair, baggy sweater, and general scowl says I want to suck you off in the chapel? He is no longer acknowledging me. As he continues to his fancy canvas chair with the cup holder Andy leans into my ear. "Tell Michelle enough."

"Kelsey's bleeding —"

"Get Kel for me."

I dial Michelle. "Hi, I have Andy for Kelsey."

"Rambo, Kel." He listens. "They're waiting on you . . . no, but it's gonna cost them if we don't — okay, then. Good girl."

"Quiet on set!"

Everyone huddles around the monitors to watch as Kelsey is nauseatingly hoisted atop the ledge and pelted with water from the rain machine used between actual downpours. Her hands jerk to where the harness must be tightest.

"Dial down the rain!" the director shouts, and the rain softens from police hose to *Perfect Storm.* "Lesslessless!" It shifts to a mist. Kelsey blinks the water out of her eyes, gripping with white knuckles at her shoulders. "More! Less! Just rain! Just fuck-me-in-the-rain rain!"

"Still too heavy," Andy mutters.

"Mmm," I say, unsure how to weigh in on what the most sex-inducing degree of precipitation for his daughter is.

"There! And . . . action!"

I watch as she shakes her oiled waves out

of her unsmudged eyes, droplets snaking down her décolletage. With a seductive look, she reaches out her right hand to nobody. According to the synopsis, this nobody will be a "guy" and "hot" and have "white *Black Swan* wings" and be CGI'd in later. The storyboard depicts this angelic hottie compelling her to run through the streets and up all five hundred and twenty-eight steps, wearing five-inch heels and dragging a ten-foot pink beaded train that could challenge a double-decker bus in a weigh-in. But her eyelashes look ah-mazing!

"Killer Kelsey! She's killing it!" The director jumps up and cups the frayed rim of his baseball hat. "Got it!"

"He's got it!"

"Moving on! Next setup in fifteen!"

"Thanks, Logan." Andy exhales. "We're good for now."

I give him a thumbs-up and grab a stale croissant from the decimated tray. Ignoring the ubiquitous NO FOOD INSIDE signs, I surreptitiously pull my sleeve over my hand like when Kelsey and I used to sneak Pop-Tarts into the Cineplex.

"Logan!" Dax comes running toward me. "She's totally losing it." He leads me to the stairs, but doesn't follow, and it only takes a few steps to see why. The staircase quickly narrows into a spindle all of two feet wide, the tight curve obscuring what's coming and what's left behind, the effect dizzying. It feels as if I'm turning in on myself as I step up and up and up.

"Kelsey?" I call, my voice echoing against a labored gasping that I don't think is my own. I arrive at her train, flowing down the stairs like sparkling Pepto-Bismol.

I turn one more step to find her ashen in the windowless, airless, brightly lit space. I grip the railing and crouch down. "Kelsey?"

Her eyes are unfocused. "I can't — breathe in here — it's too — small —"

"She needs a break!" I yell up the stairs to no one as I grab her clammy hands.

I hear Andy's frustrated voice emitting from some walkie-talkie above us. "Kel, just fucking do like he told you. Now's not the time." Something in her eyes, in my fear, in his voice — a memory flashes through my brain like lightning bringing the day back for an instant. Kelsey clutches me in her Pocahontas nightgown. Then it's gone.

"Kelsey, baby," Michelle chimes in. "Everyone needs you to keep moving —"

"Get your shit together," Andy urges over the crackling static.

"We're depending on you." Michelle is fervent. "Strong, Kelsey —"

"Oh, God." Kelsey jerks her hands from mine, and I slap the stone wall for balance. "Tell them to stop. They have to stop."

We hear the sound of someone jogging up the steps. Aaron's face appears, tight with concern.

"Look, Kelsey, it's Aaron. Aaron's here." I press myself against the wall to make room. He gathers her in, sliding his palm reassuringly to the back of her neck.

"Kelsey?"

"Momma, stop," Kelsey pleads into his shirt, her voice breaking.

Afraid I might pass out, I maneuver past them to where the other crew members wait a few stairs above, stripped to the waist and fanning themselves.

"Okay, Kelse? We gonna shoot this thing?" the director asks as gamely as he had inquired about my interest in a reacharound. Aaron starts to move out of the way.

"Aaron!"

"Right here," he calls to her from just over the camera guy's shoulder. "Right here, baby," he says softly. "Right in my eyes."

"I have to — ask you . . ." Her voice shakes. He ducks his head under the camera to her question.

"Quiet on set!"

"Yes." Aaron's answer echoes around us.

■ ■ ■ ■

The last shot they need to get before sunup is Kelsey running through scattering pigeons toward the cathedral's front doors. Ostensibly rejuvenated by the open space and solid earth, Kelsey lifts her gown as if it's not the icy albatross it must surely feel like and dashes again and again and again, all her arm muscles defined.

MTV is filming this final section of filming and E TV, *Extra, Hollywood Insider,* and their European equivalents are filming MTV. In my sweat-soaked shirt, I'm chilled to my core and ready to be somewhere that is not here. Not inside here, not outside here, not just to the left of here. Not here. Andy pulls at the bridge of his nose, and Michelle rubs the forearms of his parka. I keep turning to Aaron because he repeatedly opens his mouth to say something but doesn't.

At long last, the shot is captured, and Kelsey is hustled to her trailer. Michelle steps inside just as the stylist begins cutting her out of the dress.

"Dax?" Michelle lifts Kelsey's waiting corset from its hanger and motions for him to start blowing out her hair.

He shakes his head. "She's going to have to rinse it with all that oil."

"We don't have time." As the last stitch is broken my hands go to my mouth at the sight of the scabbing gashes where the harness has sliced her.

"I'll take a two-minute shower." Kelsey shakes feeling into her swollen feet. Michelle doesn't move from in front of the bathroom door. "I can't feel anything."

"Then we're going to have to repancake that mess on your shoulders. Kelsey, are you listening to me?"

"Momma, everyone can wait a few more minutes, or do you want me to get pneumonia, too?" Binky rapidly smears Kelsey's face in cold cream, wiping the pink gloss off to reveal purple lips.

"Kelsey!" Michelle snaps. "We're all cold! We all need a shower! Daddy's getting a migraine. Now, just —" She thrusts the corset at her. *"Come on."* Binky looks away. The stylist, caught crouched down between them, gathers up the pounds of fabric.

"Okay, Momma," Kelsey says quietly.

"Thank you."

"Of course. I'll see you in the tent."

Minutes later, her hair topped with a feather headband to mask the oil, Kelsey hops onto the director's chair between two posters of mascara tubes. "Brrr, it's freezing, isn't it?" She grins at the cameras. Billy Bush gets a last dash of powder.

"Hey, Kelsey!"

"Hey, Billy!"

"So this is a pretty exciting commercial you've been shooting here at St. Paul's Cathedral."

"Oh, my God, I'm having a blast! So much fun. But there's another reason I can't stop smiling." She strikes a coquetteish pose.

"Oh, yeah, what's that?"

"Billy, I wanted you to be the very first to know."

"Yes?"

"I'm *engaged!*"

Andy and Michelle turn to Aaron — who looks as stunned as the rest of us.

PART III

CHAPTER SEVEN

"Can I get you another?" The Chichester bartender raises his chin to my empty champagne flute. I nod, mouth full from the late dinner I'm making of wasabi peas before I head upstairs to my room. The numbers on the door change, but this L.A. hotel has become my home-away-from-tour-away-from-home since my title was tacitly reclassified from Personal Assistant to Wedding Planner.

For the last three weeks, Kelsey's been as inflated as she used to be on the Sundays following a trophy win, when it was better to steer clear or spend the day playing Lady-in-Waiting to her Queen. She hadn't even washed that oil from her hair before she appointed me to oversee the festivities that everyone on the planet wants to discuss — with the minor exception of her parents. (Michelle's response included the phrase "fool's errand.") Andy, however, jumped at the idea of booting me off the American leg of the tour, because he clearly wants to dismiss someone from Kelsey's corner, and Aaron's nonnegotiable.

I take another mouthful of peas and look around the bar. From this vantage point of relentless comparison, I've come to find L.A. disorienting in its proportions, the women having paid more than I can comprehend to look like crude cartoon caricatures. I wipe my spicy fingers on a cocktail napkin as the producer holding "auditions" in the white leather wing-back returns with his stack of eight-by-tens. If tonight is typical, a stream of nervous beauties will swap out in thirty-minute intervals, their vulnerability palpable. I wonder what his method is. Does he do this on weeknights and then invite the ones who make the cut to his room on Saturdays? Or are "call-backs" at midnight on his penis? I keep forgetting to tell Kelsey about him. But then, given her (time) consuming passion for Aaron, our brief conversations have become limited to linens and flowers. Thinking of linens and flowers, I replay the voice mail from the other fiancé. "Hey, Logan, it's Lauren. Just calling to say thank you. Missed you this weekend." Each sentence comes in a discrete burst, making it sound as if she's distracted. "The hotel was sick. We were a little crammed in, but the view was amazing. Please thank Kelsey for the spa day. I was sorry we didn't get to see her — I thought there'd be tickets to her next New York show on the bed when we checked in or something. A backstage pass. Maybe you're saving that as a wedding present? Anyway, hope you're having fun. 'Bye."

"Who did your lips?"

"Excuse me?" I ask the guy who's just sidled up.

He is not tall. Even in his absurdly thick-soled shoes. He flashes his capped teeth. "They're choice."

"Oh, I — um, actually they're mine."

"You don't need to be coy. I'm a plastic surgeon." He lays down his panty-dropper. "Whatcha drinking?" he asks.

"Thanks, but I just ordered."

The bartender slides my glass in front of me and asks, "Do you want me to put that on your husband's tab?"

"Thank you," I reply pointedly.

"Oh, uh, sorry," the surgeon says. "You should wear a ring." He flips his card to me from his blazer pocket. "I can still get you a deal if you want to do something about your breasts."

I grab his arm. "This is a *backless* top.

And if they're not made of titanium, they're not supposed to sit under your chin." Yeah, don't think the peas are doing the trick.

I ask to see the bar menu.

"The deviled eggs are awesome," another male voice says in the vacated space, and I look up with back-off eyes but am met by height and chisel.

"Care to split an order?" I ask gamely to his choppy blond hair, his visibly broken nose. Screw the erstwhile Finn and his symmetry.

"Sounds great." The guy hops onto the stool like Fred Astaire. "Staying at the hotel or just love the scene?" he asks with a smile, leaning down to rest on his palm.

"Oh, yeah, I have a warm, cozy home just around the corner, but I can't get enough of watching Bill Maher ogle escorts."

"Escorts?" he asks, feigning shock. He swivels in their direction. "Are you sure?"

"See, in New York, if you saw a woman dressed like that, with that many rubber parts, you'd be, like, okay, clearly she's on Craigslist. But here, she could be a model, an aspiring actress, or even a housewife. It's confusing."

"Mark," he says, extending his hand.

"Logan."

"Sounds like you can't wait to go home."

"Yes, home, no, definitely." I should get one of those. "Actually, I'm just in town for meetings."

"What kind of meetings?" he asks as the eggs arrive.

"Event planning. Dumb stuff."

"Shut up." He playfully pushes my bicep. "That's what I do."

"Really?"

"Yeah, corporate event planning. I'm in town doing a big launch for a new desk chair."

I laugh.

"No, seriously. It swivels, it tilts, and it ejects you on the spot if it senses you're typing drunk."

"Genius. I need one of those." I help myself to another egg.

"So, who are you meeting with?" he asks.

"Oh, I can't remember, they all have the same names. At Your Service, Your Big Event, the Main Event," I riff. "You know."

"Can I ask you a personal question?" He leans in.

"That depends." I match him, so close to letting our lips meet, so close to just letting the off-kilter nose be enough.

"What are you drinking?" he asks with mock gravity, pulling away.

"Ginger champagne cocktail," I confess.

"On Cinco de Mayo?" he balks, flagging the bartender once again. "A Corona in honor of the holiday and another ginger champagne for my friend."

For the next hour, we don't talk so much as shuttle words back and forth like a loom while I wonder how many it'll take until we've woven a link from his mouth to mine. Until finally, spun out, I put my hand on his and just say, "Do you want to go upstairs?"

"Definitely." He pays, and I swing my heels to the floor.

"Whoa, there." He catches my elbow and then slides his arm around my waist.

"Oh, I'm just tired," I say as he helps me out of the bar, through the silver-leafed lobby. He presses the elevator button.

"Too tired?" he asks.

"Oh, no, not *too* tired, just tired." The door opens, and lest he misunderstand, I tug him inside. He pins me against the far wall and plants his mouth hard against mine. In the not-Finn-ness of it all, I pull away. But I still press nine, because if I get run over in the driveway by Bill Maher getting a blow job, I cannot let the last guy I had sex with be Finn. "It's so embarrassing." The car whirs up.

"Why?"

"I shouldn't be tired," I admonish myself. "I work alongside legitimately tired people."

"Any bride will tell you." He holds up his finger like the Tin Man. "Planning a wedding is tiring."

My buzz falls to the floor like a discarded towel.

"I never said wedding." I pull my scarf up my bare arms.

"Yes, you did."

"No, I didn't." To anyone. I'm pricing out a graduation, an anniversary, and a bar mitzvah. "Who do you work for? You have to tell me."

He just shrugs, his charm gone. The doors open on nine, and, staring him down, I press lobby. We descend, while I keep my hand above the emergency button.

"We're going to find out everything, and you want us to. Those pictures are currency, and if Kelsey didn't feel that way, she'd be bussing tables in Oklahoma City and singing karaoke."

The doors open, and I stride, shaking, to the concierge. I point to Mark, standing nonchalantly by the elevator. "You need to remove *that* man from *this* building." And God bless my credit card's billing address, because they do.

■ ■ ■ ■

An hour later, a knock forces me to get up from my paralyzed ball. "Room service."

I open the door to Finn holding two In-N-Out bags.

"Thank you," I say, so grateful that he answered my call, that he just asked for my location, not an explanation.

He takes one look at my tear-streaked face and wraps me in his arms. I allow myself to sink into the comfort of his embrace for a brief moment, before I take a bag from him. "I need to talk."

"So, talk."

"No, I mean, in the larger sense, like, dusk till dawn, I need to talk. In life. When I used to watch *Sex and the City,* it wasn't the size of their apartments or their couture that filled me with jealousy, it was that they still had brunch every Sunday in their thirties." I tug out a chair against the thick pile carpet and slump down at the table. "We didn't even make it to twenty-five! Who has time for brunch when you're asleep with your fiancé or studying for the MCATs? And now I can't believe it, but I feel that same raw envy when I watch *Entourage.* I need an entourage! Kelsey needs to get an entourage. No one back home can relate. All they want is information I can't give them and free shit. So pretty much, now she's the only person I talk to, and it's my job to keep her reassured."

"She sent you back to plan the wedding," he says matter-of-factly.

"No. *Yes.*" I reach into the bag and shove a fistful of fries into my mouth in relief at finally admitting it. Finn pulls out a chocolate shake, and hands it over. "Thank you." I take a big swig. "Who wants to be responsible for ruining the biggest day of someone else's life? Kelsey leaves me all these one-word voice mails: Fireworks! Balloons! Candy! Is this a wedding or a county fair? Okay, now you tell me something I shouldn't know," I say.

He sits and takes a deep draw from his own shake as he considers. "Travis has a polyp in his sinus cavity."

"Oh, God, I'm so sorry."

"No. It's basically a wart. But it has to be removed. The downside is, if we go public, A, they'll say he's covering a nose job, which makes him sound gay, or B, they'll say he has a coke problem, or C, they just obsess about how gross a polyp is, and that kills his career right there. Hey, Bonnie, want to go see the guy with the polyp take his shirt off? Eh, I'll pass."

"Can you just not tell anyone?"

"What wakes me up in the middle of the night is the fear that Travis has used up his nine lives. He hired me to transition him out of these shit rom-coms. His clock's ticking. They're already talking about dad roles." Finn spills the fries onto the marble and squeezes the ketchup packets on the side of the bag. "So, what happened tonight?" he asks gently.

I struggle to phrase it without kicking my white knight in the groin. "This guy chatting me up at the bar turned out to be some tabloid reporter," I say casually.

"Did you sleep with him?" he asks with equal casualness.

"What? No!" I hollowly protest. "Travis did tell you I called to say I'm an asshole?"

"Oh, *you* were the asshole — that got lost."

"And yet you bought me a burger. Why are you like this?" I ask.

"I have three older sisters. You?"

"Why am I like this, or do I have siblings?"

He smiles. "Let's start with siblings and take some time to figure out why you're like this."

I draw another long sip. "I was dropped from the mother ship. I mean, it's not like my parents aren't good people." I graciously lump my dad in with my mom. "I think, actually, if I hadn't had Michelle as a comparison, it might have been easier. She was always super into the girlie glamour of us, which is why it's . . . kind of ouchie that she's not really interested in this particular event."

"Really?"

I shake my head.

"That's tough," he says in a way that lets me know he gets it. I can't ask for sympathy for Kelsey from anyone else.

"So, uh, thanks for coming and for the food. Do you want to watch *The Change-Up?*" I ask.

He stands, leaning down to kiss me. "Not even remotely."

I'm woken some time before eight by my phone vibrating across the table, cutting a path through the abandoned fries. I hop up quickly so it doesn't wake Finn, grab my robe off the floor, and take both with me onto the balcony, hoping that neither of my neighbors is already eating breakfast alfresco. "Hello?" I whisper, my voice raking its ginger claws down the backs of my eyes.

"Logan?"

"Mom?" I ask, belting the robe.

"I know we haven't talked in a while —

but a man called here last night, said he was from your office, and — I think he was a paparazzi." Oh, God.

"What did you tell him?" I rub my temples, the sound of the traffic from Sunset loud below.

"I don't know anything, Logan. I just have this accordion of a wedding invitation sitting here."

"Okay."

"I told him that must have cost a pretty penny."

"Mom, I sent an e-mail about being super-cautious to everyone, all the cousins, everyone,"

"So now Andy's expecting the entire family to screen our calls."

"It's necessary, unfortunately." I push back. "This is an unusual situation."

"I'll say."

"Mom."

"He's unstable," she says. "You don't remember —"

"I remember him throwing up at Kelsey's recital. I remember him punching Dad at Grandma's funeral. It's not like I was unconscious for thirteen years —"

"I had to look at you lying there with tubes coming out of your thin arm, while Michelle went back to her Bedazzler. Whisking her daughter off. Trotting her around some strange city. I judge her, and I judge him. Frankly, I judge Kelsey and the lifestyle she's living, and I judge —" She catches herself. "I wish I could just forbid it."

I look down and see one of the producer's prey crossing the driveway on wobbly legs, her hair and dress askew. I watch her reach shaking hands into her purse to tip the valet.

"He's sober now, Mom." I hear myself defend him. "He's not like that anymore. He doesn't get high, doesn't even drink beer."

"What am I supposed to do with this invitation?" she asks quietly.

"Come to the wedding?" I step back from the edge, where the concrete has already heated past being tolerable. "I mean, she's getting married. By a real minister. I'd think you could at least approve of that."

Silence.

"Look, it's three months away. You have time —"

"Your father and I have no intention of visiting with them. Ever."

"Okay."

"Okay."

"Well, I should probably go," I say, staring at the gray cement.

"We pray for you, Logan."

"So you've said."

She hangs up.

I know that what I need to do is start calling everyone in Oklahoma to see who else this guy got to, who else he's posing as. Maybe it's Mark, but it's probably someone else, one of legions. I can feel Mark's rough kiss, how his aftershave bled into my mouth, and my stomach sours. I look at the sliding door, but can't reach for it. Instead, I find myself crouching against the stucco between the door frame and the railing. I sit and stare as the sun thins the smog. Unable to move. Forbidden.

Minutes pass.

If Finn wakes up and comes out here looking for me, it's a sign.

If Finn thinks I've left, it's a sign.

I have no idea how much time has elapsed before I hear him moving around inside, calling for me, opening the bathroom door, then putting his clothes on. There's another long pause.

Come on, find me find me find me.

Logan, get up get up get up.

But I can't.

The door to my room swings shut.

Have you ever been in an exercise class and

you don't remember starting the situps? No one is staring at you, so you must have been following along, but a moment ago, you were upright, and now you're on the mat, the last few minutes lost to a daydream. Similarly, I don't know how I got off the Chichester's balcony, or into the cab, to the airport, or to the gate. The next moment that I'm fully, sickeningly inside myself is when I'm reading my mother's direct quote in a tabloid: "I don't like yellow myself, and I don't understand all these inserts with phone numbers on them." She seems to have read the guy the entire invitation verbatim, from the location to the phone number for the travel agent who will book the guests' flights and charge Kelsey. I'm just thankful my mother doesn't know how to text a photo.

I wheel my suitcase through the revolving doors of the Little Rock Omni and directly to the ladies' room to powder my glistening face. Knowing the pending meeting couldn't be faced with dulled wits, I denied myself the Valium I now require at take-off and instead spent the flight gripping the orange prescription bottle as if it could calm me through osmosis.

Back out, I spot GM in the lobby's Starbucks. "Hey, Princess."

"Hey!" I love being hugged by GM — it's like pulling the covers over your head. "How's it going?" I mumble into his wall of a chest.

"Well," he says as I stand back, "we've had better days." He breaks the tip off his banana. "They're gonna be on speaker with Terrance in a few. You should hustle."

I nod, my nerves like a twisted Slinky as I scurry past a faded life-size cutout of Bill Clinton. On the top floor the Presidential Suite opens to Andy, looking grim.

"I'm so sorry," I greet him. "I did everything in my power to keep this locked down. I sent out e-mails, I called —"

"You knew about this?" He squints at me, the sleeves of his sweatshirt pushed above his elbows.

"The guy who talked to my mom was a total sleazeball —"

"Your mom?"

"She feels terrible," I lie. "We both feel terrible. Is Kelsey totally crushed?" I bite my lip.

"Andy, she doesn't know," Michelle says, referring to me, and I'm confused. "Come on, Logan. We just got an order of nachos." She waves me in from a brown leather couch. "Andy, let the girl inside already."

He closes the door, staring at it for a moment before turning. "Your mother's talking to reporters?"

"No! I mean, yes, she got a call from some asshole pretending to be on our staff. But she won't make the mistake again, believe me."

"Is that what she told you?" he asks. "She said she will not talk to reporters?"

"Okay!" Michelle says as she pops a loaded chip in her mouth and reaches for a napkin. "Water under the bridge, Andy. Have a seat, Lo." Michelle pats the couch.

Aaron emerges from one of the bedrooms, eyes downcast, and grabs a soda in the kitchenette. "I'm sorry about my mom —"

"It's cool." He stares into the aluminum like he's playing through how to dive inside.

"Lo!" Kelsey comes out in her postshow sweats. "Welcome back! Did you bring the stuff?"

"I am. So sorry." I jump up. "I left you about thirty messages and am totally ready to commit hari-kari with that." I point to an antler candlestick.

"Whatever." She shrugs me off.

"Kelsey?" I push.

"Lo, I said it's fine," she says firmly. Andy scowls at the maroon carpet. "So, where're the goods?" Kelsey lifts her hands under her chin for a series of little claps. Munching, Michelle returns to her Nora Roberts.

"Okay, well, the dress is definitely the thing we should do last, but I brought you some more sketches. I've spoken to the designers personally, so there are no middlemen," I say as I lay my suitcase flat. Ignoring me, she drops to her knees to pull out the tablecloth samples, silverware designs, floral portfolios.

"Kel, focus." Andy leans over the couch and tugs her up by the elbow. "Can everyone just sit please?" Andy brings over the suite's black phone, its long cord snaking across the room from the jack, as if drawing a line between Aaron and the rest of us.

"Let's bang this out," Kelsey says, bringing her velour knees up as Andy sits next to me, his girth shifting my thigh into him. I inch away. "Then I want to see lace samples. I want to see that video of Brad and Jen's fireworks."

"Not sure we're going to be needing all that," Michelle says, licking a glob of sour cream off her thumb.

The phone rings, and Andy looks firmly to everyone before answering. "Hello, Terrance," he says, angling forward. "Thanks for taking the time tonight. We're, uh, we're real sorry for this." I am in trouble. I'm in

224

trouble, and they were just waiting for Terrance.

"Hey, Andy. Everyone there?"

"Yep."

"Terrance, I am just so sorry." I lean over the phone.

"Hey, Terrance!" Kelsey greets him playfully.

"Kelsey, it's one in the damn morning in New York." His voice cuts into the room. "I do not want to be working right now." My mouth goes dry.

Kelsey reaches her arm to Aaron, arching her back over the couch. "If you can just tell everyone here to chill —"

"First," Terrence says firmly, "I need to hear shit straight up, *then* I'm gonna make a call on what level of chill-ness we're at. Cheryl's on the line."

"Hi, guys," Cheryl, Kelsey's publicist, says in her nasal tone that manages to be simultaneously imperious and flat. A woman so strategically devoid of personality that everyone who talks to her prostrates themselves just to earn an inflection.

"Let's cut to it. Aaron, you there?" Terrance asks.

"Yes, sir." He clears his throat stepping forward. "Good evening, sir."

"Did you, or did you not, serve time for

225

dealing?"

What? I notice Andy's battered laptop sitting on the dining table. Another of TMZ's pitchfork-toting headlines. A picture of a teenage Aaron — a mug shot: "KELSEY'S EX-CON."

For a hundredth of a second, I allow myself to be relieved that this isn't about my being fired.

"I did, sir. It's a juvie record — it shoulda been wiped. I don't even know how they found it."

"If you took a shit in Antarctica, they gonna find it. Busted for selling to kids?"

Andy exhales like a bull. Kelsey tugs the elastic out of her hair and runs it between her teeth. "They're making it sound like I was selling crack to kindergartners," Aaron says.

"Were you?"

"No, sir. No way. I was sixteen selling pot to other sixteen-year-olds. I'm not proud, but it was part of a big bust, and there was a new mayor with this zero-tolerance policy. I did some time. Show me a guy from my hood who didn't."

"Fair," Terrance concedes. Andy glances up.

"But it scared me straight, and I got out. I'm a singer, sir, and that's my whole story, hand to God."

"You don't have a story," Cheryl corrects him. "There's just Kelsey's, and this taints it . . ." Cheryl trails off in a way that makes the situation feel hopeless.

"I do not want to be filling my time with this," Terrance says. Michelle looks witheringly at Kelsey, who twists the rubber band around her wrist like a tourniquet. "Cher, fix it. I gotta bounce. Later."

Aaron circles the couch to lean over the phone. "Cheryl?" he says hesitantly. "I will tell anything to whoever you want. I'll do whatever I have to do to make this right."

"Oh, we're not there yet," Cheryl scoffs as if he's independently taken this to melodrama, as if he hadn't just been told he was tainting his fiancée.

"Or Cheryl?" Michelle asks. "I've been thinking we could do the mother-daughter thing again. It's family-oriented —"

"As of this moment, Kelsey is the grown woman." Cheryl cuts her off. "Any soundbites or images linking her to childhood are only going to unconsciously make people think of Aaron selling *her* drugs. No, no-nono." Cheryl lets out a dry laugh. "As of tonight, Michelle, you're benched."

"O-kay," Michelle says, the last syllable lifting as her cheeks redden. Kelsey's eyes flit to her. "I'm . . ." Michelle stands. "I'm going to take a tub." She walks quickly out of the living room.

"Aaron, make a list of everything that could possibly be dug up on you. Have you raped anyone, stolen anything. Aaannything. I need that pronto. Aaron, big picture. There is no 'you,' there's only the brand, the idea of Kelsey people fall asleep with at night, what keeps music downloading and perfume flying off the shelves." Aaron's eyebrows rise. "Let's reconvene first thing in the morning while I get a read on how this is playing, 'kay? Get some rest. Not you, Aaron. You have work to do. 'Night."

" 'Night," we say as Andy hits the receiver and the dial tone fills the room. Aaron walks to their bedroom.

"You're fucking this up. You have *everything,* and you wanna piss it away on some . . ."

"Say it." His eyes narrow at her challenge. "Say it, Daddy."

"Don't mess with me tonight."

"You're the last person who can judge him."

Andy swipes the potpourri dish off the table, smashes it into the wall and stalks out. We stare at their door as the running water shuts off, and Michelle's voice comes through cajoling and light. ". . . wanted this over, and now it almost is! She blew it with Eric — she'll blow it with this guy. We both know she's too wrapped up in herself for a real relationship."

Kelsey crumples into Aaron, who shuts the door behind them.

Sometime in the night, I move to the floor to escape the couch buttons that seem designed to dig at all angles, then try to cover my nose to block the lingering scent of vomit and carpet cleaner that only someone sober and attempting to sleep down here would notice, and *then,* unable to stop staring at the glass shards and dusty petals, I give up and go out to the wrap-around balcony.

Aaron startles. "Hey," he says, putting out his cigarette and folding the hotel stationery he's writing on.

"Hey." I untuck my crossed arm to give him a little wave.

"Can't sleep?" he asks.

I lean against the metal balustrade, staring at the lights of downtown Little Rock. "I need a mattress — and even then, it's touch and go. Runs in the family."

"I've noticed," he says.

"You know where I slept well? On the bus."

"Maybe you need a vibrating bed," he suggests drily.

"They still make those?"

"I bet somewhere in Asia."

I smile. "How's Kelsey?"

He nods, considering. "It's tough. This is tough." He looks down between his knees, where he dangles his pen. "I'm not what they're saying," he says quietly.

"I know —"

"When I got out of juvie with forty-two bucks in my pocket, I was nothing. But I've got a solid career, a nice apartment in the Valley."

"I know."

"I love her," he says to the concrete.

"I know," I say again, because it just seems like what he really needs to hear right now — that someone in there sees him.

"How come you get that?"

"Because I find her incredibly lovable, too. Just, you know, being a goofball in her T-shirt. Especially being a goofball in her T-shirt."

"Yeah." He holds up his list. "I'm trying to think of anyone who might have shit to say to the press. I started with my parents."

"Oh."

230

The light turns on behind the curtains of their room, and Kelsey comes out in her robe, lifting lips for him to kiss as he goes inside.

"Hey, chicky," I say.

"Hey."

"I'm excited about the wedding," I offer as she leans over the balcony, the wind lifting her hair. She tugs a pack of American Spirits from her pocket and lights one. I watch as she inhales deeply. "We can pick a new venue tomorrow — I totally hear you about not wanting to do it at the house — the copters drowning out the vows. What about reconsidering the Pantheon?"

"Is she right?"

"What?"

"Am I too wrapped up in myself?" she asks, her voice deep and damp.

"You're a bride. Brides are supposed to —"

"Is that why you gave up on me?" She looks down over the railing.

"What? No —"

"Tour break is in two weeks." She stubs out the cigarette and takes my hand. "I want to do it May twentieth, on my birthday. Wherever. Let's just do it. Understand?"

I nod. Her fingers squeeze mine, and then she turns to go back inside. "Happily ever after?" she asks as she touches the glass, and in the reflection I see her looking up at me, so many ages at once, holding a broken sippy cup, hair band, tap shoe, the expression the same, my need to solve this for both of us the same.

"It'll be beautiful."

CHAPTER EIGHT

After hitting the LAX tarmac, I case the city, reassessing potential venues for vulnerabilities to aerial, land, and oceanic telephoto assault. Having exhausted the options, I pull into a parking lot to snarf a hot dog and find myself staring with caffeine-dilated eyes at a windowless single-story building. "City of Angels Bowling Alley," I sarcastically update Kelsey on the speakerphone. To my surprise, she goes nuts.

"Aaron loves to bowl! Make it home, Lo, on its most perfect day. And make it us. I lovelove*love* it. Whatever it takes!"

Translation: *no* budget. And I don't mean like it wasn't drawn up. I mean, like, get the greenhouse in Holland that can flash-harvest whatever we want. The type of no budget of which bridal dreams are made and wedding planners' spines broken. "Whatever" spiraled into an amount that, while not quite enough to restore democracy to a medium-size dictatorship, could plausibly fund an attempt at ousting the dictator. Price became weirdly meaningless. Five thousand to get it here by Tuesday? Ten thousand to have it rush-engraved? The courier is leaving for the South of France to get centerpiece pebbles, and they only have first-class tickets left? Done, done, and done. I have actually worn out the strip on an American Express Black card.

In the last fourteen days, I have located an unopened bottle of the perfume our Grandma Ruth wore that was discontinued eleven years ago, had nail polish made in the exact shade of Kelsey's Madrid hotel-room sheets, and reunited the band whose song was playing when Kelsey and Aaron first locked lips on the dance floor. And at every exchange, every transaction, every pickup and dropoff with the assistant of an assistant of an assistant, I've overseen the signing of a nondisclosure form in triplicate. It states that the signer will never mention that he or she has participated in the preparations for Kelsey Wade's "birthday party" or risk the loss of home, family, and pets. My hotel room has become a warren of boxes overflowing with these things that I continue to think would make a striking art installation.

But as I stand at the entrance to the transformed bowling alley, I have to say, it's really something. The fireproof ceiling tiles are hidden beneath yellow and white ticking, like our grandmother's porch-swing cushions, making it feel as if we're in a tent on a sunny day. The fluorescents have been swapped out for milk-painted wagon-wheel chandeliers. The walls are made of perfectly symmetrical blooms of yellow roses like Ruth grew in her backyard. I don't mean dotted, I mean packed, a full perfect bloom for every square inch. A wide plank floor has been laid over the lanes and gutters. It originates from an old barn I located outside Portland that we had deconstructed and shipped down, which was cheaper than paying the go-to faux painter guy to make a new floor look old. P.S., I'm coming back as that dude.

The piped-in smell of freshly cut hay, the Mason jars of gin fizzes, and the faint soundtrack of crickets make me think of, well, honestly . . . it's what Vegas's Venetian is to Venice.

"Only things missing are the mosquitoes," Michelle snipes before turning to greet the next round of baffled family. Hoping to keep Kelsey out of target range as long as possible, I hover near Michelle as our relatives arrive to discover they're not here for her daughter's twenty-fifth but for the event that Michelle was convinced had been averted. "That's right, it's a wedding, isn't that a riot? Now, go make yourselves at home at the bar." Michelle pivots them to the transformed shoe rental.

Her sister appears at the draped inner entrance, her youngest daughter, Caroline, in tow. "We're just so sorry Delia couldn't make it. My sister's such a workaholic," Caroline says. "Kelsey's wedding! She'll be heartbroken to miss it."

But she wasn't invited.

Michelle jumps in. "Oh, that's sweet. Now, let me look at you! Holy crap, Caroline, that Atkins has made you into a supermodel."

Through the crowd, I see Finn's profile emerge, here at Kelsey's urging that we "find our princes" in tandem. I step around my congregating relatives and see that, unlike everyone else in their jeans and khakis, he's dressed for the actual event.

"Hey," I say nervously. "Cute suit."

"Well, I'm meeting your parents." He looks around, rising on the balls of his feet.

"No, they're not coming."

"They're not? I assumed —"

"Nope! No. Another long story. How

about I push you into the path of everyone my mother might get a postmortem from?"

"You're on. I had to lie to Travis about where I was going — he's still waiting by the phone for Kelsey."

I shake my head. "Wow, only in Hollywood could he think he made a good impression."

"When you get paid ten million to play the dick who gets the girl, it's hard for him to remember that dropping someone in a fountain isn't the thing that happens at the top of Act Two that she just has to 'get past.' "

This resonates with something about today I haven't been able to quell, and I nod, lowering my voice. "Singing about true love day after day hoisted into the air on a giant silk rocking horse can't be good for your sense of — reality."

"Now you're just being cynical. I proposed to my last four wives riding a giant silk rocking horse." He steps back to take me in. "You don't look like a bridesmaid."

"Because I'm the maid of honor, bitch." I do a spin in the dress that Kelsey spotted in the window of Dallas's Roberto Cavalli boutique (in tie-dyed satin) and had them make for me (in two days) in yellow silk. "You like?"

Another group approaches before he can

answer. "There's a picnic table with place cards if you just take a right at the —"

"Go. Work," he urges gently. "I'm totally fine."

I rest my head on his shoulder for a nanosecond. "Thank you."

"Only one request."

"Sure!" I look up at him.

"If you plan to ditch me in another hotel room, don't."

"Well, look at this," Michelle says, as she forces herself behind me into the manager's office serving as Kelsey's staging area. "It's like when you two used to come to my post-office shift and set up your own store in the supply closet."

"You're so right!" I feel myself puff to fill the narrow aisle. "I'm just seeing to a last few things if you want to have a quick drink with Aunt —"

"Momma?"

Shit.

Michelle squeezes past me, and I follow her around the rented rolling mirror. Kelsey turns in her gown, her eyes wide in anticipation.

"Oh, Kel," I say, my hands on my heart. "You look beautiful."

Michelle places her champagne on a filing

cabinet but doesn't say anything. Which I'll totally take. The silent treatment is best-case scenario at this point.

"Momma, don't you recognize it?"

"The Cartier Daddy got you for the Doll-house Tour, that's sweet. He'll be so touched —"

"Yes, but this." Kelsey spreads her fingers across her beaded bodice.

Michelle pulls back. "Seed pearls?" she guesses.

"It's an exact copy of your corset." Except not polyester.

"Oh, my gosh," Michelle murmurs, bending for a closer inspection.

"Do you love it? Do you love everything?"

"It's a real party . . ."

"Does Daddy love it?" Kelsey asks. "It's just like Grandma Ruth's yard."

"Oh, you know Daddy, he's just happy to have a TV to check the score."

"There's a flat screen in the groom's lounge," she says eagerly.

Michelle takes in her daughter's expression and pulls her around the mirror. I brace myself.

"Kelsey, sweet girl." To my surprise, her tone is suddenly free of the acid that's spattered off it the last few weeks. "Life is long," Michelle continues. "The years are long."

"Okay . . ."

"You do not have to go through with this," she says carefully. "Everyone was expecting a birthday party. Let's get you changed, wheel out that cake, and dance the night away."

"Momma."

"Kel, I'm giving you the chance I never had. You don't need to rush."

"I'm not rushing."

"Are you pregnant?"

"What?"

"Because that's different. If you're pregnant, I will shut the hell up here and now, and Daddy and I will stand behind you one hundred percent."

"I — I'm not."

There's a pause.

"Then do what I couldn't. Have fun, and don't nail yourself to this cross."

"Did I . . ."

I can barely hear Kelsey, her voice is so quiet. I step closer.

"Did I nail you to a cross?"

"Oh, come now, we're not talking about the past. I always said Jesus wanted you to be here — the universe had a big plan for you. Just remember, if you run out the exit, we'll follow." We hear the door open, the music crisp and then muffled again as it closes.

Binky and I wait, but there's no sound of petticoats rustling.

"Kel?" I ask.

She comes around the mirror, tears marring Binky's makeup. "I don't know what to do. Tell me what to do." She turns to me, her hands trembling against the pristine fabric.

"I — I can't answer this for you."

Kelsey takes a deep breath before looking up at her reflection. "All I know is Aaron never makes me feel like this." Her eyes narrow with resolve as she stares back at herself. "Binky?"

"Yes, Kel."

She lowers herself in the chair and lifts her face. "Let's get my pretty back on."

After so much epic-scaled preparation for this event, the ceremony at its heart is surprisingly small. When they repeat their vows, Kelsey and Aaron are as locked in on each other as they'd been in St. Paul's. And whatever smothered reservations I've had about the speed of their courtship, it's impossible to deny their connection as they embrace in the glow of the projected sunset.

Later, everyone but Uncle Herb with his

241

bad knee gets up to do the Electric Slide. His blazer abandoned, Finn throws himself endearingly into the moves. I think it's safe to say, as she pivots and spins alongside Michelle and Aaron, that Kelsey has never looked so genuinely happy. Even Andy is doing the white man's overbite on the dance floor's periphery with an older guy I can't place. Kelsey was adamant that there be no industry here, just family and close friends, but he's been at Andy's side all night.

As we're walking out to the tented driveway at the evening's end, Kelsey pulls me into a hug. "Oh, Lo, you did it! It was perfect! Wasn't it perfect?" she asks Michelle.

"Perfect," Michelle says with the hint of a slur as she leans on Aaron's steadying arm, puckering the wool of his tux.

"Happily ever after!" Kelsey lifts her shoulders and squeals.

"Yes!" I cheer.

"I, uh, was kinda hoping to talk to you and Andy before we left. Just to say how much I respect your daughter and feel honored to join your family —"

"Aren't you the cutest." Michelle dismisses him, patting at her own hand.

"Where is Daddy?" Kelsey asks.

"You'll see him when you get home from

Hawaii. Go on, now."

"But Aaron wants to talk to him. Logan, can you go grab him?"

"Oh, Kelsey."

"Just to say what I missed the chance for —" Aaron jumps in. "In not properly asking for Kelsey's hand."

"Daddy's busy."

"Who's that man with him?" Kelsey asks.

"His sponsor." Michelle feels pointlessly for a diamond-crusted comb that was a Bon Jovi head-banging casualty. "Daddy thought he might need the extra support. This was a real trial for him," Michelle states with bleary finality.

The car honks.

"Okay, well, see you in a week!" she says, her usual smile back in place, the one that stops just beneath her eyes. I pack in the swaths of satin and carefully shut the door. As we wave them off, I notice that some guests, heedless of the waiting paparazzi, have jerry-rigged cans of bowling-shoe polish to the rear fender.

And of all the night's artful sights, sounds, tastes, and smells that could have lodged themselves in my memory, it's the clank of metal bouncing on the asphalt that rings in my ears for days.

■ ■ ■ ■

Sitting on the edge of Travis Moynihan's pool, I'm still unsure if Finn inviting me to "crash" at the guesthouse where he resides while Kelsey is on her honeymoon was the kind of spontaneous request that leads to a charming story for the grandkids or an annoyed boyfriend finding a stray Tampax wrapper and announcing he was just kidding. The two-story casita is predominantly occupied by a pool table custom-fitted with a felt mural of its owner's tanned chest. The kitchenette's equipped to make a mean margarita and nothing else, and the upstairs is essentially a giant bed beneath a retractable ceiling, which is initially super-sexy until you realize that those are not birds circling between you and the stars but bats. Another libidinous challenge is that the walls are covered in posters for Travis's movies in every language you can think of. Essentially, the house is a sun-filled storage locker for the Travis Moynihan memorabilia that people have either bestowed upon him (the pool table) or he has come across and can't resist ordering (toilet paper bearing his image).

My phone rings, and, and hoping the

blocked number is Kelsey, I lunge for it. "Oh, I was just going to leave you a voice mail," Lauren says, sounding put out that I answered.

"No, I wanted to talk to you!" I say, glad she's finally returned my calls. "How are you?"

"Good. You're probably lying by the pool in some Hollywood mansion."

"Well, funnily, yes — but this is the first break I've had since I started. Usually, I'm lounging by the Formica in some sub-basement," I hasten to add. How was the honeymoon?"

"Mexico's the gift that keeps on giving, if you know what I mean."

"Oof. Good to know. I'm heading there this fall."

"Well, you won't have to worry — I'm sure the kind of place you'll be staying hand-washes your fruit in Evian."

"Only Kelsey's. I'm also her taster."

She doesn't laugh.

"Oh, I saw the pictures on Facebook today — the reception looked *beautiful.*"

"It should. Scott's been sitting with Quicken all night, telling me what we're not doing for the next five years, which is pretty much everything."

"Yeah," I commiserate. "Weddings are crazy."

She snorts. "What did *People* say your floral budget was — two hundred thousand —"

"Well, it wasn't really *my* floral budget."

"Right. Anyway, I just wanted to let you know we got your present."

"They're not floor seats," I say apologetically.

"I know."

Because I bought them on StubHub, along with the rest of America looking for tickets to a sold-out show. "But they were the best we had left. Listen, Lauren, I'm really sick about missing your wedding. There was just no way to fly back to New York the weekend before Kelsey's —"

"No, I totally get it. Well, enjoy the pool!"

I toss my phone into the grass.

The pool filter gurgles nearby, and I close my eyes. After Kelsey left when we were kids, when no one could tell me how to reach her, I rode my bike over there every day as soon as the doctor cleared it. I would stand across the street in the shade of the neighbor's tree, and try to screw up the courage to ask Andy. I'd lean against the scratchy bark and then slide down and finally sit, doing sweaty battle with myself to just go over. Just go ring the bell. And then, one day, Andy was gone, too. And there was nothing to confront but the For Sale sign stuck into the browned lawn. Those last few weeks of August, there was nowhere to go that didn't remind me of where she wasn't. Finally, school started, and it was real. The drawn-out acceptance of her departure set fast into the shock that this was forever.

The door opens and Finn jogs out, pulling a fresh T-shirt over his wet hair. I drop back onto my elbows, trying to look relaxed. "Good shower?"

"Lonely." He smiles. "I'm going to run out and get Supreme." He refers to Travis's pet iguana, who has just been groomed.

"Don't forget to tip the shampoo girl," I quip.

"I don't know what the fuck one does to clean an iguana." He swipes a fresh rolled towel from the terra-cotta urn and tosses it to me as he passes. "You're getting crispy."

"Thanks." I wrap it around my reddening shoulders.

"You okay?"

"Yeah, totally." I climb to my feet with purpose. "I'll see you later."

It's not like I don't have friends. Or even like I don't have Finn. But if I could just

call the bride, even for two seconds, and tell
her I was spending her honeymoon wiping
my ass with Travis's face, she would just get
it.

When Mr. and Mrs. Watts arrive at LAX's
private hangar, they're as rested as I've seen
them. To my surprise, Michelle makes a
beeline for her son-in-law. "Aaron, I down-
loaded *Ghostbusters*. Didn't you say you'd
never watched it? You'll have to come sit
next to me." She hooks her arm through
his, regaining its spot from when they last
parted.

"We're kinda tired from the flight." Kelsey
tries to intercede.

"He's only watching a movie, not acting
in it. If you're sleepy, you take a nap."

"Kel," Andy says, "You can sit next to me.
Tell me about Hawaii."

"Logan and I haven't talked in days, but
I'll catch you after the show." She evades
him.

"Actually, I have a bunch of stuff I need
to go over. Logan, back of the plane," he
orders.

So the summer evolves with our seating ar-
rangements, Michelle Netflixing Aaron into
an adopted son and Andy doubling down

on the details. Finn and I are, as he predicted, on opposite schedules. I land, he departs. I wake, he goes to sleep. He did manage to meet me in Atlanta on a layover, where we got intimately acquainted with a janitor's closet at the Philips Arena.

At the end of June, Kelsey, Aaron, and I fly home for a night so she can be a presenter at the MTV Movie Awards, their first red-carpet appearance as a couple.

With Aaron in the city, catching up with his friends for the day, I'm geekily excited to have a few hours together, just the two of us. I push open her bedroom door with a full breakfast tray to find the bed empty.

"Good morning!" I call, sliding it down on the chaise.

No answer.

"Kel?"

I don't hear anything, no water running, no rifling of hangers — I think at this point, I even know what it sounds like when she tweezes. The door to the bathroom is open, but she isn't there. "Kel?" I call again, walking into her dressing room. I'm about to push the panic button when I spot her bare feet sticking out from beneath a row of gowns. I crouch to find her sitting with her knees tucked up under one of Aaron's T-shirts.

"Can I play?" I ask. She points at the island in the middle of the room. I'm not sure what I'm looking for. But amid the sparkling costume jewelry, the white plastic wand unquestionably stands out. As does the pink cross in its window. "Oh, my God," I say.

"Oh. My. God."

"Oh, my God." I spin to her. "Are you in shock? Do you want juice?"

"Holy shit," she says, her face limp, as if she's just come offstage from the most killer performance of her career. She stares at the trellis-patterned carpet, a slow smile spreading across her face. "Oh, my God."

"Okay, it's going to be okay."

She scrambles up. "I have to tell Aaron. No. I should wait till tonight, in person. Am I a bad wife? Maybe I should've waited. Oh, my God, pretend you don't know, okay?"

"Okay." We stare at each other, our hands on our cheeks.

"I've been peeing on those ovu-predictor sticks every morning, but nothing, so I thought, I haven't ovulated, I'm two weeks late, I'll just pee on the other sticks — I didn't think — oh, my God."

"So, you were trying?" I ask, catching up.

"Since the wedding. Oh, Logan, I want a

baby so bad. But holy shit." Her face flushes.

"You're in shock. I'm in shock. Let me get us juice."

She grabs my wrist. "Logan, you have to find us a house in the city. By the end of tour, so we can move right in and start planning for the baby." She does a little jog of excitement, her fists clenched. "I'm pregnant!"

"A baby!" The enormity of it hits me. I put my hands over hers, and she beams, her eyes tearing with unadulterated joy. "Logan Wade, lozenge holder, wedding planner, and real estate truffle pig, at your service."

I lead Finn on the full tour of the Malibu house while Kelsey puts the finishing touches on our Labor Day feast. "That is an incredible view," he says, one hand gesturing to the wall of glass doors, the other sliding up the back of my shirt. I point to the hovering electronic eye at the cornice. "Travis doesn't have security cameras."

"Travis also doesn't have big male fans who still live with their mothers and want to wear his underwear as a mask."

"That we know of. Can I wash up?"

I point him to the powder room. "Meet you in the kitchen — just through there." I follow the smell of blueberry pie. "Wow," I say as Kelsey takes off her apron.

"What?" she asks, bending over the cutting board to peel the carrots.

"I swear your boobs are bigger than they were this morning."

"See?" Aaron calls from where he's playing Wii in the breakfast atrium. "I told you."

"Well, you heard what the doc said." She pushes back her hair with her forearm. "On someone my size, it's gonna show quicker." We all flew home last night for Kelsey's ten-week checkup, where they officially declare you pregnant.

Michelle comes in carrying placemats. "What are you two gabbing about?"

"Kelsey's boobs." I fill her in.

"I thought we agreed loose clothing until after we're done with the South American leg."

"Momma, nothing's as tight as my costumes. Someone's gonna notice."

"We've gotten a sweet pass from the press since the wedding, and Daddy wants to ride it as long as possible." Michelle sticks her head in to Aaron. "Dinner's almost ready. Please don't put your big ol' feet on the coffee table."

"Momma," Kelsey says, pulling out the Hellmann's. "I've licked that table with so many coats of lemon oil he'd have to run a tractor over it to scuff it." She unscrews the top, and is over the sink before we can register what's happening. "Shit," Kelsey murmurs as I rush around the island to rub her back. Aaron's paralyzed, as he is every time, because he wants to help but is as unnerved by vomit as I am by snakes. "I puked on the potatoes." She runs her hand across her mouth, her lips whiter than the mayonnaise. "Sorry, guys."

Michelle keeps setting the table. "I never had morning sickness."

"You okay?" Aaron asks, twisting the leather cord at his wrist.

"Yes, I'm, uh, all good." I pull out a stool for Kelsey and put the jar away before rinsing the sink.

"Sweetie," Michelle queries, "you ready to say uncle and get Angela back?"

"Normal families do not have chefs. I can do it. I want to do it." Kelsey pushes herself off the stool, landing back on her platform espadrilles.

"Do I smell pie?" Finn asks as he strolls in.

Kelsey gives him a hug. "Did you have any trouble finding the place?"

"I just followed the seagulls in hot pants." He squeezes my waist and a warm flush comes over me as I bask in the closest I'll probably ever get to bringing him home.

"So, what do you think?" Michelle asks, gesturing to the mansion.

"Logan has three green purses." Apparently his takeaway from the tour.

Everyone looks at me.

"What? One is leather for winter, one is canvas for summer, and one is pleather for when we travel to places where they steal your purse."

"You don't have to explain it to me," Kelsey says.

I feel myself turn pink. "I don't know, okay! I don't know where all that stuff came from!"

Kelsey circles the breakfast bar and puts her hand on my shoulder. "Logan," she says solemnly, "we're acquirers."

"Not like Great-aunt Gemma," Michelle reassures me.

"Not hoarders, just acquirers," Kelsey clarifies.

"Because," I protest, I don't have, like, a flat cat between my turtlenecks."

"Okay, let's get seated." Andy walks in and drops down at the head of the table, relegating Aaron to the side. "I got a bunch of questions I need answered." We all move to our chairs while he gets back up and goes to the fridge, returning with the mayonnaise. Beads of perspiration form on Kelsey's upper lip, but no one, including me, says anything. "Okay. This morning, I heard a lot of well-ya-coulds and no-need-to-just-yets from that doctor. What I need to know is how are we going to hold up our commitments?"

"Commitments?" Kelsey repeats.

"Hundreds of thousands of people have bought their tickets. They're expecting a full show, and I've got a daughter that's barely keeping down her breakfast."

I feel Finn glance at me.

"I'll give them full shows." She rushes to reassure him. "No question. I can totally do three more months."

"You have to fly back for the check-ups. And from Asia? Or Brazil? That's a full day right there. Will they let you get on a plane? Is that even safe?" he asks accusingly. Michelle sees that Finn is missing his dessert fork and reaches with a frown to pass him hers.

"I can see someone local."

"In Japan?"

"Lo, you can put a list together for me, right?" Kelsey asks.

"Sure."

"Dammit, that's just scratching the surface

here." Andy explodes. "Beyond keeping that baby healthy, what's this gonna cost us if we have to spread dates or cancel shows? You were single when this tour started; we're not insured for this. You're asking me to keep a shitload of balls in the air."

"It'll be like . . ." Kelsey's voice is small. "I'm not pregnant. I'll be just fine. You don't need to worry about it, Daddy. Okay?"

Not giving an answer, Andy moves into serving himself, unscrewing the mayoniase lid.

Kelsey goes running back to the sink, retching.

Andy puts down his fork, pushes back from the table, and walks out. I don't see him again before we leave.

Finn curls his naked body around me under the stars — and occasional bat. I threw myself into seducing him the second we got in the door, trying to fuck the embarrassment away. "Can I ask you a question?" He speaks first.

"Shoot."

"If Kel's moving, do you go with her?"

"Delia always did."

He adjusts the pillow back under our heads. "But she's married now."

"I'm staff — I go where she goes."

"You're not *really* staff."

"Well, yeah, I kinda am. I mean, I have to be good at my job."

"That's not what I'm saying." He slips his hand up to my breast. "I'm just psyched you'll be in the city. And, you know, if you did ever end up at loose ends, you could crash here permanently."

"Permanently? I could grow old with you in Travis's pool house?" I tease, trying to cover for the sudden grip of claustrophobia.

"Well, you know, see how it goes, whatever."

"Thanks, but I could no more move out of there than you could move out of here."

He pushes my hair up off my neck, holding me closer. "How'd you get that scar?" He runs his lips over it, and I instinctively hunch. "Sorry. Does it hurt?" he asks.

"No, just — a little sensitive," I answer, meaning the subject, not the flesh. "Finn, I'm kind of mortified about dinner."

"Don't be. Families are weird. My aunt adopts decrepit rescue dogs — she has enough to do the Iditarod now — it's totally crazy."

"Really? Once, our grandmother knocked her pitcher out of my hand to keep me from helping myself — didn't place the smell till college — half Minute Maid, half Smirnoff."

"Oh."

"Yeah," I say, needing him to know just what it is he's inviting to crash. "And, believe it or not, compared to my dad, Andy was actually the fun one — one year, we shut down the state fair." I flash to the excitement and then that feeling in my stomach. Was that the start of the twist I get — that instinct there was something off in Andy's need to keep us going around on the wheel, ignoring his sleeping daughter, the rides going dark one by one?

"The next summer Kelsey and I were in the backseat of their station wagon. I'd snuck out. By that point I was forbidden from sleeping over. My parents didn't tell me much. Just that there'd been an accident. By the time I was discharged, Kelsey and Michelle had left to do *Kids, Incorporated,* and I didn't see them again until this year."

"Wow. So . . ."

"Andy ran me into a tree when I was thirteen."

He's quiet.

I roll away from him flat on my stomach.

"Shit."

"Yeah."

He rises on one elbow and strokes the hair off my face. "Hey."

258

"Yeah?"

"My aunt bogarts the dogs' phenobarbital."

"Really?"

"She makes them five-star meals from scratch — and steals their meds." I muster a smile, letting Finn pull me back into him. His breathing slows as I replay the night. Maybe that's why I'm so impressed by Kelsey. It's not just that she goes out there and does back flips and sings till she's hoarse, it's that so much misery could funnel down to someone who brings so much joy.

CHAPTER NINE

Everyone exhales as The Dollhouse Tour reaches the finish line on November first and Kelsey takes her final curtsy at the Hollywood Bowl. There's no denying her baby bump, and the media has responded much the way Michelle did in Europe, with a testy dismay that they're officially stuck with Aaron. As if she's theirs.

"Stop following me," Aaron jokes as we step out of separate bathrooms to find each other at the communal sink of the restaurant Terrance has chosen to celebrate.

"Don't want you to miss me too much." I take a hand towel from beside a menacing-looking spiky plant. "Wendy's or Taco Bell?" I ask our stock question following these dinners.

"Pizza. You?"

"Driving straight out of here to get a burger." Chefs get so excited upon hearing of Kelsey's arrival that they start sending out their diminutive masterpieces unbidden: quail on a bed of quail with a quail gelée, topped with quail foam and garnished with a quail reduction. Two courses in, I'm always nauseated and starving.

"What did you do today?" I ask, availing myself of the Bulgari hand lotion.

"Rocked it hard. Helped Andy take the pool filter apart while Michelle got Kelsey to look at inspirational baby lines for Kelsey Kids. That girl does not need to be inspired. She needs to sleep and eat cheese."

We exchange looks in the mirror.

"I'm really sorry I haven't found you guys a house yet. There's a shocking lack of inventory that meets Michelle's criteria." A mansion with fringe on top, as our real estate agent has taken to calling it.

"Whatever, dude, it's all good. Our little girl will be here soon," he says, sweetly fitting "little girl" into every conversation since they found out. "And we got plans." He opens the door for me, and we walk back to the private garden. The air is heavy with the scent of magnolia as the dessert course lands on the table — quail brûlée.

"To the Wades!" Terrance raises his glass. "The hardest-working family in the business!"

"That's you, too, hon," Andy whispers as

261

Cheryl snaps a picture to applause from the table.

"E-mail me a copy?" Michelle asks, tapping the hard sugar with her spoon. "I want to frame that."

"So." Terrance rests his glass, and the table quiets. "What's up next?"

"Uh." Kelsey mugs, putting her finger to her chin, and then pointing to her budding belly. Everyone laughs.

"And?" Terrance asks.

"Well." She lifts her hair over her shoulder, her abdomen grazing the table's edge. "I don't really want to be one of those L.A. moms, so we've talked about heading back to Oklahoma. Building a house." *What?*

Michelle coughs up her wine.

"A few years of being a momma and a wife should give me a ton of new material. I'm looking forward to having a whole new well of stuff to draw on —"

Terrance cracks up as if she's building upon her original joke. Everyone follows his lead. Am I really hearing about this with Terrance and Cheryl? Is this what Aaron meant by plans? Why wouldn't she tell me?

"Eric's wound down over the last year." Kelsey continues with determined poise. "I think it makes sense for me. Of course, all the merchandising lines will still —"

"Girl, those hormones gone to your head? You'll be bored in five minutes. Seen it a thousand times. *Oh, T, get me back in the studio, this kid's driving me crazy!*"

"I think what Kelsey is trying to say." Her agent leans forward in the awkward silence, her pavé bracelets clinking. "Is that she's a little baby-brained at the moment. She knows we owe you three more albums, right, Kel?"

Kelsey opens her mouth, but Andy speaks. " 'Course she does."

"We want to hear what *you'd* like to see next, Terrance." The agent's silk top flops to reveal the tape unsuccessfully holding it to her bony sternum.

Aaron clears his throat. "I think Kelsey was talking about scaling back mostly on touring."

Michelle shoots him a silencing look.

Terrance reclines in his chair, his palm flat on the table. "Well, that's LiveNation's problem. How many mil you owe them, Andy?"

"Seventy," he says, folding in the edges of his placemat.

"That was the right contract for someone her age. Madonna, Beyoncé, Pink — they worked the hell outta their twenties."

■ ■ ■ ■

A month later, I'm on the set of the video shoot for the Christmas single, which we've been told is going to be a "tasteful" take on "Away in a Manger." I'm immediately met with a flurry of questions that are morphing my job into something I'm terming Gestational Psychic.

"Logan!" the assistant director shouts. "Will the mom-to-be want to stand or sit — need to focus the lights one way or the other!"

I don't even bother texting Kelsey, because she will say both are fine. That it is all fine. Even though both will, at some point today, become untenable. Which I'll only be able to guess when the blood has drained from her face, we have to beg the producer to take a break, and Andy smacks something in frustration.

"Let's start standing!" I gamble. Today I've requested extra ice packs — apparently, this Mary had a thing for Alexander McQueen platforms.

"Logan says standing!" he calls out so everyone knows whose fault the expensive delay will be if she arrives lightheaded and needing to sit.

A girl with random piercings — her face looks as if someone blindfolded chased her around the room with a stud gun — calls out to the crew, "Kelsey arrives in twenty!" Maybe it's a constellation, I think, as my butt pocket vibrates. A text from Michelle. "K gone AWOL. Needs pick up in Laurel Canyon. ? ? ? Stuck in traffic. Can you? Don't tell Andy."

Awesome.

I look to where he's going over the storyboards and try to dash nonchalantly for the exit. "Just grabbing a sweater from the car!"

I take as many side streets as I can to avoid rush hour, repeatedly dialing Kelsey, but she isn't answering. I finally make the turn into the wealthy bohemian neighborhood of Mid-century Modern homes. Is she meeting a birthing coach, getting her cards read?

Pulling up to a two-story teak house I hop across the pebbled drive. "Hello?" I call, pushing into a sun-baked room.

"Well, that's the offer."

I turn to see a woman wearing a black bouclé suit, her French tips pressing her phone to her ear.

"Kelsey?" I ask.

"And I'm telling you, if you can get an engineer here today, we'll pay him double."

Without pausing her conversation, she points at the open-sided staircase.

I tread quickly past a Cy Twombly, resisting the urge to grab it in lieu of a banister, and pause above the double-height room. "Sorry, where?"

The French tip, like a weather vane, swings left. In the master suite I spot Kelsey standing on the edge of the balcony, a jetty of whitewashed concrete, below which the Canyon dizzily unspools. "Logan, what are you doing here?"

"Your mom sent me. We have to go."

"She isn't coming?"

"It's rush hour. Kelsey, you're due on the set, like, now."

"I have to wait for her."

"Why?" I pull out my phone, my temples pounding as I see no fewer than five texts from Andy.

"This is my new house."

"Your house," I repeat stupidly. "What do you mean, your house?"

"Logan, I love it." Her face breaks open. "I mean, we have to put in a gate and a guard booth and make those stairs safe and fence the pool, but otherwise, it's perfect. It's not too big. You don't need an intercom. I made Linda downstairs call my name from every corner, and you can hear everyone

266

everywhere. No need for yelling — ever. I'm so sick of sparkly frames and crystal figurines and trophy walls. All that freakin' stuff in every room. No more. Just a comfy couch, a dining table, and the piano. And toys everywhere. I can be a mom here, I can feel it."

"Oh. Okay . . ."

"What?"

"No, I'm just sorry. I swear to you, I've seen every available listing that fit what your mom —"

"Oh, and this ledge will be a terrace. The glass blew away in that last storm, but they'll fix it or give me an adjustment."

"What does that look like?" I ask, trying not to glance at the treetops sloping down the steep drop, trying to make my tone as enthused as she's asking for. "A few thousand off a few million?"

"I suppose. I'll start her college fund."

"Cuz I hear that's getting expensive."

"Okay." She crosses her arms. "What?"

"What?" I say.

"I thought you'd be happy for me."

I let out a frustrated breath. "I am. I mean, how is that not obvious? I am."

"You seem pissed."

The corners of my mouth twitch stupidly as my failure sinks in. "Kelsey, you know

267

what I was really doing when your first single went to number one?"

She shakes her head.

"Rooting for you. If I don't know that you want to move to Oklahoma or like Mid-century or need to sit down, then I can't do my job."

"Sorry. Is my getting married and having a baby hard for you? Are you having feelings about that? Because you can take a number and get in line behind, you know, *America*."

"Okay, that's not at all what I'm saying." I shove my hands in my back pockets, hunching against the sting. "And I didn't think I was America."

"I didn't think I was a job," she responds evenly. I can't humble myself to clarify the statement. It's not what I meant to hit her with, but at the same time, it is.

"Kelsey!" Michelle calls from downstairs. Kelsey brushes past me. "What're we doing here?" Michelle asks as we descend to the living room. "Buying art? Your dad's head has blown clear off. Why didn't you return my calls?"

"Ta-dah!" Kelsey declares, splaying her arms like she's shooting rays from her fingers.

"Ta-dah what?"

"I own it," Kelsey says simply, taking a seat on a kitchen stool as if it were a throne. "Or I will in a few days. We still need a survey before we take the deed."

"Here?" Michelle scowls, bewildered.

"I love it." Kelsey rests her palms on her bump.

"But it's so small."

"Yep."

"How many bedrooms?"

"Just four."

"How can you do this — buy a house? So fast."

"I'm an all-cash buyer." Kelsey looks at the counter as if a stack of contracts waited there. "I spoke to Rich this morning, and he's ready to transfer the funds."

"You can do that?"

She fixes her mother with a look I've only seen on set. "With one phone call, yes."

"But where will *we* live?"

Kelsey takes Michelle by the elbow and leads her to the wall of windows, where, a few hundred feet down the Canyon, sits a wood guesthouse nestled in the trees. "Isn't it perfect? You even have your own driveway."

"But it looks so dark. Where's the ocean view? I don't like it. No, I don't like it at all. This is all wrong —"

"Well." Kelsey swings to her. "This is our home, mine and Aaron's." Her eyes flash over her mother's shoulder, spraying her meaning. "And if you want to live with us, you live there. If you don't want to live with us, that woman on her cell phone is Linda. Linda?" Kelsey calls. "My momma's looking to buy herself a house."

CHAPTER TEN

Kelsey's there. She's sitting next to me in the backseat of a car. It's night. The tan seats — it's Michelle's car. Kelsey's in her Pocahontas nightgown. People are yelling in the front seat. Grown-ups. Screaming at each other. Kelsey climbs to her feet and starts to sing, but I can't watch because all at once, I'm frantically trying to pull a shower curtain to block us off from the front seat. Everything depends on my getting this green plastic curtain closed, but it's impossible. I pull it to one side, and the other opens. Smoke starts to pour in from above, then the sides, then the seams. Kelsey keeps singing, and I don't understand how she isn't coughing as I try to keep my grip on the plastic while my nostrils, my mouth, my eyes are burning, and I'm choking on the smoke — and —

— I open my eyes to a mess of white sheets, moving instantly from the frantic adrenaline of my dream to realizing that I really am coughing. I abruptly sit up to reach for water. I gulp, only to inhale another wave of burning air. "Finn?" I jog down the steps, tug a dishtowel from the bar, and cover my mouth as I yank the door open.

In the bright December morning my eyes instantly tear. But I stand under a clear sky. Birds singing. No flames.

"Well, good morning, sunshine!" Travis whirs over on his Segway, the top of his wet-suit hanging off his bare waist.

"What's on fire?"

"Huh?" He grins.

I yank the towel away. "What's on fire?"

"The bison I shot! My sous is cumin-searing the carcass in the garage to kick off the holiday season — get some good solstice energy going." He taps his handlebars, and the intro to the *Bonanza* theme blasts the property from every foliage-obscured speaker. "You lookin' for Finn?"

"Here," Finn says, coming through the break in the hedge.

"You have pulled off some neat shit today." Travis bows, the sleeves of his suit grazing his feet. "You're in the groove, little grass-hopper."

Finn salutes him.

272

Travis backs the machine up to turn around. "Lo, do not, I repeat, do not eat anything this week. No lunch, no dinner, nothing. We've got to let Friday's Bison Fest be consummate, comprende? Da, da-da-da, da-da-da-da-da-da BONANZA!" he yells as he lurches away.

"Seal it up," I say, turning toward the house. "I have back-to-back interior-design meetings, and I can't face Thomas O'Brien looking like I've just been dumped."

"Uncontrollable tearing could be hot on you," Finn says, wiping his eyes on his sleeves as he pulls the windows shut, helping me to Ziploc ourselves in with the flaming air.

"So, you've already pulled off neat shit?" I sneeze.

"The project that's going to transition Travis —"

"I remember." I prod with a smile, as this is pretty much all Finn talks about.

"The writer I was trying to get signed on!"

I throw my arms around him. "Yea!"

"Thanks." He squeezes me tight, his hands sliding up under my shirt. "No bra and still in pajama pants, which means no panties . . ."

"Sorry, dude, gotta get going. Can I take a rain check for your casting couch?"

"You okay?"

"Yeah, just . . . still having these crazy intense dreams," I say dismissively, even as the flutter of adrenaline returns.

"Where the pool table's trying to eat you?"

"Yeah," I fib, as their actual content makes even less sense. "I have to stop having chocolate cake at bedtime."

He kisses me as the air starts to clear. "Listen, I had a crazy idea."

"Travis should cut an album."

"You should come with us to New York."

"Really?" I ask as I fill the coffee pot.

"I'll be booked with Travis leading up to the premiere —"

"A.K.A. Christmas Day."

"But I'll have the next week off and we can do it up in style. Travis is taking a block of suites for his family, and my family's coming down."

"I'm in!" I say, jumping at the chance to avoid Christmas in Oklahoma saturated with my parents' disapproval — not that I've been invited.

"Awesome." He grins. "I know this great little bar in Midtown, near the hotel. You're gonna love it. They have these old murals on the wall."

And rather than tell him that's where I spent my most depressing birthday to date,

I circle the island to peel off his sweatshirt, deciding that Thomas O'Brien can wait a little longer to meet my sexy tearing eyes.

By Friday morning, my thoughts thump across my brain in wagon-train rhythm as I wait outside Chez Watts for Kelsey, doing a last inventory of fabric samples. I never knew there were so many shades of white.

Kelsey, intent on driving home what "just being a job" can feel like, has relegated me to assisting the renovation.

It's point-blank jarring to look at her across Vicente's latest sketch of their new bedroom and reconcile the intensity of our connection replaying nightly in my dreams with the generic politeness she makes available to me in real time.

She comes out carrying her travel mug. "It's a sick joke of nature that leading up to a baby, when you should be sleeping, you can't sleep. I just don't get it," she says with a nod of greeting to Peter in the driver's seat as I open the car door for her. "An album has ten tracks. This is one single. It should be one-tenth the work."

"It should," I agree.

"Make a note about holiday decorations, would you? I don't want to ask Momma who she used for Malibu, all that flashing color like friggin' Times Square. I'm thinkin' steady white lights on the trees and white poinsettias for the front walk."

"Mornin', Lo," Aaron calls as he jogs down the front steps, swinging his car keys.

"Break a leg, baby." Kelsey blows him a kiss.

"I've got my girl," Aaron croons in a low drawl, walking backward to the Porsche that was his wedding present, much to Andy's disapproval.

"This is the one — I can feel it!" Kelsey pulls her door closed. "Fourth audition since tour ended," she says under her breath, surprisingly sharing something more personal than a paint preference. "Some shit about his new notoriety upstaging the headliners, which is ridiculous. Aaron's too professional for that." He answers his cell as he opens his car door.

"I had no idea," I say carefully, as if trying not to startle a doe in the woods.

"It'll be fine." She reaches for the seatbelt, her eyes still on her husband. "Okay, trees. I want a real one. Not gi-normous, like Momma . . ." Her voice trails as Aaron gets back out of the car. He slams the door hard. Kelsey rolls down her window. "Babe?"

"They, uh, canceled my audition, so . . ."

"Fuck them. This just wasn't the gig for —"

"My agent doesn't want to send me out for a while, says things need to 'cool.' "

"What's 'a while?' " she asks, her face pleated in concern.

"Didn't say." Aaron shakes his head and walks back into the house.

"Dammit."

"I'm so sorry," I say, wanting to squeeze her hand.

She turns away from me as Peter backs down the drive.

Hours later, Kelsey is still repeating her same love of all that is Christmas in back-to-back three-minute intervals to different radio stations.

I stand on the other side of the sound booth holding Kelsey's remicrowaved fries and wait for the next sixty-second break, in which she'll attempt to pound them before they grow cold again.

Michelle chats happily behind me to yet another licensing agent about Kelsey Kids. "Sing nursery rhymes together? Me? Well, you know, there was 'Itsy Bitsy Spider.' The standards."

"Michelle," Andy says with blatant annoyance. "Take it in the hall."

"Oh, that's sweet, people always said I was good with a tune," she continues.

"Michelle."

"I will do just that . . . Okay. 'Bye now!" She hangs up. "Phew, I am just about losing my voice!"

"Doubt it," Andy mutters.

"Everyone." Michelle prickles, and I am surprised to hear her continue, given his obvious mood. "Is calling me, everyone."

"I know, I hear you talking to them all the damn day. She's distracted enough."

"And . . . clear." The producer waves me into the claustrophobic chamber, and I lead with a fry right into Kelsey's mouth.

"Forty-five seconds," the producer warns.

"I can't go this long without eating."

"Logan." Andy leans on the intercom. "Your cell."

"Be right there."

"Get me a smoothie, something I can chug."

"Sorry — I'm sorry — just let me grab my phone, and I'll, uh, one minute." I dash back out to lunge into my bag.

"GM?"

"We got a situation."

Kelsey's hands are wrapped protectively around her belly as GM swerves our Suburban in and out of traffic. "I wish y'all would let me handle this," GM says to Kelsey in the passenger seat beside him. "You shouldn't be here. You just shouldn't."

She sucks in her lips as she searches the crowded stretch of road. "There." Kelsey points at the approaching Walmart sign. GM peels in, checking his rear mirror to make sure that Andy and Michelle made the light. We haul past the SUVs and wagons to the nauseating string of — "Motorcycles," Kelsey says, the same way she says, "Turbulence," when we hit rocky air.

"Stay here," GM instructs as he tugs out the keys. But Kelsey has already thrown off her seatbelt. He clamps his arm over her. "Kelsey. You can*not* go into this." She struggles.

"Kelsey." I scoot forward.

"You want me to get him, right? Get him out of here?" GM asks.

She nods.

"I cannot focus on doing that if I'm keeping those shutters off you. Stay. Here."

She whips to me. "Logan, go. Please go. Please?"

I follow GM through the crowd as he appraises possible retrieval points. "Okay, you'll be able to get the closest to him without drawing attention. Tell him to walk directly to the employee exit." He points to a door on the side of the building. "Go."

The barren checkout lanes are unmanned. The aisles are empty. In the packed snack bar there's about a five-foot radius of space around Aaron maintained by the unmistakable "fuck off" vibe he's emitting. I take a breath and in three steps am sitting across from him, setting off fresh flashes. He jerks his face up, and I recoil from a look of such rage that it knocks out my breath like a sparking power line.

"Logan," he says with surprise, dropping his gaze to his sweating wax-paper cup.

"GM is waiting at the edge of this crowd."

"*This* crowd?"

"There's, uh, another outside. Okay, on the count of three, we're going to get up and go."

"I have to pay for the lights."

"What?"

He nods down, and I see a jumbo pack of white Christmas-tree lights between his feet.

"Aaron, I'll call the florist."

"I need to get these." His lip quivers, and cameras flash once again. "I need to pay for these. Myself."

"Aaron, seriously."

"I just wanted to run an errand on my

own. I used to spend whole days on my own."

"How long have you been here?"

"I don't know. Two hours? It started in the decorations aisle, then I went to check out, but everyone was leaving their lines to take a picture. My card was declined — it was my fault — I grabbed the wrong card — but I didn't want more pics of me pulling out more cards, how that would look. So I came over, ordered a soda, but all the servers started taking pictures. I thought maybe if I just sat, acted normal —"

"Why didn't you text us earlier?" I can't help asking.

"I used to get myself outta my own shit."

"But this isn't your own. Aaron, we have to go. Kelsey's in the car —"

"She's here? You brought her here? Are you fucking crazy?" He jumps to his feet, and I leap to follow as we are bombarded by flashes.

"Fuckin' pussy!" someone shouts. The crowd grabs at whatever part of him they can reach. Then GM has his arm around both of us and runs us straight into the back of his car. Andy peels away. I right myself on the seat as I turn to see GM hop into the car driven by Michelle behind us.

"Aaron!" Kelsey twists in the front seat to

281

reach to him. "Baby, you okay?"

"Kelsey." Andy tugs her back around. The brakes screech as the car in front stops short, and we all brace for an eluded impact. "Sit fucking still, and keep your seatbelt fucking on. Aaron, FUCK were you thinking?" Aaron stares out the window. "You pull a stunt like this again, so help me God, I will fucking —"

"I was trying to decorate my family's house for Christmas." Aaron's steel tone cuts through Andy's histrionics. "There's not a thing you can say to me that I have not said to myself in the last two hours, so if you don't mind, sir, could we please." Aaron clenches his jaw. "Get home."

That night marks Bison Fest. It's what I imagine Burning Man might be if it took place at a mansion and had staff. Instead of dish towels, Travis's guests are armed against the smoke with all manner of designer scarves as if we're about to shoot a rap video. Just as Travis is readying for "old-timey fire chants," my cell rings.

"Hi," I answer. "Sorry, with all the craziness this afternoon, I didn't connect with the florist, but I will tomorrow."

"Oh," Kelsey says. "That's fine, whatever."

"Okay," I say uncertainly as Finn triages

the dwindling Wild Turkey reserves.

"Aaron felt like he needed to get out."

"Sure," I say, marveling that he would venture beyond the driveway.

"Just to meet up with some of his buds. Get a drink or whatever. GM's with him."

"Cool."

"And I was wondering . . . want to watch a movie or something? I mean, if you're not doing anything."

Travis walks past, smearing something gaggingly pungent under his eyes that I'd venture came out of one end or the other of that bison. "On my way."

"Aw, you look so cuddly," Kelsey says as she leans against the the guest room door.

"*You* look cuddly." I smile as I close the last button on my borrowed pajamas. It was eleven by the time I arrived, so Kelsey made hot cocoa and conversation while I drank in her openness with every steaming slurp.

"I love when I can take my bra off." She hunches in Aaron's sweatshirt. "Taking off my bra is the highlight of my day. Didn't see that coming."

"But soon a beautiful baby girl will be the highlight of your day." I switch off the bathroom light and flip back the duvet. "So it's all worth it."

"I don't know. It's going to be hard to upstage this bra thing."

"What time is Aaron due back?" I ask as she curls up at the foot of the bed.

She's quiet for a moment "Howard Stern's calling him Twatts, and today it trended. His agent messengered over termination papers."

"Oh, man."

"Yeah, so whenever he's ready to call it a night is fine by me." She rolls onto her back. "It's not like he needs to work."

"But he needs to work."

"And I love that about him."

"He came to L.A. to have a solo career. So, maybe that? Or he could open a club or a restaurant or something?" I feel my eyes getting heavy.

"I'm glad you're here," she says.

"I missed ya, chica." I nudge her from under the comforter.

"Well, you really hurt me," she says with a severity I hadn't anticipated.

"I . . . I'm sorry."

She turns on her side, her hands tucked together to form a pillow. "When I was sick in Amsterdam, you told me I wouldn't have to entertain you."

"You don't, but that doesn't mean —"

"I need one person I don't have to sell it

to." She sits up.

"Kelsey, you don't have to sell me, but it kinda sucks to be in the last-to-know category. You have to tell me what's going on."

"But you said I didn't have to *anything* with you."

I open my mouth, stunned by her interpretation of support.

"Okay, good." She pulls a bolster into what's left of her lap and smushes it. "I'm glad we talked. I just want things to go back to how they were."

"Yes. No, I do, too." I think.

"You're spending Christmas with us, right? Remember Daddy dragging us on the sled to cut down the tree? And when he dresses up with the Santa beard? You'll be here, won't you, Lo?" she asks with a look that tells me this is the moment to show that I've heard her.

"How can I pass up Andy in a Santa suit?"

"Yea!" She claps and climbs off the bed as visions of hot rum at the Carlyle recede. "All right, then, happy faces in the morning."

I reach for the lamp, my hand freezing at the distinct sound of a twig breaking outside the window. I flick off the light. Another twig. Branches moving and then the sound of heavy footsteps on the porch.

"You're sure it's not Aaron?"

"Did you hear a car?"

"What about your parents?"

"At a movie." She grabs my hand, and we run. Kelsey tugs open a kitchen drawer and fumbles for a knife as I race to the security panel, and the front door opens to — Andy.

"Daddy," Kelsey gasps.

"You okay?" I turn to Kelsey. "Is the baby okay?"

"Come on out." Andy waves to us.

"When did you get back?" Kelsey asks, breathing hard. "We thought somebody was out there."

"Come on, it'll be quick."

Kelsey grips my hand as Andy futzes with something. The front bushes light up in a mish-mash of multicolored blinking lights.

"Oh," Kelsey says.

"And check this out." A motor comes on, and a trio of ten-foot blow-up snowmen whip frenetically to and fro. "You know," Andy says sheepishly to his sneakers. "Like y'all wanted."

"Thanks, Daddy." Kelsey holds her belly. "It's just what I pictured."

Later, the rainbow flickers across the guest-room ceiling and into my looping dreams. I wake with a start and realize I'm listening to the dull thud of Andy's hammer, still pounding in his decorations on the back of the house. Hearing a car doom slam, I look out the window. Gripping his coat in one hand, Aaron takes in the decorations while a taxi U-turns around him. He lifts a middle finger at seemingly the entire property, his frame swerving before his arm falls slack. With a dropped head, he stumbles out of view.

CHAPTER ELEVEN

I wasn't the only one whose holiday was hijacked. Travis's movie spiraled on Rotten Tomatoes, so to shield himself from "the bad juju," he transferred to an unfinished Tribeca condo, for which he asked Finn to purchase — wait for it — pup tents for the arriving families. Finn warded his parents off at the pass. "Not telling Nana this is carry-in carry-out," was his best text of the week.

On my end, Christmas had the foretold effect on Andy — from his tinsel to his Turducken, he was uncharacteristically jovial, reviving memories of childhood holiday antics. Michelle basked in his mood and parked herself in front of the fireplace to fantasize about next year's candy-cane-themed capsule collection for Kelsey Kids.

Aaron marginalized by Andy's holiday spirit announced Christmas Eve that he's going to record a solo album. As I plated the bird(s), I overheard Michelle whisper, "Well, we don't really understand why her stuff sells — maybe he'll be huge." To which Andy conceded, "It could help him grow a pair."

Finn got a pass from Camp Moynihan and we met for a New Year's weekend of low-lit drinks, museum kisses, and our very own penthouse suite, complete with plumbing. When I returned, Kelsey informed me that I'd just missed Aaron at LAX because he's decided that the best producers for him to work with are based in London.

"Here, let me hold your water," I say, reaching for the bottle as Kelsey walks backward up the stairs, holding her laptop. In the two months since Aaron's departure Kelsey's been subsisting on Skype dates.

"Those cool egg chairs you liked haven't arrived yet, but Logan calls the store every day to follow up, and, see, I got your painting —"

"Baby, are you sure this is safe?" Aaron's voice comes out of the speaker as Kelsey gives him a tour.

"Logan's got me, right, Lo?"

Lifting the hem of her low-slung skirt, I wave. "Hey, Aaron. How's London?"

"Cold. And damp. Shit, is it damp. My

socks won't dry."

"It's seventy-six here today," Kelsey can't help letting him know. She tilts the laptop to the sun streaming through the skylights.

"How's the recording coming?" I ask.

"Off the hook. This producer's really letting me steer the ship. I'm writing lyrics, using my voice in a whole new way. Damn, you look sexy." He interrupts himself as she steps fully into frame.

"No." I register my daily protest. "Do not encourage her."

"She does! Every time I run out for some smokes and see a picture of her with her belly busting out — full wood, I swear."

"Aaron!" she squeals.

"You're biased," I tell him. "She looks like a pregnant prostitute, and that is arguably the saddest kind of prostitute."

"One-legged," Kelsey challenges. "So much sadder. Aaron?"

"No hands."

"You two deserve each other."

We step into the chamber beside the master suite. *"Candy kisses on a sunny day,"* Madonna's lyrics to "Dear Jessie" are painted over the door. "And this is Jessie's room!" Kelsey slowly leads the Macbook past every surface like a Geiger counter. "These are her books, this is her *Sleep*

Sheep, isn't it cute? This is her crib with a view of the pool, see, this is her view —"

"Baby, I remember her view. I gotta get back." We can hear a drum track start up.

"This is the swing. It has lamb ears. Logan helped me put it together." Between Lamaze classes.

"Kel," Aaron says testily, "I told you I'd do it my next trip back. It's only two weeks before the single drops."

"But what if I'm early?"

"I was having a manly moment," I say to restore a playful mood.

"Come on, baby, you've hit every target you've ever been given. You think our little girl's gonna be any different? I'll be pulling my half, and that boo of ours will come into this world on schedule with two stars looking out for her."

"I know." Kelsey's gaze softens at this vision.

"Well, hold me up to her, won't you?" he requests, and Kelsey lowers the screen to the bump bared below her knit bra top. "I love you, little girl. Daddy misses you and can't wait to come home and give that belly some proper lovin'."

"Friday?"

"Kel, we're so close. I don't want to break everyone's flow."

"I miss you. I need you."

"Baby?" he asks, his voice low. "I'm one of the guys here. I cannot just jet off to see my famous wife. It wouldn't be good for morale."

"So if you had a pregnant wife no one had heard of, you could go visit her and rub her back and help her put the crib together."

"It's together!" he says. "I just saw it!"

"That's not the point."

"I have to go. I'll really try, okay?"

"Okay. And there's too much treble on that bass," she tosses off without even thinking. The screen turns black.

I hold up the tissues from where I sit wedged between two stuffed elephants.

"Ew." She dabs her eyes. "I'm so hormonal."

"You're allowed to be sad that he's missing this, Kel," I say as a tiny foot visibly pushes at its confines.

"But he really isn't." She smiles and rubs over it. "I'm right in his face every time he goes to the corner," she says, pleased. Neither of us mentions that *his* movements are chronicled with equal attention stateside — including nightly forays into London's club scene. I strain my neck to see that she's typing her name into Google UK.

"*What* are you doing?"

"Just want to see what they like over there so I can plan my wardrobe for the week." She lowers herself down beside me on the thick carpeting. "And he's just trying to be a good dad, so we can be a normal family. I get that. It's all for us." She looks to the molding, where a chain of elephants lead each other by the tail. "Just have to be strong a little longer."

The page fills with nine images of her pole dancer maternity wear and the assorted snarky commentary, but the banner headline is, "Sad Kelsey All Alone While Hubby Enjoys Our Shores."

"Kel, what? Is it the baby? Are you okay?"

She shuts the lid. "They've never been right before."

I'm standing in Spago with Andy as we wait on a trio of very unathletic-looking athletic-apparel executives. Respectfully steering clear of the house now that Aaron's returned home to promote his single, I'm surprised when he calls. "Hello?"

Andy follows the maître d'.

"Is that Logan? Did you get Logan?" I hear Kelsey beseech in the background.

"Aaron?"

"Yeah. She wanted me to call you."

"What's wrong?" I turn to the wall.

"It's happening. She's early. We're going in."

"Oh, my God. Andy!" I wave him back.

"*Don't* tell them."

I drop my hand, then hear her moan my name, and he clicks off.

"What?" Andy asks, doubling back. "Kel okay?"

"The, um, the pool house had a flood, and Finn is away, so, I'm so sorry — would you mind if I — ?"

I blow out the door, valet ticket in hand.

I'm informed by a nurse that Aaron's restricted me to stay in the waiting area. By the time Finn arrives, my fingers are pressed to my ears to drown out the sound of her calling my name from across the hall.

"Finn, go ask them, ask them what's taking so long."

"I think that's just having a baby," he tries to hold me.

Sometime around two AM Aaron sticks his head in to hoarsely inform us that the baby is stuck. I want to tell him she has pressure points and breath patterns and rankles at the phrase "You can do it."

Finn eventually pushes a few chairs together and tries to get some rest. I can only pace the linoleum, remembering when I was a patient, the headache when I came to, the bruise in my arm from the IV, lying in that private, public place with the enormous sense of Kelsey — the physical separation from her — and yet the engine of my will to bridge the divide, the bottomless ache to wrap protectively around her. But all my mother would tell me was that it was over.

Even then, I couldn't connect Mom's summation to the car accident that my father informed me I'd been in. We'd been in. I still can't.

"Bullshit!" The sound of Michelle screeching above the slap of her sandals brings me to a halt. "Making us wait down there like we were paparazzi! As if she wouldn't want her own momma by her side."

"Logan, what in the hell?" Andy storms at me. Finn jerks up as I back into the chairs. "For fuck's sake!"

"We have to find out about this on the damn news ticker?" Coming in behind him, Michelle jerks open the blinds, revealing throngs of reporters hungrily standing vigil in the parking lot as if waiting for smoke to come out of the Vatican. "I was so flustered I didn't even have my wallet. That security thug made me go all the way home. All the way! Where is she?"

"Good, you're here." We turn to see Aaron

beaming in the doorway. "Come meet our daughter."

I recount Kelsey's bags while Aaron hands out roses to the blushing nurses, going on about how great they've been to his family. Andy idles the car, not trusting Jessie Logan Watts's first drive to Peter — or Aaron. We wait for Michelle, who has insisted on helping get Kelsey camera-ready for her mandatory wheelchair-assisted departure.

"That's you!" One of the nurses squeals, and I look up to see Aaron on the TV over the snack machines.

"Shit!" He blushes as one of the nurses scrapes a chair over to adjust the volume.

"— an unprecedented amount of cover videos on YouTube in the last forty-eight hours making fun of what can definitely be called Poppa Wade's failed attempt —"

I hear the double doors behind us as the screen goes to footage of Aaron recording in the studio. "It made E! Oh, Aaron, I'm so psyched!" Kelsey cheers as she and Jessie are wheeled in to watch low-grade footage of people parodying Aaron.

"And the blogger commentary can best be summed up by Kelfan4eveah: 'I hope for its sake the baby's deaf.' Aaron, stick to what you do best, selling drugs to kids. Now on to which star's going to be the voice of the next animated —"

"What are you all standing around for?" A harried Michelle pushes through the doors, the massive stuffed elephant Aaron brought in her arms. "Shake a leg! Aaron, Andy's waiting. We're going to have to send a car back for this thing. It's never going to fit with the rest of us. What? Why's everyone —"

"Nothing." Kelsey cuts her off.

"I can — I'll get the elephant home," I say to Michelle.

The nurses return to their stations.

The next day I ferry Kelsey's coconut water to the couch in the narrow aisle I've created between gift boxes.

"No more. I can't," she protests as she adjusts the muslin nursing cover.

"It'll make you feel better."

"I have stitches in my vag, I pee every time I move, and my nipples are bleeding, but no, coconut water — sure." She winces, her pallor anemically white.

"Should I get the lactation consultant back?"

"No, just when Jessie tugs on a scab with her gums —"

"Ay!" I raise my shoulder to my ear. "That

feels wrong."

"You don't have to nurse, Kelsey," Michelle says. "If you switch to formula, Daddy and I can feed her."

"Anyone want some chips?" Andy calls over from the kitchen, digging his hand into a bag. "Kel, at least put a TV over here next to the fridge. I can't be running to the den every time I need to check the news."

"No TV," she says firmly. Especially now that Letterman, Leno, Chelsea, Kathy, the guy at Coffee Bean and Tea Leaf, everyone is making cruel jokes at Aaron's expense. "Baby, you okay?" she asks him carefully. He doesn't answer.

"Ooh, Kel, this one next." Michelle tries to pass her yet another Tiffany's box.

"Momma, why don't we wait till later?"

"Don't you want to know what —" Michelle opens the card for her. "Elton John sent?" I kind of want to know.

"Ooh, maybe it's a tiny dancer," Michelle guesses. "Andy, Elton John sent the baby a gift!"

He grunts at his BlackBerry.

"Or you do it?" Kelsey offers, and Michelle unties the white ribbon while I add the robin's-egg bag to the mountain Michelle is saving for — what, I have no idea. "Ooh." She pops open the navy velvet box to a pair of huge diamond earrings. Elizabeth Taylor–size.

"Wow," Kelsey says.

"What?" Aaron looks up.

Michelle models the earrings. "I may have to borrow these."

"Fucking unbelievable," Aaron scoffs.

Kelsey hastily takes the earrings from her mom with her free hand and puts them on the pile with the rest of the jewelry.

"What, hon?" Michelle asks him.

"I just, you know." Aaron scowls. "Thought it'd be a level playing field for at least a few years. She has every fucking thing a girl could ever ask for right through her fucking wedding tiara, and she's only four days old. I'm useless."

"You're her daddy," Andy says simply.

"Yes!" Kelsey rushes to agree, and Andy looks surprised. "No one's more important than her daddy."

Aaron kicks the pyramid of jewelry boxes, and they tinkle as they scatter. "Fuck ever happened to sending a blanket?"

I spot a small striped bag with fur sticking out and hand it off to him. "Look, here!"

He pulls a stuffed rabbit by its floppy ears.

"It's a Frankenbunny." Andy laughs in response to the exaggerated stitching from its forehead to its nose.

"Who's it from?" Michelle asks.

Aaron opens the card, then flings it at Kelsey before striding to the stairs he takes two at a time.

"Aaron!" Michelle calls him back.

"Aaron, for Christ's sake," Andy adds as their bedroom door slams and Jessie starts crying.

Kelsey scrambles to get the card open.

"What, what is it?" Michelle asks.

"It's from Eric," she says. "Here's what you can't do when you're nursing — chase your husband." Jessie lets out a piercing wail. Kelsey fumbles under the blanket, wincing and cooing.

"I don't get it. So Eric sent Jessie a stuffed animal — so what?" Michelle dismisses the drama. "Now who's being a baby?"

I pick it off the floor. The tag dangling from its ear flips over and I realize it's the Velveteen Rabbit.

CHAPTER TWELVE

"Can I show you anything else?" Professionalism straining, the woman behind Fred Segal's cufflink counter stares at Kelsey with the same intensity that Kelsey peers through the glass at an array of skull-themed options. She is obviously hoping that Kelsey will say no, so we'll leave and take our colicky infant with us — let the sneering bleached lollipops shop in peace. The store is steadily raising the music to drown out Jessie's wails, Joy Division sounding more joyless with every added decibel.

With the baby strapped to her chest, Kelsey bounces continuously. It feels like she's been bouncing for two straight months — downward swaying being the only of the Five S's to buy us a respite. I now totally get why recordings of an inconsolable infant are used to torture suspected terrorists.

Kelsey bites her lip as she contemplates platinum poker-chip cufflinks. "I don't know, I don't know."

I study the case, aware that this anniversary gift has to be as perfect as the elaborately planned day it will cap off. "Lo, how we doing on time?" she asks, adding quietly, "I was so wrong about coming here. This feels all wrong. Can we swing by Rodeo on our way — it needs to feel special — these don't feel special."

"We have to be at the studio in half an hour, and Aaron's plane should be landing soon." Bringing him home for the first time since Jessie was born. My mind races to make sure we hit all her marks — that the Annie Leibovitz angel-themed family portrait doesn't run late, ensuring that they have time to play with Jessie at home, give her a bath together, put her to bed, and still make their dinner reservation and first-kiss re-creation at the club.

"And don't forget about traffic," Michelle says as she returns from the dressing room with a green Eres maillot in hand.

"But none of these is right." Kelsey rubs Jessie's feet.

"I could hear that child clear across ladies' intimates. Maybe it's something you're eating, Kelsey," Michelle helpfully observes as she takes a seat on a converted surfboard and picks up a tabloid. "She's pretty lippy.

You never screamed like this."

"Can I see those little gold revolvers?" Kelsey asks the salesgirl. "The food thing is an old wives' tale, Momma."

"What we call folk wisdom."

"Okay." Kelsey lets out a jittery breath as she takes the guns. "I'm just going to have to figure this out while she screams."

"Oooh." Michelle looks up from the magazine. The very one that's been avidly chronicling Jessie's colic, and the opinions of "experts" who assess where Kelsey is failing. It started a month ago, when one morning, after driving Jessie around for hours, she had finally fallen asleep, and Kelsey desperately needed to pee. Panicked and leaking, she left Jessie in her car seat for less than a minute while she dashed into a gas-station bathroom. What the pictures didn't show was that Jessie was still under the watchful eye of about a hundred paparazzi and GM parked a few feet away. Now the tabloids are trying to one-up each other chronicling Kelsey as a bad mom. Which, to anyone who knows the strain her knees are taking as a one-woman cradle, is ludicrous.

"Baby Gap is looking for models."

"No. You have your clothing line to focus on, right, Momma?"

"Not even Kathie Lee and Hoda's Beautiful Baby contest?"

Kelsey clanks the revolvers down and turns to her mother. *"Why?"*

"She's so beautiful — we should give her opportunities."

"For *what?*" Kelsey raises her voice to be heard, rubbing Jessie's back as the screams escalate. "Momma, I don't want her to have to think about anything but having fun until she graduates college."

"And that's a dig at me." Michelle turns the page. "You didn't *want* to go to college, Miss Thing — what use would college have been?"

"I don't know. Logan, what did you learn at NYU?"

"Use a condom." I slide the gold guns back to the salesgirl.

"Oh, please." Michelle dismisses her. "It just about wore me out keeping up with you. You loved performing. You loved the contests."

"Because it got us away from Daddy."

In a lull between songs, between screams, Kelsey's words echo off the tiled ceilings. Michelle lowers her beating face, wordlessly untucks her legs, and walks out the door. Kelsey watches, as everyone watches, her hands momentarily still on her daughter.

I push the tray back to the salesgirl. "How

about I have Cartier pull a few things and run them to set?"

Kelsey nods, wrapping her arms around the tiny bundle on her chest. "I know, baby," she whispers. "It hurts. Your tummy hurts. I know."

In pursuit of Kelsey's heavenly vision, the set feels like a chicken coop as we all sneeze, blow, and sneeze again, our eyes, ears, and mouths filled with the spray of hundreds of bags of feathers.

Today Andy and Kelsey's aspirations are in alignment. Andy wants this *Vanity Fair* shoot to shift public perspective from questioning Aaron's fidelity to a wholesome family bond. Kelsey wants the wholesome family bond.

My phone rings. "Aaron, everything okay?" I ask, trying to find a spot out of the way.

"Yeah."

"Your flight land?"

"Yeah."

"You in the limo?"

"Yeah."

"On your way here?"

"Yeah."

"Okay, great," I say, having checked off my immediate fears. "Happy anniversary."

"I, uh, wanted to see what I could do for that. We're doing something tonight, right?"

You're shitting me. "Yep."

"I don't have anything up my sleeve, but I could have flowers sent . . ."

"Um, Kel got some roses," I say, underplaying the yellow blooms blanketing their home.

"Okay. Well, what about getting a friend to DJ at the house, make that fun?"

"I think you guys are going out."

"Oh. Okay, well, whatever. It's not like this is our tenth. I'm sure she didn't sweat it, what with the baby 'n' all. Okay, see you."

Fuckfuckfuck.

I immediately call Cartier and add the canary diamond rose brooch Kelsey admired. A pin might be an odd gift for a twenty-five-year-old, especially one she's technically buying for herself, but the reference to her bridal bouquet should beat the nothing that's been planned for her.

"Please keep the door shut!" Kelsey cries, sneezing as I enter. "I can't take Jessie out there." I glance at the sleeping baby, praying this nap holds out. "How is this gonna work?"

Annie's studio manager bites his pencil. "She's gonna shoot the baby separately at the end and Photoshop her in."

"What? No," Kelsey protests. "I wanted, like, like, the Cruises or the Testino spread with Lola sitting on her stomach. This is supposed to be our family portrait — *ah-choo!*"

"I hear we're having a crisis?" The stylist sticks her head in.

The assistant flaps his arms. "I tried elastics, I tried clamps, I can't get anything to close. I can't get her arms through the sleeves, I can't get the pants past her hips, I —"

"Well, she's fat," The stylist says matter-of-factly.

"I had a baby."

"What about using what she came in?" I ask. The sound of everyone's nostrils flaring is audible. "Or running to H&M and getting her some normal-size clothes? These are like Build-a-Bear outfits."

The stylist scowls. "Percy, call the office, see if we have any of that stuff we pulled for Queen Latifah."

Kelsey is handed a robe. The hairstylist flags the studio manager over. "And *psst.*" He points unsubtly at her scalp.

"I'm shedding, I know," Kelsey says loudly, blinking as her irritated eyes water. "And I'm breaking out. But my stitches have healed — too bad this isn't for *Hustler.*"

Kelsey is already hoisted into her harness when Aaron arrives, forcing them to greet each other from a distance. He first refuses the outfit they've chosen, then the meal on offer, followed by the drinks in the cooler, and is generally surly and difficult with everyone, as if trying to ensure they walk away saying that Aaron is such a dick and not, hey, I worked with the loser who sings "Zigging When It Should Be Zagging."

"Okay, now, Aaron." The room quiets as Annie finally speaks in the thin voice of someone whose every word is hung on. "I want you to look at Kelsey like you love her." She stares down at the screen, analyzing the image. Then up, analyzing Aaron. "Love her." Down to the image. Up to Aaron. "More love." Again. "More love *in the eyes*." Again. "She's the best thing that ever happened to you."

A determined Kelsey makes a joke when we arrive at the club that Aaron should carry her to the VIP lounge to complete the reenactment. But, by design, there are no douchey guys to maul her this evening. I thought it would feel more special if we rented out the VIP area, but, devoid of Hollywood heirs and the randy twenty-somethings looking to bag them, the empty booths have a dampening effect on what little enthusiasm the two guests of honor seem to muster. Jessie slept through tummy time and was hungry early, precluding the bath, leaving Kelsey alone to nurse while Aaron succumbed to jet lag. Even with Aaron's friends, Kelsey's dancers, and the handful of buddies Finn was able to wrangle, the party is slow to get going. Honestly, I have to keep reminding myself that we didn't just load in for another video shoot. But then, at Finn's suggestion, I tell the manager to reopen his VIP list. And once everyone gets a cocktail in them, dancing starts in earnest.

Nursing her spritzer, Kelsey gamely watches Aaron do shots with some friends, and I have to wait until she excuses herself to the bathroom to catch him. "She didn't need to go to so much trouble," he says.

"Well, you know Kelsey."

He nods.

"Anyway," I continue, "I left a red leather box under your side of the bed."

"Of course you did." He knocks back another shot. "Well, thanks, I guess," he says.

I excuse myself to find Finn.

"Happy Someone Else's Anniversary." Finn, a little buzzed, pulls me against him into one of the velvet booths.

"You, too." I smile, fingering his collar.

"How 'bout we go to the bathroom and have a re-creation of our own?"

"If you'll recall, what we bonded over was the bathroom being disgusting." I take a sip of my drink. "And technically, I'm on duty. Oh, and we have a really comfortable bed now."

He gives me an acknowledging smile. "You sound old and married."

"You love it."

He separates the damp napkin from the base of his sweating highball. "I do."

Aaron unsteadily pulls Kelsey in to dance, people making a circle around the pair, cheering them on. Kelsey snaps into show mode, flipping her hair back and rhythmically snaking up her husband. He lifts his hat, turning it around as he drops his hands behind his back. I watch as the shrinking distance between their pulsating movements once again sparks. Kelsey looks up at him, into him, lifting her arms languorously over her head and swiveling her hips. He bends his knees and starts to dance down her when he trips. She reaches for his arm, but he tugs it away.

He stumbles off the floor, and then, seemingly remembering that they're being observed, she resumes dancing, albeit distractedly as a new song comes on. Suddenly, her forearms brace her chest and she scurries out of sight.

"Be right back," I say.

"Meet you in a stall?" Finn squeezes my bare thigh.

"Hold that thought." I follow the booths until I find Kelsey in the corner of the last one. "You okay?" I yell over the music, but she doesn't hear me. She slides cocktail napkins into the gold triangle tops of her dress. "Hey." I put my hand on her shoulder as I realize that Kanye's latest single samples a baby crying.

"I'm engorged," she says into my ear. "It's so painful. I didn't bring the pump. I didn't think of it. My dress is soaked. How am I going to say good-bye to everyone?" She clenches her eyes.

"They'll understand. We're out of here." I grab a stack of napkins.

Mortified, she won't let my arm go, and I end up in the backseat of my car behind Aaron, whose head lolls on the seat rest. Kelsey holds bracing palms to her breasts, her forehead resting against the glass as she takes little breaths. The second we pull up at their house, she flings her door open to race inside, her heels fighting against the suck of the pebbles.

"Thanks for chauffeuring." Aaron pats Finn's shoulder. "And rustling up your bros."

"Sure thing. Hope she feels better, man."

"Yeah." Aaron opens his eyes wide. "Jet lag and Hennessy do not mix." Finn responds with a knowing laugh. "Thanks, Logan," Aaron's voice empties as he gets out. "Party was awesome."

I move up front, and Finn turns the car around in the driveway, the headlights cutting a swath of dimension into the black profiles of the trees. I focus on the broken yellow line, reminding myself that I can, should, clock out.

Suddenly, tires screech and the horn blares. I spin to see the stop sign Finn just ran as the other driver screams, "Asshole!" and continues on.

"Pull over."

"We're almost home."

"Finn, pull over, you're drunk." I catch my breath.

"I'm tired."

"You ran a stop sign!"

"I'm fine. You're fine."

"Pull over!" I scream. He slams on the brakes.

"Fine! Fuck!"

My beaded clutch vibrates between us.

A few minutes later I run past a bewildered Michelle, stretching awake on the couch. Upstairs Aaron is standing awkwardly over Kelsey in the far corner of their bathroom. He backs out of the way, and I crouch where she's curled between the bidet and the wall, a towel clenched around her shivering shoulders. The top of her dress is undone under the terrycloth, its gold strings pooling between her legs.

"She just started hyperventilating."

"Kelsey." I look into her face, but she's staring down, her eyes large O's.

"I — I can't do it. I can't —"

"Okay. It's okay. You don't have to do anything," I say, trying to reach her. Her teeth are chattering. I go to take her hand, but she jerks back, bracing her feet against the porcelain as if to burrow away from us through the marble.

"What happened?" I turn to Aaron as Finn comes to the door.

"I have no idea." Aaron points at the bottle of milk on the counter. "She was pumping, and she started apologizing about making us leave, and I said it was nothing, and then —"

"What's all this?" Michelle leans around Finn. "Kelsey?" Kelsey jerks her face up, her whole body tremoring. "Oh, she's just drunk."

"She's not," I say.

"She didn't drink barely anything." Aaron corrects Michelle. "A glass of wine, that's all."

"Kelsey." Michelle grips the vanity and bends her knees. "You're scaring your husband half to death. Is that what you want? What kind of welcome home is that?"

Kelsey grabs the bidet, twists her head, and heaves the last contents of her stomach into the porcelain.

"Tell me that's not drunk." Michelle *tsks*.

"I can't." Kelsey lifts her palm defensively, as if Michelle is about to spit on her. "I can't, please. Just go, Momma. I can't have you here." Kelsey's voice thickens.

Michelle's eyes narrow, and she spins to leave. "Your daughter fell asleep just fine, in case you're wondering," she calls over her shoulder.

"I'm sorry. I'm sorry," Kelsey murmurs as I nudge Aaron forward to scoop her up in his arms.

"You're welcome!" Michelle yells before we all hear the back door slam.

"We should call someone. A doctor," Aaron says to us, the veins in his arms popping.

"I kinda agree." Finn leans on the wall.

"No, baby, please, just lie down with me. Hold me. I'm freezing."

Aaron carries her shivering into their dark bedroom, and that's when I realize my own hands are shaking. I'm surprised by a rolling lightheadedness as my vision tunnels to a cone, my mouth drying as if I've opened it in front of an industrial fan.

"Now what?" Finn asks quietly.

I tuck my palms out of sight. "I need to stay in case the baby wakes up."

Nodding, he follows me out to the hall. "It's not like I hit the guy," he begins again. "Nothing happened."

"Finn, I can't. Please." As we descend I'm unsettled by the sensation that my feet aren't making contact, as if with each step, I really drop. Holding the wall, I lead him to the guest room. I force myself to check that the front door is locked and security on and then shakily take the baby monitor from where Michelle left it on the coffee table. *It's okay. She's going to be okay. I'm going to be okay.* Back in the guest room, I curl away from Finn's snoring and somehow, at some hour, pass out myself.

I come to, sweaty and dehydrated, the patch in the skylight still an inky black. For once, the dream that woke me is gone entirely, like a wave, but in its wake — certainty.

I push off the covers, grab my phone and tread to the kitchen. "Hello?" my mother answers, sounding panicked.

"I don't remember the accident." I lean against the glass that looks over the pool.

"Logan, go back to sleep."

"I don't remember it," I say emphatically.

"What have they been telling you?"

"I'm calling you."

"I . . . you were spared."

"The memory?" I ask, confused.

"He spared you. And that's all that matters —"

"I don't think there was a car accident," I say before I realize I'm going to, before I realize I even think it.

"Are you calling me a liar?"

I hear the cicadas outside, and the rush of blood in my ears. "I think I am."

She hangs up on me.

At the yard's edge there's a blue glow coming through the leaves. I listen to the whir of the AC and the faint gurgle of the pool filter, and realize it's coming from the guesthouse. From Andy's TVs. My mind trips back to the bathroom. To Kelsey.

Shit — the breast milk. Still sitting on the vanity.

Upstairs the light from the bathroom still spills onto the carpet. Kelsey, her dress unzipped, lies across the bed, asleep with her hand flung out for a garbage can Aaron holds. His back against the side of the bed, the jewelry box at his feet, he is wide awake.

Hours later I stir as Jessie's gurgles shoot the illuminated green dots up the monitor. Grabbing the guest bathrobe, I drop it in my pocket. I make a bottle and snuggle up to feed Jessie on one of the lounge chairs outside.

"You're going to wake her?" I hear Kelsey hiss, and look behind me before realizing that her voice is emitting from the terry-cloth folds at my hip.

"I'm not going to just jet without saying good-bye," Aaron whispers. "Dammit. Michelle's already grabbed her."

"You can't go away again."

"I have to get this album wrapped."

"Why?" she asks plaintively.

"Why couldn't you hang out last night?" he retorts.

"That's just mean. I told you my boobs were —"

"The hell happened to you when we got back here, Kelsey?"

"I — I don't know. It was a long day, with the shoot — maybe I ate something. It won't happen again. You have to stay, you have to —"

"I told you, I'm not living off you. That's not the father I'm gonna be."

"You think I don't see the pictures, Aaron?"

"I'm making connections, doing what I have to do. Some of us work at this. We didn't have it all handed to us at sixteen."

I inhale sharply.

"Fuck you. So, that means you don't want to use my producers?" Kelsey's voice grows brittle like Michelle's. "Or drive my car, fly on my ticket, stay in my hotels? I mean, I wouldn't want to *hand* anything to you."

Jessie's face scrunches to cry. Embarrassed, I fumble for the device.

"That's what you think?" He sounds like she's punched him in the gut.

"I'm just —"

"You're just forgetting *you* called me. *You* proposed to me. If you really think that's what I'm in this for, you can go fuck yourself."

I find the off button and click it.

Following almost a whole month of consoling her through Aaron's terse texts, canceled Skype dates, and no homecoming in sight, I arrived at Kelsey's this morning to find her in the living room, hovering on the edge of the couch with a tapping foot. She looked as if she'd been up for hours, but her mood was frenetically energized. She told me she'd had a brainstorm, that she needed to make a play like the one that got Aaron to fly to her in the first place. Then she passed off a manila envelope to hand-deliver. She was so eager for me to make the flight she'd booked that she didn't want to slow to tell me anything more, even when I called to press her from the car.

"I don't want to talk about it and lose my nerve, Logan, start second-guessing myself. Just go."

I'm guessing it's a ticket to meet her somewhere romantic. Maybe that island. She was talking about this the way she does when she gets one of her big video ideas, before the details have to be reality-tested by budgets and physics. I sense she has a half-sketched storyboard in her mind, including a drawing of my limo drive to south London.

At the studio, I'm told Aaron has moved to another facility, and we drive even farther into the labyrinth of municipal council estates.

"Sorry, can you repeat your name?" the voice requests as I stand by the rusting buzzer on the desolate street of brick row houses.

"Logan. Logan Wade. I'm Aaron's wife's assistant."

"I guess you can come up . . ." A skinny teenager is waiting as I huff to the top floor. "He's in back." I follow a curving warren of egg-crate-covered walls to a small room saturated with the aroma of cigarette butts floating in congealing coffee.

"Aaron?" I tentatively call, only to realize he has headphones on. I wave in front of him, and he leaps back, the taut cord jerking the headset.

"Shit." He catches them before they hit the floor. "Hey!" His face lifting, he smooths his hair as he darts around me toward the hall.

"I'm —" I go to stop him. "No, I'm on my own."

"Oh." He slouches. "You, uh, here for work? I could've met you in town. You didn't have to drag your ass all the way out here."

320

"Where is everyone?" I can't help but asking. "They told me you were shifted to this place?"

He drops back into the wheeling office chair. "Those assholes were totally useless."

"The producers?"

"The label needed them for another gig, and I was just, like, see ya."

"When?"

"Sometime after the single dropped." He makes a little explosion sound and blows apart his hands with a feeble laugh.

"You're finishing this alone?"

"Well, I've got Douglas out there. He can pick up smokes and carry-out fish and chips like a fucking pro. Seriously, will.i.am could do no better. Dang, I've got to tell you, it's nice to see a familiar face."

"You, too," I say automatically, covering my surprise that he seems to genuinely mean it. It's been weeks since there've been any pictures of him going out. I guess no one wants to risk a contact case of public stink. "You look great," I lie. His skin makes Kelsey's look sun-kissed.

"How're my girls?"

"Good. Missing you. I'm here to give you this, actually." I whip out the envelope and hand it over my arm with flourish. "From my lady."

"Nice." He grins. "That's cool of her. I just felt like I had to get this in better shape before we talked. You know, have something to share." Taking it, he walks away from me the few feet the room will allow where I see he's taped up photos of Jessie and Kelsey. There's a picture of Kelsey getting coffee only two days ago. He eagerly rips into the manila, pulling out the document that doesn't look like an itinerary.

"What is it?"

He hurls the papers onto the board, and grabs a pen. "Fuck. *Fuck!*" He throws it at the wall. "Do you have a pen?"

I dig into my bag and hand it to him. "Aaron, please, I honestly don't know what it is. What is it?"

Seething, he scrawls across the bottom and flings the pages at me. "You won. All y'all."

I clutch at them as they scatter across my chest, lifting one to read: "Petition for Divorce." "Oh, my God — I'm sure she doesn't mean this. She's just hurt —"

He glares at me with black eyes. "She's yours."

It was only when I checked in for my return flight hours later that I learned the seat next to me had been optimistically booked for

322

Mr. Watts.

I dropped my bag into it and asked for a stiff drink. And then another.

She comes from the house to greet the car, hair done, Jessie in her arms, the scent of her cinnamon rolls wafting out to greet me. When I emerge unaccompanied, her face collapses for a brief moment. "He's coming." She turns around, and I see the yellow rose brooch has been pinned to her ponytail. She returns to the kitchen and puts Jessie in her exersaucer.

"Kelsey, he's really — that was just — I'm sorry, but *what* were you thinking?"

"He'll see I want him with us or not at all. That I love him that much." She ties her apron. "He'll come."

She bakes and checks her phone and refreshes her makeup and scans the drive-way. Finally, after two full days of silence, she says she has to get out. At the corner coffee bar, I hang by the door with Jessie while Kelsey places her order. A guy in a rumpled suit jog-trots to the entrance with a singular look of purpose. I hold Jessie close as he passes. Then I see that he isn't carrying a camera but an envelope that he hands to Kelsey.

We somehow get Kelsey calmly, expressionlessly into the car, as if, to onlookers, she was supposed to meet this man for this very exchange. He's an old friend, bringing an expected document — a contract, maybe. Nothing going on here, folks, keep moving.

As the motorcycles escort us home we don't rip it open. I grip the wheel, and she makes herself sing "Old MacDonald."

We pass through the safety of the gates, and, obscured from the road, I immediately stop the car. She hands me the envelope with tremoring hands.

"It's a countersuit," I read quickly. "Petition."

"What? What is he suing me for?"

"Divorce." I puzzle, my eyes scanning down. "No." I grab her wrist. "For Jessie."

PART IV

CHAPTER THIRTEEN

The next morning I stand outside Kelsey's bedroom door as I hear her team greeting one another downstairs, low voices repeating my question: *What* was she thinking? Even I still don't get it. But Aaron's move — that I get. I saw him crouched on that balcony in Little Rock when his privacy was sucked away into the air. In the eye of that funnel, he said he loved her like I did. The girl being goofy in her T-shirt. And we both know, if you want to hit this girl in the heart, if you want to break her like you felt her world had broken you, you would come for her baby. I wish I could call him, but the first thing Kelsey learned was that he cancelled his phone.

I crack Kelsey's door to find her lying in Michelle's arms in the king-size bed. The curtains are drawn against the paparazzi, who have doubled in strength outside the gate. Every time so much as the mail arrives, the sky lights up like Michael Bay is filming a battle sequence in Laurel Canyon.

"Sorry, but the lawyer just got here," I whisper, and she nods, nudging her mother.

"He's here," she mouths to Michelle. Kelsey carefully gets up, shifting her swaddled daughter to the mattress.

"It's for real down there," I say quietly as Kelsey goes to the bathroom to splash her face. "There's seriously no way to call this thing off?"

"Maybe his lawyers will tell us where he's staying." She grabs a towel.

"And then you're going to tell him you made a mistake."

"Logan, things were so bad when Momma took me to L.A. — when we left Daddy." She scrapes congealed soap off the dish. "God, it was so shady — the motels, the guys we'd have to meet in their dingy offices. We were down to cereal and powdered milk. And then it just . . ." She lifts her shoulders. "Came out okay."

"It did," I say uncertainly.

"He came back! She threw down the ultimatum, and he got his crap together and showed up, and it all came out okay."

"But he didn't get sober for, like, years after that, right?"

"Well, he's sober now," she says tartly,

picking up a rubber band and twisting her hair into a topknot. "And Momma just had to be brave. She *was* brave."

Michelle comes in, tying her robe over her nightgown. "Holy mess." She sees herself in the mirror and Kelsey hands her a brush.

"So, were you in on the strategy here?" I ask her.

"What?" Michelle looks at me as if I'm nuts.

"I didn't talk to anyone about it, Logan," Kelsey says. "And it still can work. It'll work. He's just being a guy."

Michelle nods supportively. And while at a fundamental level, it is true, she's also just being a girl, playing at a high-school level with adult ammunition.

At the dining table Bob, her divorce attorney, passes out a packet to Cheryl, Kelsey's agent, and a few other suits.

"Honey, want some eggs?" Michelle asks Kelsey as we seat ourselves. "Or a bagel?"

"Can't eat." At the head of the table, with her mom beside her, she looks expectantly at the assembled, and it strikes me that this is the first time I've seen her open a meeting without her choreography of smiles.

Bob clears his throat. "Now, before we dive into the nitty-gritty of what they're asking for and what we're prepared to give —"

"Nothing," Andy states. "She's already given him way more than he deserves."

"Andy, I know we're only a day in here, but, to set your expectations, this is a long process. You should know Aaron's hired a very high-end team."

"How?" Kelsey asks, and Michelle covers her hand with hers. "He's broke."

Bob shrugs. "Banking on a future cut of a big payout."

"Think again," Andy interjects.

"Okay, this is totally out of hand," Kelsey says. "I appreciate that you came all the way up here to meet with me, but I only wanted him to come home. So, if you can please communicate to his attorney that we just need to talk, there's no need for —" Kelsey lifts the heavy packet and drops it.

"Yes," Michelle agrees. "They just need a pastor. You know, some good old-fashioned guidance."

"He's *suing* her." Andy repeats what he shouted all day yesterday in disbelief. "I am not fucking slow-dancing with that redneck piece of shit."

"But, baby," Michelle entreats. "We're performing an autopsy on a breathing person."

"If that was the case, he'd agree to mediation." Bob's mouth is pressed into a line.

"Which he has unequivocally refused."

"He wants to take Jessie from me?" Kelsey seeks confirmation.

"He wants to take money from you," Andy corrects her.

"He can want a lot of things. He has absolutely no grounds. The prenup was very clear." Bob tugs off his wire-rims. "Custody will fall along a seventy/thirty split in your favor. You can set it up how you like, but typically, it's a weeknight and every other weekend."

"Without me?" Kelsey's stunned. "But he's never even been alone with her. He's been gone from the beginning. She won't even know where she is." Kelsey can't catch up. "I think I should just take her back to Oklahoma until he calms down and we can —"

"You can't cross state lines with the baby, and the judge will not be impressed if you leave the city. Really," Bob continues, "your dad's right. This is about hitting you where it hurts. Pursuing custody is just a strategy to get you to break the prenup."

"Over my dead fucking body," Andy says.

"I need him to take my call." Kelsey repeats herself in vain.

"Can't you just talk the other guy into getting these two together?" Michelle tries yet

331

again. "You still get paid."

Bob snaps his briefcase shut. "My retainer notwithstanding, given the case his team is hustling to compile, these two should not be together." He hits the side of his palm against the table. "No e-mail, no calls, no texts, unfriend him, unfriend his family. I cannot emphasize this enough. The person you fell in love with is gone. Your husband is gone. From this point forward, he's just someone out there who wishes you harm."

When the custody arrangement is finalized, it grants Aaron every Wednesday night and every other weekend, as Bob had predicted. The following Wednesday at four o'clock, Kelsey brushes Jessie's downy brown hairs and dresses her in a strawberry-patterned jumper. And then puts on full makeup, painstakingly picking out earrings, her skinny jeans and halter top hanging loosely on her emaciated frame. We see the sky light up at the gate, and she opens Jessie's bag yet again to run through its contents. "Diapers, wipes, pajamas, swaddles, pacifiers, bottles — where's Blue Bear?"

As the bell rings, I lean over and lift the onesie to remind her where she snuggled Blue Bear first.

"Okay." Pressing her lips together to

refresh her gloss, she picks up Jessie from her bouncer, and I follow them down the stairs with the bag. "Who are *you?*" she abruptly asks the woman in the white starched uniform waiting by the door.

"I'm Mr. Watts's nanny, ma'am. I'll be bringing her to him."

"We agreed no nannies," Kelsey says, her composure evaporating as her arms tighten protectively.

"I'm sorry." The woman shrugs, embarrassed, confused. "I'm just supposed to take the baby."

"I don't know you." She grips Jessie against her. "You could be anyone."

"Kel." I put a hand on her shoulder. "I'm sure he was nervous having her all to himself — he hasn't exactly changed a diaper yet."

"I'll call him —"

"No," I say firmly, stepping between her and the phone. "I will call our lawyer, who will call his lawyer, who will call him."

Twenty minutes later, Kelsey and I wave manically to the receding taillights.

"What do you want to do?" I ask gently as she wipes under her eyes. "Order in? Catch up on Bravo?"

Michelle comes through the back door

with a nightgown folded under her elbow and a Walmart bag straining in her hands. "Did Jessie get off okay?" she asks as I go to help her. "Daddy's right behind me —"

"Here I am," he says, wrestling the door open with the popcorn machine in his arms.

"We'll watch a movie," Michelle says. "And then I want to show you the pieces of Kelsey Kids that Walmart ordered."

Kelsey takes in the empty house. She looks forlornly overhead, where raw wires hang, waiting for the chandelier Aaron picked out that is still being blown in Venice. She crosses to Jessie's activity mat and picks up the purple pig she jingles for her amusement. "Okay."

"You choose." I wait for her command. With Finn in Toronto for the next month, I'm ready to camp out. Michelle pulls Kelsey down next to her on the couch, shifting to braid Kelsey's hair. Not knowing what else to do, I take Michelle's nightgown up to Kelsey's room, where she's been sleeping. As I return, I hear Andy and Michelle in the den, fiddling with the TV.

"Pass me my phone," Kelsey says quietly.

"What are you doing?" I ask. She looks flatly at me, her hair reminiscent of her fifth-grade picture.

"I want sushi."

"Great — let's order sushi."

"I want to go out."

"Okay, let me grab my bag."

She puts up a hand to pause me, dropping her voice. "Logan, I need a break from this house." She gestures with the pig and then visibly forces herself to put it down. "From everything." She starts to tug her hair loose. "I want to have a drink and a cigarette. With girls who have lives of their own with sex and islands and not popcorn and their parents. Divorced girls whose friends are divorced, whose dogs are divorced, and they won't look at me like you — like I'm dying."

"Okay," I say, shrugging casually against the hurt.

She jumps up, shaking out the last of the braid. "Tell them I needed some air. I'll be back by eleven." Throwing her phone and keys into her bag, she leaves the wipes and a pacifier on the chest. "I am, though," she says softly, chin angled slightly, her hand on the doorknob.

"What?" I ask.

"Dying."

Midnight comes and goes. I persuade a perturbed Michelle to sleep down the hill in her own bed and promise to text when Kelsey gets home. I pass out on the couch watching HGTV, and daylight is breaking when I hear her key in the door. She's only wearing a mini-dress and sweat.

"Hey," I say, stretching up. "Did you come home and change?"

"I borrowed it. Sshh," she says, utterly drained. "It's Thursday. I made it. Just wake me when Jessie gets home."

A few weeks later, Michelle and I have spent the morning looking for snapshots of Kelsey being a "regular" girl for the upcoming Walmart campaign. Michelle wanted Kelsey to do this with us, but she's still asleep.

The nights of Jessie's departures have fallen into a routine. Without ever asking me to join her, Kelsey is through the door on the heels of Aaron's nanny, their cars only a few convertibles apart. To the tabloids, it looks as if she can't wait until Jessie's gone to head out and party, but really, it's her unbearable absence that drives Kelsey from the house. She dances and drinks until her limbs are so heavy and her head so thick that she can manage to pass out only a wall apart from the empty crib.

"Can my seventh-grade perm be Photoshopped out?" I ask, since I have my bony arm around her in almost every picture that wasn't taken at some contest. It's comforting to discover that a record of those years remains. Especially given that my dad took everything off the walls one afternoon and threw it onto a smoldering leaf pile.

"What about this one?" I ask, holding up six-year-old Kelsey with a hula hoop.

"She has to look contemporary yet classic. I don't think kids even know what hula hoops are now."

"So, one where she's playing Xbox in pearls?"

Michelle laughs. "Thanks for doing this, Lo. I couldn't get Kelsey to sit still with these for one freakin' minute." I flip to a Christmas picture where Kelsey has scrawled out Andy's face with a crayon.

"Hello? I need a ride!" Kelsey calls from the garage beneath us.

"Uch, she wants to go meet those bitchy girls." Michelle clucks.

"I know." I share her derision.

"Mom! Logan!"

"Up here!" we yell.

I hear her jog the outside staircase. The door opens, and she leans in the doorway in cutoff jeans, the white pockets hanging below the frayed denim.

"What can we do you for, Kel?" Michelle asks.

"I stepped on my last contact, and I can't drive."

"Well, where are your glasses?" Michelle reaches for the next album.

"In the diaper bag, I think." With Jessie at Aaron's. "So, is there any way you can drive me?"

"Can't this Sage pick you up? She's got three cars." Michelle aggressively flips pages. "That I've seen."

"It's out of her way. Logan, please?"

"I need Logan to help me." Michelle lays her palm on my arm. "This has to be done by Monday. Sit down, pick an album. We're having a hoot, aren't we, Lo?"

"I'm rediscovering my suspenders phase," I offer.

Kelsey sticks a scabbed cuticle into her mouth.

"Can't Peter drive you?" I ask.

"I don't want to roll up like that. I already have GM tailing me. It's weird enough."

"Don't be so antsy." Michelle peers at a photo. "How 'bout you pull what Jessie's grown out of? That closet of hers is getting totally out of hand."

Kelsey releases the door, and we hear her wood platforms clatter down the slats.

Michelle uses tweezers to take a contender from the toddler album. "The first time I met Eric, he shook my hand — all of eleven years old, mind you — shook my hand, said, nice to meet you. I found Sage putting my La Mer on her elbows! Wasn't even embarrassed — just said, 'Kelsey said I could,' and walked out."

"At least you've met them. I'm never here when she invites them over."

"Count yourself lucky. I know they're rich and all, but they walk around this place looking like they're gonna slip her panties in their pocket. Which I suppose is better than keeping her out till all hours." Michelle returns the album marked "first grade" and picks up "second." "Like I wouldn't have loved to get out of the house when I was separated? I was new to L.A., *all* the men we were meeting were asking. What I wouldn't have given to get a drink, get a little wild." She pulls her glasses back down with a frown. "I had responsibilities. As always, Miss Thing's only thinking about herself. She'd better focus on Jessie soon, remind Aaron what a great wife and mother she can be, so he gets over this B.S."

"I think it's just hard to be here," I say. "You know, when Jessie isn't."

Her disdain doesn't waver. "That's what parenting is, Logan. Learning to let go."

"Of a four-month-old?"

"Oh, you know what I mean. Jesus, *look* at me." Michelle passes the album over. "Look at those legs!" It's a shot of Michelle in a miniskirt and Kelsey beside her in a leotard, squinting at the camera in front of their beaten-up hatchback.

"Hot," I acknowledge.

"Thank you." She tilts her head with a grin. "Oh God, that sack of crap! I'm amazed it survived. We left in the middle of the night — made it in a day and a half. Even lost a hubcap outside Albuquerque, but that didn't slow me down."

"The middle of the night," I repeat.

"Like a house on fire," she says with a hard glint of pride.

"So, that's why you didn't say good-bye?" I ask without turning.

"Well, it's not like I was going to stop at the hospital!"

"Dad says I was in a car accident." My throat is dry. "I don't think it was a car accident."

"Well," she says.

"Yes?"

"Your daddy is a . . ." She slides the album off my lap and onto hers. "Good Christian man," she answers with careful finality. "I, for sure, should've been a Nair model." She resumes flipping.

We hear the engine of the convertible rev below us. "Dammit!" She slaps her palm on the floor. "She can't see!"

I race down the steps.

Luckily I catch up before she hits the highway, abandoning my car to get into her driver's seat.

"What the fuck?" I say as I pull us back into traffic with the motocycles in tow, knowing that whatever the tabloids make of this won't be good.

"I can do it! Everything's just a little blurry, but I was going super-slow."

When we pull up at the strip of boutiques on Melrose, Kelsey perfunctorily invites me in to meet her new friends, but we both know it's just because she'll need a ride home. Standing in her Hanky Panky, holding a beaded sarong, Sage Kopelman immediately informs me that she's the heiress to America's number one mattress company. Her friends, Brooke and Jodie, say the word *Daddy* an awful lot for women in their twenties. Other than that, I cannot get a handle on what they actually *do*. Brooke seems to be generally frustrated by wait lists — for handbags, restaurants, and yoga classes — and Jodie alludes to a jewelry line, but it sounds more like an excuse to peruse display cases than an actual business. Ultimately, judging from their speckled chests, deeply lined foreheads and preoccupation with chemical peels, they seem to spend half their time traveling to fry themselves and the other half paying people to correct it.

The paparazzi are starting to block the sidewalk, "Is Aaron fucking someone else with your baby there?" they shout. The flashbulbs *click click click.*

Kelsey keeps her head down, face locked, until she's released into the refuge of the next store, not giving them the expression of hurt or shock worth a hundred thousand dollars. Once inside, her companions stare at her expectantly, awaiting a private show. "You know what's totally weird?" she asks, grabbing a pinstripe hat. "They write about my shopping like it's this crime, like I have a problem." She tosses it next to the cash register without even trying it on. "I'm paid by the American people. You don't like me, don't download my work, don't wear my perfume, stay home." She has Sage's undivided attention. "What would suck is to hoard it like Scrooge McDuck. Take all that cash out of circulation." She swipes up a scarf. "I'm helping this boutique owner pay her bills and the manufacturer pay his. I keep businesses running. But nobody ever writes that."

Sage pats her. "That was amazing. You're so right. Can I tell you something, as a friend?"

Kelsey nods.

"You should talk more like that in public. People think you're stupid. *I* thought you were stupid until we met."

"Me, too," Jodie and Brooke echo, trying on matching parachute pants.

"Oh," Kelsey says, nodding. "I mean, there's a brand — I was really young, and I've had to balance — it's hard to transition."

Sage nods. "Just something to think about. Oh, no," she says in response to the red top Kelsey has picked up. "Not while you're sallow. Let's find something flattering for tonight."

"What's tonight?" I ask.

"Oh." Kelsey's eyes dart to Sage's. "Nothing."

"Right." Sage smiles. "Just a quiet night in."

"They just suck." I fill Finn in that evening as we follow the Chateau Marmont's maître 'd to our table. "I swear I heard Sage talking to her dealer. Her *dealer,* like some eighties movie. Do you really want to be *that* person?"

"What does Kelsey see in them?" he asks, waving as he spots the studio exec we'll be dining with — and trying to impress — on Travis's behalf.

"Well, she didn't go to high school, re-member, so it's probably fulfilling some latent seventh-grade need to be talked to like shit."

We take our seats, and I try to focus as the executive and Finn trad insider gossip and film reviews fresh from the festival circuit. Then I spot Less Than Sage leading a tanned processional to a long table by the patio's edge. "Sage," I mouth to Finn, just as the last of her party weaves into sight — Kelsey.

As Sage's dinner party, consisting pre-dominantly of cigarettes and gin, progresses, Sage gradually slouches until she's almost parallel with the tiled floor. Then, as dessert is served, she climbs up, and Kelsey slides back her chair, spotting me. I excuse myself and follow her into the ladies' room.

"Oh, hi," Kelsey says, nonchalant.

"Really?"

"Uch, Logan." She tosses her arm as if I'm a weighted handbag she's dropping.

Sage comes out of the stall without flush-ing. She wipes at her nose. "I'm texting anyone who can get their hands on a case of Cristal and some party favors. Wait, you're two-three-two or three-two-three — I can never remember."

"Two-three-two," Kelsey confirms.

"Yea." Sage pushes back into the restaurant as Kelsey pulls out her lip gloss.

"You really want to open your house to Sage's iPhone contacts?" I ask her reflection.

Her eyes flash. "Are you fucking kidding me, Logan? Are you seriously questioning me right now?"

"She talks to you like an asshole."

"Oh, go be with your boyfriend, Logan. I'm twenty-five. I'm not spending the rest of my life stuck in that house with pictures of the year I was happy." She opens the door. "I have to live, *I have to*. And I *definitely* don't need your — or anyone's — judgment."

I shakily reseat myself as the executive takes a last swig of his scotch. "If we're talking about a sports team that gets dropped in the Andes, I'd cast Travis as the Saint Bernard who comes to the rescue."

"But he started in drama," Finn reminds him.

"She started in porn." He flicks his thumb

at his wife. "Doesn't matter. He needs to be texturized. Get Tarantino to give him a cameo. Soot him up and win an Oscar, then your field's wide open." He raises his hand for the check.

"Well, at least now the boobs make sense." I try to cheer Finn up as our car inches along Sunset.

He doesn't smile.

"You're a guy, and you love Travis. I'm sure other guys feel the same."

"Apparently, they see him as two hours they have to sit through to get laid. This is an absurd amount of traffic." An ambulance siren wails in our wake, and Finn steers hard to the right, clearing a path. Then we see the motorcycles weaving through the idling cars, and another block on, we pull level with the wreckage. "Stop the car," I say as Finn is focused on clearing to the other side of the rubberneckers. "Stop the car!" I scream. I bolt out my door.

"Miss." A cop tries to catch me, but I struggle past him to the woman standing in the torn dress amid an assault of flashbulbs, her black shins bleeding, shoes in her hands. I wrap Kelsey in my arms, and she sobs. Sobs like the world is coming to an end.

CHAPTER FOURTEEN

Sitting on the edge of Kelsey's couch, as if staying rigidly alert will somehow help her, I watch the navy sky shift to gray and then orange, waiting for Andy and Michelle to bring Kelsey home from the police station. Finn found his way to the guest room at around three AM after conceding that persuading me to join him was pointless. I press my phone again for the time. I can't believe that with everything at her disposal, it's taken this long for her to be released.

Hearing a car in the driveway, I run to open the door, finding only Cheryl climbing out of her Audi in silk pajamas, clenching her laptop and cell. "Shit," she says, blowing past me, stink face at full throttle. "I lost the signal." She sets her computer on the dining table.

"What's happening?"

"Cocaine was found in the car. Coffee. Now." She starts scrolling the blogs, watching the story break. "Jumbled up with all the shit that fell out of that Sage's purse. But it's Kel's car, and any second now, Nancy Grace is gonna say just that."

I hand Cheryl a mug as we hear the SUV approach. Michelle blows right past me to the fridge. Kelsey is behind her in a sweatsuit, the gash on her forehead bandaged, her bloodied dress in a Ziploc. Cheryl looks from the pictures on her laptop to Kelsey and back. "I wouldn't have gone with gray," she actually says.

Andy's cell's on speaker. "Dan? Dan? Can you hear me?"

"I don't know what to tell you," responds the newest addition to Kelsey's legal team, a criminal specialist. "These charges aren't going away."

"Fuck." Andy spits.

"But I swerved because that paparazzi lost control of his bike." Kelsey protests. "I saved his life."

"We'll get to that," Cheryl adds as Michelle slaps the whisk loudly through the eggs.

Andy gives her a silencing glare. "Dan? You still there?"

"Andy, Michelle, I don't want to make today worse, but you need to know that Aaron's lawyer is at court reopening his claim for custody."

"What!" Kelsey cries.

Michelle slams the omelet pan onto the range.

"How can he — he can just do that? It was finalized!" Kelsey pulls the phone to her mouth. "Custody can be reopened?"

The phone crackles. "I'm going to try to buy us some time for you to shift the public discourse."

"On it, Dan," Cheryl says from the couch.

"Public discourse?" I ask, not sure how the public enters into it.

"The fact is," Dan clarifies, "our judge waits to buy her milk in front of the same magazines as everyone else, and it's colored her opinion. She's really hung up on that whole fountain incident. I promise I'm doing everything on my end. I'll call you as soon as the official tox screens come back. Hang in there, and please, Kelsey, do not go out."

Michelle jostles the cast iron pointlessly against the burner as the eggs singe.

"Momma," Kelsey says, licking her chapped lips. "Momma, do you think maybe you could —"

Michelle lands the pan heavily and turns off the flame. "No, I can't. I can't do a fucking thing. You weren't even out of finger-

349

printing before Walmart called. The Wade name is 'tainted.' That's the word they used. Tainted by the spectacle you've made of yourself." She pulls a plate out of the cupboard and bangs it onto the counter.

"Your deal's canceled?" Kelsey asks, touching where blood is starting to seap through her bandage. "I'm sorry —"

"I *finally* get something, just a little something of my own, and you go and pull this shit." Her eyes narrow in her flushing face, and I remember how she'd look when Andy came home high, primed to strike. "You have had *everything*," she says, her body jackknifing at the waist as if the sight of Kelsey was punching her.

"Now, let's just calm down." Andy interjects.

"I've been calm. And patient like a saint."

"I — I." Kelsey tries to respond. "I just —"

"You just *what?*"

"This is not the time," Andy barks, and Michelle drops onto the bottom step of the nearby staircase. "Cheryl?"

"You're making them want to root for him. We have to shift the conversation. No more dumb slut who can't manage one baby. Let's remind everyone why they fell in love in with you."

Andy steps in between Kelsey and Michelle to get his daughter's attention. "Terrance wants you to open the European Music Awards in Stockholm, and Dan and Bob think it's the right strategy. Show the judge what's what."

"Yes," Cheryl says. "Love it."

"Um, really?" Kelsey asks in dazed disbelief. "I guess I could do 'Chemistry Lesson'?"

"No," Cheryl states. "This needs to be big. Same girl-woman-virgin-whore we love but, you know, fresh."

"The world premiere of the first single off your new album," Andy announces triumphantly.

"But I don't have one due for a year. I haven't been writing."

"The single's the important thing," Andy says. "It has to be huge, it has to be — a lot of things, I don't know, Terrance said it real good. We're meeting at the label tomorrow." He claps. "Twenty-four-seven, baby, you're living, eating, and breathing this."

Only weeks later, I'm already sitting in rehearsal for the new single, "You Can't Tell Me." With custody at stake, Kelsey hasn't left the house except to go to the studios, leaving the paparazzi to stalk this unassuming one-story building as if it were the Ed Sullivan Theater.

Terrance sits between Andy and Michelle, waiting to be wowed. "Got to check this one out for myself," he says. "Make sure baby girl here knows it backward and forward." Kelsey nods, still chasing her breath from the last run-through.

"Oh, you'll be impressed," Duane says, wiping his glasses on the hem of his tank.

"And what you can't tighten up we'll Spanx."

Duane seems unsure how to respond, so he just starts the music. It's been decided that because the choreography is so aerobic, Kelsey's going to do a full lip-sync, no overlay.

"Okay, everybody!" Duane shouts. "From the top!"

Terrance fixes her with an appraising stare, and she stares back, something long absent locking into place. She throws her head hard to the left and her arms hard to the right, and she's off, flying against the dancers. It is dynamically intoxicating. And then something suddenly shifts — the dancers seem confused and stop following the choreography. Breaking the fourth wall, they look to Duane, but Kelsey just keeps dancing new steps with equal ferocity and precision. It doesn't hit us until she ends where she started, throwing her head hard to the right and her arms hard to the left. She did it forward — and backward.

Two days later, Terrance arranges a private plane to fly us discreetly to Stockholm and a black-windowed car to ferry us directly to the stage door, skipping the red carpet. We're welcomed in the dressing room with a magnum of chilled champagne.

While she takes off her K necklace I pull out her travel picture of Jessie.

There's a knock.

"Come in," she trills. "I'm decent."

Eric is blushing before he can even get in the door.

"Oh, my God." Kelsey throws her arms open. He gathers her against his leather jacket, and I see her lip trembling in the mirror. She playfully pushes him away. "What are you doing here?" she asks.

He tucks his hair behind his ear. "Well, my bachelor party's next week, and I hear you put on quite a show."

To my profound relief, she laughs. A deep belly guffaw I haven't heard from her in months. "Thanks," she says, "I needed that. Sorry, this is my cousin, Logan."

"This is Cousin Logan?"

"Hi!"

"Nice to finally meet you. And that's her?" he asks, pointing to the picture.

"That's my girl."

"Beautiful. She looks just like you."

Kelsey smiles gratefully at him.

"Well, I better get back. Have a great show. I'll be out there."

Suddenly shy, she waves her fingers by her face. He pushes the door open —

"Oh, thanks for the bunny!"

He turns to look deeply at her from across the years. "Are you talking to someone?"

"What?"

"You should talk to someone, you know, professional," he says with concern, but she closes like a prodded anemone.

"Thanks. Enjoy the show."

Acknowledging that it's become awkward, he raises his palm and leaves.

She sucks in her lips, then claps as if trying to jump-start herself.

Binky and I take our seats in the audience, and it feels like hours before the auditorium goes black for the live broadcast. Kelsey's voice comes over the speakers. "You think you can tell me, but you can't tell me." The lights rise on the sexy opening tableau, but as soon as the music starts, it's as if she and the dancers are records being played at different speeds. They cut across the stage, while she seems to meander, neither dancing nor trying to lip-sync. Clearly drunk, she is walking through the routine, her eyes flat.

And then it happens.

As Duane and Pita lift her for what should be a tucked spin, she doesn't draw her legs in fast enough, ending instead in a spread-eagle, the fabric at her bikini line gaping. A split-second in our time, but I sense DVRs the world over freeze-framing.

Binky squeezes my hand while discomfort rolls over the celebrity-packed audience. "I'm calling time of death," Terrance says loudly, already distancing himself. The second we're cleared for commercial break, I run the aisle and bound the steps reserved for celebrity presenters, dashing across the stage after Kelsey. A flat drops in my path.

"Akta!" one of the crew yells.

I double back to the other wing — skidding straight into a woman carrying a clipboard. "Delia!" I exclaim. "What are you doing here?"

"I'm with Fergie. Oh, Lo." She's crying.

"Come with me to talk to her."

She shakes her head. "Fergie's up next — then we leave for the airport." She scribbles something on a corner of her paper and rips it off. "This is my new number. Give her my love?"

I pull her into a fast hug, aware that the Duchess is hovering. "Wait, Delia!" I have to know.

She turns back.

"What did you say to Andy?"

She stares at me a long moment. "If she kept going like this, she was going to break."

CHAPTER FIFTEEN

Kelsey cracks the passenger window and inhales the few inches of air that she can get without giving the paparazzi a view of more than the top of her head — although they could probably even find a way to turn her sunglasses into a scandal. Since she stepped offstage in Stockholm, the dominos have not so much fallen as been pelted in her face. The label dropped her so fast Terrance actually billed her for the flight back. Her management e-faxed dissolution papers to my phone. Her agency "released her from her contract." Cheryl not only quit but has been extremely publicly vocal about quitting for, you know, a publicist. And her entertainment lawyer calls hourly to inform me of yet another corporation executing its out clause.

Andy and I brief each other in the driveway. Like a funeral where the deceased passed away banging a hooker, these somber meetings address everything but the cause. He then plods back to the guesthouse, to Michelle, whom we haven't seen at all.

I try to remember when this family started communicating through avoidance. I picture my dad opening our front door at all hours. I'd peek around his pant leg to see Kelsey on her mother's jutted hip, Michelle wild-eyed because Andy had been on some three-day bender. His absence punished with theirs.

I guide the Suburban's steering wheel along the GPS-dictated twists and turns, while we watch the houses modernize and their acreage shrink.

Kelsey sucks on her iced coffee. "Thanks for not letting me take another Xanax this morning."

"You're welcome."

"I lose track," she says, embarrassed. But I prefer it to finding her balled up at the base of the empty crib, crying because she can't stand for Jessie to think that she wants it like this. "I just can't face being up in the middle of the night. I look out the window and see his TV on, and I can't —" She catches herself. "I'm gonna get him that new Benz. Start there. Maybe he can persuade Momma to forgive me."

"Look, you're out of bed"

"And you're still here," she says softly to the glass.

"Of course," I reply, although at this point there's no of course about it.

"I think this is it." I steer us into a cul-de-sac.

"Well, this isn't an apartment in the Valley," Kelsey says snidely. Legitimately. Marrying her was the most money this guy could make in a year without taking out a bank.

A couple of kids are playing soccer on the pavement. "Should I honk?" I ask Kelsey. "We're kind of leading the *War of the Worlds* right into their playground."

"Definitely, yes, honk." The kids look over, and their jaws drop as the motorcycles swerve around the vans trying to swerve around the news trucks trying to get the closest spot to us. Kelsey cringes as a mother comes running down her front steps and calls her kids inside.

"I wish you'd let GM come along."

"I told you, no," she says with frustration. "Daddy doesn't need a bodyguard." She inadequately compares herself to Aaron. "Is that his house?" She points at the porch, with a baby swing next to a wicker glider, a little bucket of toys on its seat. "It's just so . . ."

"Normal." I finish her sentence as I get out into the crush.

Aaron's nanny lets us inside. She glances out at the barrage of cameras, and I apologetically pull the drapes closed. "From now on, GM comes."

"Yes." Kelsey collects herself as we both take in the living room. A far cry from a bachelor pad — there are even throw pillows on the boxy blue couch. I guess he got his white phase out of his system.

"The baby's still sleeping," the nanny informs Kelsey. "I didn't want to wake her until you got here."

"No, that's good, thank you," Kelsey says, but her gaze is flitting from the basket of stuffed animals to the pile of freshly folded men's T-shirts on the dining table.

"I'll get her." The nanny turns toward a hallway.

Kelsey goes to follow. The nanny looks uncertain. "She's my daughter, and I'd like to wake her," Kelsey says firmly. The nanny nods reluctantly and leads us to a door with a pink polka-dot plaque that says *Jessie*. Kelsey pushes it open and smiles, her hands crossing over her heart as she walks to the crib. "Hey, little girl," she coos quietly. "It's Momma." Jessie wriggles awake, a smile breaking when she looks up. "Hi, bunny, hi.

Oh, I missed you." Kelsey scoops Jessie up and nuzzles her. "You smell delicious."

"She smells like she's got something in that diaper," the nanny adds, flicking on the overhead.

"Well, Momma can fix that right up, can't she?" Kelsey takes Jessie to the changing table and gingerly lays her down. Reaching for a diaper she freezes. "Logan."

I see the framed picture of Jessie with Michelle, Andy, and Aaron. They sit on the porch we were on just moments ago. With a bracing palm on Jessie's belly, Kelsey turns to the nanny. "When were my parents here?"

"I have no idea, miss."

Kelsey looks over to the bookcase, and I see it with her, a photo of Michelle holding Jessie with the ocean behind her. "We haven't taken her to a beach," Kelsey says faintly.

"Let's, um." I step in to seal the diaper. "Let's just get Jessie together, and we can discuss this at home." Kelsey nods.

In the living room I now recognize Michelle's coordinating hand in everything from the picture frames to the lampshades to the needlepoint pillow nestled on the armchair, *Bless This Mess.*

The nanny clears her throat. "All right, then. You'll have her back by six. She'll be wanting a bottle as soon as possible, and she probably won't need another nap for three hours or so. I can write it down."

"I got it." Kelsey flings open the door and, gripping Jessie against her, muscles through the scrum. The diaper bag over my shoulder, I attempt to make space for her to move and, at the same time, pull out the car keys. Kelsey's gaze is cast down as she shields Jessie's head against her chest.

"Watch it!" I cry as her foot lands on the soccer ball.

"She's dropping the kid!"

"Shoot the kid!"

I dive to grab her wrist just in time.

As soon as we pull in, Kelsey tugs Jessie from her seat and slams through the front door. I catch up as she lays Jessie on the bed and dumps out the diaper bag. "Kelsey, what're you doing?"

She storms into her closet, punching in the code of her jewelry safe, and sweeps the boxes into the elephant-patterned bag. She scoops Jessie up. "Logan, come on!"

I follow her down to the guesthouse. Andy looks up in surprise as Kelsey swipes the remote from the coffee table and spins at the screens, pushing every button until they all go black.

"Kelsey, what the hell?"

"Momma!" she yells. Michelle walks in from the bedroom, carrying a book, her thumb holding her place. Pointedly ignoring Kelsey, she reaches her arms out for Jessie. "How's my little princess?"

Kelsey swings her away. "Have you been giving him money?"

"Now, just hold up a minute," Andy says.

"You're helping him take her away?"

"No. Absolutely not." Andy slices the air.

"Logan was there. She saw it."

"It's strange," I attest.

"What did you expect him to do, for God's sake?" Michelle's incredulous. "That baby deserves a proper parent, and you've been —"

"Doing every fucking thing you've ever asked me to."

"Now, don't go turning this around." Andy crosses his arms, his chest puffing. "You put us in this situation. Your partying left us cut out of that baby's life, and Aaron was good enough —"

"Good enough?" she shouts back in disbelief.

"We can help him give that baby a stable environment," Michelle says.

Kelsey snorts. "Like when I used your bag of coke in my Easy Bake brownies? What was I, six?"

"Now you're just trying to get attention."

"See it from our point of view." Andy fumbles to recover his ground. "You're going to have to let this go, Kelsey Anne."

"Like all the times I had to let it go when Momma had a black eye?" She thrusts Jessie into my arms and dumps the jewelry boxes onto the couch. "Take this fucking stuff — I never wanted it. I can sing till I bleed. Smile till I black out. But I can't make this shit you've pulled with Aaron okay. It's impossible. I have *nothing left.* She catches her breath as Jessie breaks into a full wail. "It's okay, baby. It's okay." She bounces her as she turns back to the door. "You have a day to get off my property. You're officially fucking fired from Kelsey, Inc."

CHAPTER SIXTEEN

"You're *where?*"

"Vegas," I repeat to Finn that night as I hand a twenty to the distracted bellboy. Kelsey crosses the onyx-floored penthouse to a switch by the two-story windows. The immense curtain panels whir, blocking out the city lights below.

"I thought you were coming with me tomorrow morning. The breakfast with the charity consultants — I wanted your two cents."

"I'm sorry," I say as Kelsey studies the gold drapes in consternation. "We'll be home tomorrow night." When Andy and Michelle are gone.

"A family vacation?"

"No. No, just us." The sole remaining members of Kelsey, Inc.

Kelsey lifts the heavy lamé, and I see her moving under it until she finds the switch. The schizophrenic skyline returns, the

Statue of Liberty, the Eiffel Tower.

"Okay . . ." Finn answers. "Should I be concerned?"

"No. No. It's all good. You'll be great tomorrow. I wasn't going to be much help, anyway. I've got a lot going on."

"In Vegas."

"Yup." I strain not to scream at him, *I know!* I get it, thanks. Kelsey circles the party pit to stand beside me in the foyer. "Gotta go."

"Right."

"I love you," I say.

"You could leave, you know. Let her make her own mistakes. There are people who'd kill to hire someone with your experience and discretion. Just, you haven't even mentioned it, and I thought I should put it out there. It's your life, too."

"I — I —"

"What?"

"No, you, too!" I disconnect, and stare at the device in my hand. "How we doing?" We are reflected back at each other in infinite telescopes in the mirrored walls.

"I remember this different."

"Okay . . ." I walk away from the prism effect. "Is this not the hotel?"

"No, it is. I just . . . I thought it would feel different."

"It's been a big day, Kel." An understatement. "Maybe if you took a bath. Got some sleep." I rest on the edge of the lacquer dining table. She looks down the gold hallway leading to the bedrooms.

"No," she says simply.

"A cheesy movie and room service?"

Her brow furrows. "I thought if they weren't here. If I wasn't working. But it's just big and cold and —"

"Let's go." I swing my finger in the air and turn to the vestibule, my voice echoing.

"What? No! I'm not going back until they're out of there."

"We're not going back." I swipe up the keycards. "But we're not staying here."

"All the paparazzi downstairs? I can't go home —"

"Kel, there's a middle ground between Versailles and defeat." I pick up the house phone.

Three hours later, we've finally found it — in a king-size bed in a standard-size room. We've polished off two bottles of wine, macaroni and cheese, and a chocolate molten cake. I unlock the door and roll the ravaged cart into the hall.

"You got a lot of potential, Kit De Luca," Kelsey murmurs from under the bedspread.

"Ya think?" we say together as I pad back in, slip off my jeans, and hop in next to her. Opera music fills the room as Richard Gere comes to his senses on the glowing screen. Kelsey smiles drowsily, her eyes closing.

"This was good, Lo. A good night."

"You deserve it." I squeeze her arm, and then, clicking off the TV, nestle down and give in to Bordeaux-sodden exhaustion.

I awaken to the sound of the door clicking closed. Four twenty-eight — shit. With a thick head I kick off the covers, and run to the door, yanking it open and squinting in the bright light. But there's only a guy at the elevator bank, pulling a pack of cigarettes from his pocket. He glances back at me as the car arrives, and I shut the door, confused. I hear the shower turn on and push into the bathroom — it takes a moment to readjust to the dimness — Kelsey is hunched over the toilet bowl.

"What happened?" I ask.

She whips around, holding the wall. I realize I smell vomit and that she's only wearing her tank top. "Are you okay?" Panic wells up from the cold tile. I flick on the light.

"No." Her hand slams over mine, shutting it off, but I've already seen the discarded

Trojan wrapper.

"Kelsey, what did you do?"

"I couldn't sleep. I felt like they were gonna show up. My heart pounding a million miles a minute. And I needed . . . I needed . . ." She starts to dry-heave, spinning to the sink. My brain fully revved now, I sickeningly place the tattoo on the forearm of the guy in the hall.

"That guy was paparazzi."

"Get out, Logan." She trembles, steam filling around us. "*Get out.* I'm taking a shower. Just, please." I throw my hands up and back away. The door closes behind me, and I sit down hard on the bed.

Oh, my God. *Oh, my God.*

I should leave.

I can't leave.

I mean, obviously, I can't leave.

Or can I?

Let her make her own mistakes?

No. That's not my job.

Or is it?

What the fuck *is* my job, exactly?

Finn's face in my mind's eye, I dare myself to just get dressed and walk out the door.

Hearing the bathroom door clicking open, I feel her pull the covers up. I have crystallized all of my questions down to one so

369

pressing I was asking it in my restless sleep.

"Are you looking for someone to beat you up?" I say quietly.

"What?" She speaks into the pillow, her head turned away.

"If you want someone to beat you up, at least have me do it, because I won't kill you."

A luggage cart rolls by outside.

"I don't want to get beat up."

"Good."

"This is all new, Logan."

"I know. I just . . . want you to be okay. I want to know that you're going to be okay."

She props herself up on her elbows and faces me. "I waited my whole life for that love, for everything I thought I was getting." Her eyes clench against tears, and she blows out. "But I'm not . . . whatever *that* was." She points to the bathroom. "I'm not. I'm going to be fine, I promise."

We opt to drive back, making it through the gate just after three, the hour of Kelsey's stated deadline. Even though the guard said the moving van had left, neither of us quite believes it when we round the oaks to see their cars aren't there. She pauses before twisting the handle of the guesthouse. I nod encouragingly, and she goes inside while I wait, looking up to where the breeze is ruffling the tops of the trees, the branches below untouched.

"They're gone!" She throws her arms around my shoulders. "Really gone! And they didn't break anything or take everything or kill themselves. Oh, my God, Logan. Oh, my God." She grips my hands. "Could it be this easy? Did I just have to fire them?"

"I guess." I can't help but smile at her euphoria.

"It's going to be okay. It's really going to be okay! I've been thinking all day, I'm going to figure this out, do whatever it takes to get Jessie back. Something different — no more touring. Something on my terms. Let's make a picnic and sit on the lawn, and just, holy shit, I don't even know where to start."

"You should've seen her," I marvel to Finn that evening, leaning in Travis's kitchen doorway with a glass of wine. High off Kelsey's victory lap, we're taking advantage of Travis's absence. "Within an hour, she'd gotten on the phone with the head of comedy programming at NBC —"

"Impressive," Finn says as he plates the salmon.

"And he said she can have a cameo on any sitcom she wants. She's going to be fine," I say, believing it for the first time. "So, this whole time we've been living without a kitchen, you can actually cook," I say, admiring the bowls of rosemary grilled vegetables and wild rice.

"You haven't tasted any of it yet."

"How did your meeting with the charity consultants go?"

"Leo has water, but they said no one has air yet, so Travis could take air. Make air his thing."

"And for two hundred and fifty thousand dollars a year, this couple will help Travis navigate becoming air?"

"Yep."

"Genius," I say as I set our places at the mahogany table painted down the middle with the racing stripes of the Indianapolis driver Travis sponsors. Finn is just pulling my dining chair out when both our phones start ringing and pinging at the same time.

"Ignore it," he says. "If James Franco is dead, he'll still be dead when we finish dessert."

"Finn," I say, immediately nervous.

He pulls my napkin out of its numbered ring and waves it onto my lap. "So? David Duchovny joined a monastery. Charlie

Sheen helped a seeing-eye dog cross the street. I don't care. How often do we get to have dinner together?"

But I can't stop myself. "TV on!" I say loudly, bringing the flat screen to life with Kelsey's image — her bloody mug shot. The reporter is saying something about paparazzi.

"It's just some new shit about the crash, Lo. The fish's getting cold."

"— reportedly had sex with her in her Las Vegas hotel room."

I'm going to be sick.

"According to this gentleman, Pedro Gutierrez, she invited him to her room, where he alleges they had sexual relations." Pedro comes on the screen. He's saying something about loving her for a really long time. And then there's a picture of her posing for him in the bathroom like a pinup. Her body in position but her eyes are drunk and sad.

"She really let me in," Pedro says. "Like most people don't know that tattoo on her ass — it's the Velveteen Rabbit."

"I have to go," I say.

"No, you really don't." The camera pans over photos of the darkened room. *"Oh my God,"* Finn says. "That's you." Asleep in bed, my bare ass black-barred.

"I can't just sit here." I rush to the front door.

"What if this guy had been a rapist?" He grabs my wrist, putting himself between me and the door. "You look pretty naked and pretty passed-out."

"Finn, don't — I have to — I'm scared for her."

"I'm scared for you. What if you'd been in that car she totaled? You can't see this clearly — you're too close."

"You're jealous."

"Wow." He releases me. "Okay."

"Finn —"

"No, if you go to her now after the danger she put you in —"

"It wasn't like that —"

He shakes his head. "Then you're on your own."

"Are you forbidding me?"

"Yeah, I think I am."

And I can't slam the door hard enough.

"It's the cousin!" The reporters and paparazzi blind me with their flashes, crushing against the car, slapping the windows, hurling questions until it's a singular indiscernible din of need. "Is it true you had a three-way with Pedro Gutierrez?" I try to hold on to the awareness that I am an employed grown-up, surrounded by a throng of other employed grown-ups. Yet I still take a shuddering breath once the gate shuts behind me. Finn, I don't know.

I see Andy's car and run up the steps. Kelsey stands on the stairs, facing off with him, while Michelle sits on the couch, eyes on her lap.

I hear a small cough and step inside to find, perched by the fireplace, a middle-aged woman with a platinum bob.

"Thank you." Kelsey is trying to muster civility. "But I'm really okay, and you can really go."

"Kelsey," Andy presses, "you're pissed at us, fine. But at least listen to what the doctor has to say. You let a paparazzi into your hotel room."

"It's none of your business, Daddy, remember? You made Aaron your business."

"How you can look at us like that?" Michelle asks. "With such contempt. I was there for *everything*." Her hurt is palpable. "Pounding Five-hour Energy so I could drive you half a day to some mall where I was the only one clapping. I'm not one of those bitch mothers who didn't give a shit. The ones who complained and read their magazines and looked at their own nails." She wipes her nose as tears stream. "I was front-row center, Kelsey. Sewing, driving, saving. I just hope." She palms off her cheeks. "I hope for your sake that your daughter doesn't ever make you feel so small."

"That's not —" Kelsey shakes her head in frustration.

"Kelsey, your parents are the two people who love you most in the world." The doctor leans forward and takes a Tic-Tac from her purse. "This is a safe space."

Kelsey's entire body flares, a visible rigidity spreading from her nostrils down through her flexed toes. "Please leave."

"Kelsey," she replies evenly, crunching the Tic-Tac. "I want you to hear how your behavior has hurt them."

"My behavior."

"You used to be so happy," Michelle says, grappling. She wipes her nose. "You were always smiling, always." She leans forward, struggling to make herself understood. "But it's not your fault, Kel. We get that, we do. It wasn't Daddy's fault, either. The doctor here has helped us to understand it's in your genes."

"*What*'s in my genes?"

Michelle looks to the doctor, who nods for her to continue. "One minute you're laughing backstage, then you're crying in your closet. Logan knows. She's seen it."

"That's my *job*," Kelsey says, disbelieving what she's being accused of. "I have no space to react to anything *except* in my closet."

"Kelsey," the doctor starts again, "your parents only want to see *you* get the help you deserve."

"Okay." Kelsey stares at her, seeming to calculate how to counter being called crazy without seeming crazy. "I will look into it."

"Thank you," Michelle says softly, reaching for Andy's hand.

"Now, if you'll excuse me." Kelsey gestures for them to leave.

"The doctor carries her quilted purse to the door. "I'll wait in the car. So nice to meet you, Kelsey. I look forward to our first session."

Andy pulls two prescription bottles out of Michelle's tote.

"What're those?" Kelsey asks, eyeing them.

"My lithium," he says.

"And your chlorpromazine," Michelle adds.

"I have extra. Try 'em for a few days, it'll level you out. I get it, the coke brings you up, the booze brings you —"

"Hear me from the sanest part of my

377

everything. For the last time. Get! Out!" They don't move. "GM!" she calls, and he rushes in from the den.

She turns to climb the stairs, but Andy roughly grabs her ankle, and before I know it, GM has apologetically picked him up and shoved him toward the door like they're both on skates, Michelle scurrying behind.

As we catch our breath we hear Kelsey's name from the den TV. "From what we're being told, Dr. Laura will be addressing us from the Wades' home." We run to the doorway.

"Kelsey's parents have asked me here today to counsel them in their time of need." Kelsey grabs my hand. "Kelsey is obviously deeply disturbed and in need of our help. In my professional opinion," the doctor says, "Kelsey's behavior has all the hallmarks of being bipolar."

The text below her face immediately changes to "Kelsey Wade is Bipolar."

Her knees buckle.

The questions drown one another out, and Andy jostles closer to the microphone. "Bipolar's serious, but it's treatable. We hope that with God's help and the proper medication, she'll get the care she deserves. We ask America to pray for our little girl."

Chapter Seventeen

A few torturously miserable days later, I stand behind Kelsey in what was her and Aaron's closet. Across from her customized racks and shoe cubbies sit the barren shelves and rods where Aaron's things briefly lived. I keep waiting for her to spread her wardrobe around the room, try, at least, to minimize the specter that makes it feel as if the floor is tilting ever so slightly from the weight of her belongings.

Kelsey's diagnosis has commandeered the news cycle — Republican front-runners, international crises, and even Pedro have been bumped. The cable channels have been rerunning her old interviews, going back to age sixteen, while talking heads who took one psych class in college analyze them for signs of a "split." They're even playing her bubbly dance videos up against her wistful ballads, proving that she was always struggling with a "duality."

"I still don't understand who she is," Kelsey says as she clenches her towel around her damp chest with one hand and pushes through each hanging item with the other.

"The social worker?" I clarify as I make a note to get more Band-Aids. Her nail beds are raw and infected.

"Yeah. Who is she, exactly?" She tugs out a sun dress and holds it up, her brow contracted.

"I like that one," I say, but she's already returned it and continues flattening garment bags with quick swipes to identify their contents. "What's wrong with the white dress?"

"I never wore it with Jessie. And it's already been cleaned. I want her to recognize my scent."

"It's only been a week," I say gently. "I mean, I'm not that versed in babies, but —"

"Please. Who is she?" She returns to the dresses.

"Sorry, the social worker is the court-appointed observer." I read through the letter from Kelsey's lawyer outlining the conditions of her newly restricted visitation. "Andrea Salazar."

"And we're picking this social-worker observer woman up?"

"At Aaron's, yes."

"She has to be in the car with us?" She turns to me, her hair sticking to her face from her shower.

"Yes." I look pointlessly at the memo as the rules are not vague. Ms. Wade is not to interact with the observer. She is not to be alone with Jessie at any time. She is not to exhibit any indication of being on a substance of any kind. She is not to exhibit any angry or hostile behavior or the indication of angry or hostile behavior. "If Jessie's there, the observer has to be there." I summarize rather than force her to hear the requirements yet again.

Tightening her lips, she turns back to the rack and continues to swipe, the sound of the metal scraping the rod gaining momentum. "Here." Kelsey tugs a bright red T-shirt dress off a hanger.

"That's a full boob show when you lean over. Not an issue on a plane or in a studio, but in real life . . ."

"I won't lean. She needs to remember me. And it's bright and cheerful." Kelsey tugs open a drawer and withdraws underwear, pulling it up under her towel. "We're going somewhere bright and cheerful." She opens another drawer and whips out a bra. "I want to be somewhere bright and cheerful. With

Jessie." She snaps it on and then pulls her dress overhead. "The observer wants to observe me being bright and cheerful, so if you could please just call the nanny and remind her to have Jessie up and changed by the time we get there, it will be —"

"Bright and cheerful," I say under my breath as I reach for the land line on her makeup table. I dial Aaron's house and click it to speaker, awaiting the nanny.

"Hello?"

We both freeze at the sound of his voice.

"Aaron." Kelsey takes the phone from me, gripping it with both hands. "Aaron?"

"Hey."

"Aaron, I —" She falters as she stares at it. "I'm not crazy."

Silence.

"I'm not. You can't believe what my parents are telling you."

"No one has to tell me." He sighs. "Jesus, I've seen the pictures."

"But you know how those guys are, I know you do. Walmart, Aaron. I was there —"

"Kelsey."

"I just don't know how this got so out of hand. I would never hurt Jessie, never."

"I don't know anymore."

"But I wouldn't!"

"We're not supposed to be talking. I thought it was about the pickup. I can't talk to you —"

"Wait!" Silence. Her eyes are wide as she hunches around the phone. "Aaron? Aaron!"

"What?"

"Why are you doing this to me?"

"Get it through your damn head. You've done it all yourself." The line goes dead.

Kelsey insists on driving. She has reframed the afternoon as the audition of her life, which is evident as she chatters to me with an enthusiasm normally reserved for morning television. I can feel Andrea sitting behind me in her boxy blazer, gripping her pen, her expression maddeningly impassive. Jessie lets out a moan in her sleep as she shifts in her seat, and Kelsey issues a string of reassuring murmurs to the Suburban's ceiling. We hear Andrea scribbling. I realize Kelsey has hit her turn signal to get off the highway.

"Rest stop?" I ask through the smile we've both had in place for the last hour.

"Just need to pick something up. I'll be quicker than a rabbit hump," she apologizes over her shoulder, getting nothing in return. We roll past a Subway, a Michael's, and a

Dress Barn before she turns a hard right into a parking space in front of a Designer Shoe Warehouse. "I'm realizing these sandals are a little snug for walking. Be right back!" She jumps out and dodges the paparazzi to dart between the sliding doors. I look down; she's left her bag.

I turn around, still smiling for Andrea, as Jessie starts to shift awake. "Be right back." Andrea lifts her eyebrows. The papparazi race to the store, lifting their cameras into place and yelling to one another as if they're Special Ops. I run past the dumbfound shoppers.

"Kelsey Wade?" I ask a salesgirl whose lower teeth keep her gum in while her mouth hangs open.

"Here. Right here," she marvels.

"Yes. Where is she?"

"In the evening aisle. Oh, my God. Oh, my God. Kelsey Wade is in our evening aisle!"

I dash away from the photographers covering the windows like some Stephen King fog. I turn around the last row and spot her crouched against the rear wall. "What the fuck?" I hiss. "I'll give you my shoes —"

She looks up at me, and I see that her jaw is chattering. The sparse customers are starting to get braver and inch their way toward us. I bend to take her hands into mine. "You're doing great, Kel. Perfect, honestly."

The air comes into her in little sucks. She scans my eyes, her pupils darting back and forth.

"I can't."

"You can," I say. "You *can* do this. But we have to leave right now. Right now."

"The shoes — if I come back without shoes, she'll write it down."

I scan the stack to grab the first box with a seven on it. We stand to find the customers now less than an aisle away. I hold her hand tightly as we walk speedily past.

"Hey!" she manages. "I love this place, don't you?"

I reach into her bag, pull up her wallet, and slip a hundred-dollar bill into the stunned hand of the cashier. Facing the windows blackened with the swarm, Kelsey tugs me back. She takes the box and opens it. We both blink for an instant at the Lucite heels and rhinestone straps before she steps out of her sandals and ties them on.

Jessie is sobbingly awake by the time we get through the flashes and back into the car. Kelsey asks Andrea if she will sit in the passenger seat so that she can comfort

Jessie. Andrea says nothing but undoes her seatbelt and sits down beside me. I glance at her pad as I try to back us up. "SHOP-PING," it says, underlined twice.

The air is thick and humid by the time we make it through the Disneyland turnstiles. Kelsey has settled Jessie, who is fussily gnawing at the knot adorning the shoulder of her mother's dress. It is ridiculously satisfying to see the paparazzi slowed to a human pace as they're forced to wait and pay to enter the park alongside the other families.

"Isn't this fun?" Kelsey rubs noses with Jessie as she jostles her in her arms. Jessie's lips lift into a smile as her gums work the fabric. Teetering on her ridiculous heels, her neckline shifting precariously with her daughter's movements, she heads into the park, chattering to Jessie as she points out the fountains and flowers and life-size characters who stand as stunned in our wake as the little kids who spot them. Andrea walks behind her in her sensible flats and nude hose. I look to see a wedding band and then steal a glance at her unlined features. I bet we're the same age. "Oh, my gosh, Sleeping Beauty's Castle!"

"Wow, she didn't leave the baby in the car

this time."

Kelsey's face drops as a sneering couple strolls past, each holding a mammoth turkey leg.

"Lead the way," I encourage Kelsey just as the husband mutters under his breath, "Stupid bitch."

The wife nods in agreement as they're subsumed into the growing march of photographers following us.

"Miss Wade." A man in a red blazer and a Mickey Mouse print tie makes his way over to us. "I'm so sorry, we had no idea we'd be so fortunate as to have you with us this afternoon. I'm Craig Winterson, director of the park, and on behalf of everyone here at Disneyland" — he turns out for the cameras — "I want to say what an honor it is."

"Thanks, Craig." Jessie starts to push against Kelsey's chest.

"Now, Miss Wade, if you'll indulge me, we would like to give you a guided tour."

"I think she's hungry." Kelsey turns to me. "I need to feed her."

"Perfect!" Craig extends his arm toward a wood plank door. "Our Princess VIP courtesy lounge is just up the stairs here to the turret. That way, you can have some privacy, and we can, uh, . . . prepare a proper itinerary for you to maximize the fun while you're with us." He glances over his shoulder at the cameramen, pushing between children and the gift-shop windows. I am not so sure that ours is the fun he's concerned with. Kelsey's heels click against the stone as we twist up the staircase. "It's a bit of a climb, but it has its charms."

He slides his ID in front of a box, and a door unclicks to a circular room awash in the same pastel-hued fabrics as the stones of the castle. Craig flips on a pink chandelier because the small windows let in minimal light. And are sealed shut — it is utterly airless.

"Make yourselves at home. I'll just get the air conditioning going. Again, if we knew you were coming . . . Well, our castle is your castle! I'll be back." The door slams, startling Jessie. Her face scrunches red and then opens into a wail as Kelsey tugs the bottle from the bag. Jessie stops crying as she sees it.

"He didn't put the cold pack in." Kelsey holds the bottle to her cheek to check the temperature. "I don't know when he packed it. I don't know how long it's been sitting out —"

"I'll get some water from the sink, and we'll make a fresh one."

"It's coming, baby, it's coming," Kelsey

murmurs as I prop the bathroom door open with my foot so Jessie can keep it in her sight while Kelsey sways with her. "She hasn't been like this in months. I don't know what it is. Do you think she's just too hot?" She stops in her tracks to twist her head and see what Andrea has written. "Teething? Teething," she repeats as Andrea stares past her. "You hear that, Logan? Andrea thinks Jessie is teething. She is officially making note of the fact that I did not know that."

"Okay, Kelsey, I'll have it in one minute." I splash my hand under the hot tap, waiting for the icy water to warm.

"It's true. I didn't expect her to be teething. I also didn't expect her daddy to leave us. Or take her away from me. Or a judge who uses TMZ like it's documentation from God himself. Or my crazy fucking parents to call *me* crazy. I did not see myself standing here hovering over Fantasyland in an oven with the very important Princess Andrea who I have to pretend isn't here. No, I didn't see *this* being the way I realized my baby girl was teething."

Andrea stands up. I turn off the sink and come out.

"She's hot," I say apologetically as Andrea roots in her purse. "We're all just hot. She's not angry —"

"Why would I be angry? Just because the whole world — and some people say that, but I get to really fucking mean it — the whole world thinks I'm a shit mother. A stupid bitch mother." Kelsey tries to keep hold of a hysterical Jessie. "I would die for this baby, Andrea. I *am* dying for this baby. I don't want to eat or sleep or sing. I don't want to take air into my lungs. But I'm doing all of it. I'm getting through the day so I can get to see her, and I'll take her any way I can. Even with you."

Andrea fingers in three digits to her phone, and with an eye on both of us, she finally speaks. "Yes, my name is Andrea Salazar. I am a court-appointed social worker with the State of California, and I need to request an emergency removal."

"What?" I cry as Kelsey's arms tighten around her baby. "She's just hot, and the photographers —"

"Yes, I can." Andrea walks to the slim window and looks down. "Disneyland. The castle. There's a VIP room —"

In three long steps, Kelsey grabs my arm and tosses me into the bathroom. She slams the door and locks it and then thrusts Jessie at me as she spins around, grabs a pink chair, and wedges it under the knob.

"Kelsey, what're you doing? Open the door."

"No, Logan."

Andrea pounds from the other side. "Open up!"

"Kelsey, open the door." I step forward.

"They'll take Jessie," she says frantically, looking around for something heavier to barricade us.

"Miss Wade, open up!"

She starts shoving the pink dresser from under the window.

"Come on, Kel." I grab the chair.

"Logan," she says, her voice slicing. "If you open that door, I swear on Jessie I will never talk to you again."

The hot room rapidly feels dwarf-size, and I find my breath coming in pants. I drop onto the pink toilet lid with Jessie and dig around in the diaper bag for something for her to gnaw on. In a side pocket, I find three teethers. Nice of Aaron's nanny to keep Kelsey updated.

"Miss Wade, the police are on their way — please open the door."

"There," she says as she pushes the dresser the final inch to brace the chair holding the knob. "We have diapers and formula enough for hours."

"Kelsey," I say, fanning the baby, my own

panic pulsating in the confined space. "What's the plan here?"

Kelsey opens her arms for Jessie, who quiets as soon as Kelsey gives her the teether. She lifts Jessie's face over her shoulder and bounces.

"This is security, open the door!" a man's voice bellows.

"Hush, little baby, don't say a word, Momma's gonna buy you a mockingbird." She holds Jessie's head, her eyes shut. She presses her face into Jessie's little neck and takes a deep breath through her nose. "I'm never letting you go," she whispers.

We hear that sound that's become so familiar that I don't even notice it until I notice it, like a refrigerator hum, the din of a crowd gathering below the parapet.

Then we hear the short siren bursts of police cars inching their way through that crowd, a bullhorned request to step back. Please step back.

"Kelsey, what do you want?" I ask again, my vision tunneling, the claustrophobia winning, my tremoring hands locked under me.

She looks up from the baby, her face so open, so gentle, as if we're just home, as if we're okay. "This."

"I know. But we need to make a plan —"

THUD! The door shakes on its hinges. *"Anaheim PD, open up!"*

Kelsey suddenly grabs me and pulls us under the skirt of the vanity. I cough from the dust as she tugs the curtain closed —

My brain splits —

"We were together," I say urgently as the image from my dreams fills in behind my eyes, Kelsy in her Pocahontas nightgown. "In the bathroom."

Jessie starts to cry. "I've left the bottle," Kelsey says. "Out there, I left it out there." She peers through the skirt, seeing the stacked furniture jostling — THUD!

"Your dad was tearing the house apart." The memory replays itself with cutting clarity. "Your mom pulled us into the bathtub." I can hear the sound of Andy smashing Kelsey's trophies against the door.

"Anaheim PD! Stand back!"

Kelsey's eyes lock on mine, and I remember us trapped. She shook — shook uncontrollably as Andy had hurled his body over and over at the door. I could see the lock giving, hear the wood splinter.

"Sing, Kelsey," Michelle had whispered. "Sing so he stops."

" 'Stars shining bright above you,' " Kelsey choked out.

"Sing!"

" 'Night breezes seem to whisper I love you.' "

"Ms. Wade, we're coming in on the count of ten!"

"You threw up," I say. I had scrambled out of the tub to grab a towel.

Jessie screams. I dart my hand out for her bottle.

"Logan, no!" And I don't know if it's ten-year-old Kelsey in my memory or Kelsey with me now.

"Two, one!"

The Disney door bursts off its hinges, the cops rush in — the Wade door burst off its hinges — Andy grabbed me up and smashed me hard into the tile wall — I slid to the floor — my blood splattered the porcelain — "I'm sorry, oh, Jesus, I'm sorry," Andy had said, taking me in his arms. "I thought you were Kelsey."

PART V

CHAPTER EIGHTEEN

I halt my pacing on the hospital hallway's linoleum because I sense, the way you do when someone across a crowd is staring at your back, that on the other side of this security door, a psychiatric patient is shuffling in rhythm with me, tuning into my movements and mirroring them.

I rest my hands on my aching hips and look up into the fluorescents until black spots float, making censorship dots over Andy's and Michelle's menacing faces in my memory. Now that it's finally been unearthed, I can't stop seeing that night compressed into a kaleidoscope of locks, curtains, eyes, towels, and blood. Once again, I raise my face to the small mesh window, peering to see if she's among the gaunt figures in gowns that drip down shoulders like old candles — whoever's moaning moans again.

I wish I could sit. But there are no chairs.

Because no one is supposed to wait here.

"Logan!" Andy rounds the corner from the elevator landing. "Thank God." Michelle comes into view over his shoulder, looking drained and small and, for the first time, unequal to her surroundings.

"We were so damn scared she was alone," Andy says as he goes to the door.

"No, I was there." I find my voice, anticipating Michelle's demand for an explanation.

She looks around at the soiled gurneys waiting to be stripped, her sweater folded over her crossed hands. "Aaron called us to —"

"Don't touch me!" a man screams violently on the other side, and Michelle flinches.

"I can't see her," I say, watching Andy crane his head at the window.

He drops back on his heels. "Is this really — does she have to be in there?" he asks.

"She was committed by the time I got here, and no one will talk to me."

"They'll talk to *me,*" he says. But then he looks around helplessly as I had — there isn't even a call button. "Dan'll be here soon," he sounds more hopeful than convinced. "He'll get us back in front of the judge. He'll fix this." He catches Michelle's wandering eye, and she nods.

"Today was all a huge mistake. I can testify. It was hot, and she got rattled by the observer — she got frustrated —" I'm distracted by Michelle absently touching a pile of sheets. "But she's *not* crazy."

"Thank you, Logan." Andy turns away, placing both hands on the door, dropping his head, and I realize he's crying. Soon someone on the other side meets him and matches him, their grief entwining as Michelle seats herself on the gurney and stares at the wall.

It takes two days for Dan to get Kelsey a hearing. Andy's been on the phone, accomplishing a transfer from Anaheim to Mount Sinai in L.A., pleading with anyone who can help, any celebrity who has donated to that hospital, any doctor who has a pet cause we can fund, but there is no upgrade from involuntary incarceration, no VIP area, no private anything. We have not seen her, do not know how she is, only that she's been heavily sedated.

Under siege from the media, to the point where I don't know how any of them are reporting a word over the grind of the generators, I'm effectively trapped in Kelsey's house. I don't answer when Finn calls, magically hoping he can sense that I grip the phone when I see his name, as if I were squeezing him tight to me. I can't talk to him, because a reassuring explanation doesn't exist. Michelle's taken to the glider in Jessie's room with her needlepoint, leaving me to watch as the dining table is cleared of Kelsey's own optimistic career map and buried under a mound of legal files. And Andy's so uncharacteristically quiet, so obviously scared as he pores over them, that I override my need to confront him with my need to believe that despite all that's happened, he has a plan, a strategy for making her okay.

When the car pulls up at the courthouse the morning of the hearing, GM and three colleagues form a human chain to allow our passage through the roiling sea of journalistic excrement.

Dan is waiting on the second floor, wordlessly holding open the door to the courtroom. It isn't at all what I expected. A drab little chamber with water-stained ceiling tiles and only two rows of benches. We take the seats behind Dan.

"All rise. The honorable Judge Borenstein presiding."

"Be seated." She smooths her robes beneath her.

"Inmate entering!" the bailiff yells, and

Kelsey shuffles in wearing a white jumpsuit that drapes her laceless sneakers. Her hair is pulled into a greasy ponytail, and her eyes are glassy. Andy purses his lips to keep from breaking.

The prosecution makes its case — that Kelsey is a danger to herself and others. That she should be kept indefinitely in a psychiatric facility. He is prepared to call the Anaheim police, Sage and everyone involved with the crash, the head of the Swedish F.C.C. even Aaron's nanny, who apparently is now a foremost expert on Kelsey's deficiencies as a mother.

Dan stands. "Your Honor, Ms. Wade has been through a tough time —"

And I swear the judge snorts. So fast it's barely perceptible.

"The circus outside your courtroom today would drive anyone to distraction. Ms. Wade lives with that night and day. She's had no peace to recuperate from her painful divorce, from the emotional distress inflicted on her by Mr. Watts."

"Ms. Wade," the judge asks, shuffling manila folders. "Do you have anything to say to this?"

She stands carefully, a steadying hand on the desk. "Thank you, Your Honor." Her speech is slow. "I have not handled this

401

divorce like I could have." There's a pause, as if she isn't sure what to say next. "But I want to take care of my baby and be a full-time momma." The judge looks unimpressed, but I'm not sure why she even asked Kelsey to speak in this condition. "I just need a few days to think straight," she adds, the "s" in *straight* an embarrassing "sh."

"Ms. Wade has multiple charges pending against her," the judge says, looking down.

"No one is served by prolonging Ms. Wade's incarceration in a psychiatric facility," Dan continues. "Certainly not the taxpayers. Mr. and Mrs. Wade are proposing to take over as her temporary conservators. We have a report from the county mental health representative supporting our petition."

The judge waves him up to the bench.

"What does that mean?" Kelsey asks the room.

"Counsel, please quiet your client," the judge cautions.

"What does it mean?" I whisper as both lawyers convene with Borenstein.

"It means this is over," Andy says quietly.

Kelsey spins around in her seat. "I don't understand."

"Kelsey." Michelle addresses her daughter

for the first time. "Face the judge." Kelsey nods and returns her foot to the floor, taking her body with it.

The lawyers resume their positions. "After careful examination of the relevant documents, this court hereby grants the temporary conservatorship of Kelsey Wade to her parents, Mr. and Mrs. Andrew and Michelle Wade. To be reviewed in sixty days." The judge bangs her gavel and rises. She pauses to look us over. "Good luck."

A few mornings later, I park the borrowed pickup truck and climb down into the cloud of dust outside the kitchen door. An AA friend of Andy's has given us his ranch in the Santa Barbara hills for Kelsey to recoup, as far off the beaten track as we could get and still keep Andy in driving distance of L.A. He's been back every day for meetings to "keep things moving in the right direction." He's trying to settle out of court with everyone, including Sage, who, along with the loss of her cocaine, apparently suffered grave, seven-figure emotional harm.

"There's nobody out there this morning," I marvel.

"Simple economics," Andy replies, sliding a pie crust from the oven. I hand off his Dunkin' Donuts coffee and pass the other to Michelle, who's been studying plastic-surgery web sites. "A pic of Kel's worth, what? Half a mil right now? Those maggots'll sit out by the fence a day or two, but eventually, there's nothing to see and nothing else to snap but a buncha cows. Don't fuck with me."

"Does that mean she can walk outside now?" I ask, since we did get a few flyovers the first day.

"Maybe." Andy hesitates. "Whatever the doc says."

"About what?" Dr. Flannery asks, coming from his morning run. Another recommendation from Andy's sobriety circle, he apparently has a lot of experience with this kind of hush-hush outpatient treatment. So far, he seems to be a stellar choice, inasmuch as Kelsey lets him in to check on her.

"Can she walk outside today, Tom?" Andy asks.

The doctor takes a biscuit off the table. "Let's see how she's doing when she wakes up. How far did she make it yesterday?" he asks.

"She sat on the porch for a while." Andy gives an optimistic description of what was really a pass-through that they weren't even here for.

"Well," Tom continues, "she's transitioning off the hospital's tranquilizers onto a sustainable med program, and that takes time." He plucks his coffee from the cardboard tray. "I'm going to shower. Holler when she wakes."

"Will do," Andy says. He pours the peach slices into the crust.

"Med program?" I ask.

Andy lays the top on the pie and starts pinching the dough the way Grandma Ruth taught us. "Everything she wants depends on getting her leveled out."

"Right . . ." I wander into the living room and stare above the fireplace, where someone has laid the Serenity Prayer in mosaic tiles. And I ask to be granted the wisdom.

Sometime after lunch, I hear a door on the second floor open. "Logan?" Kelsey calls, and I run to the bottom of the stairs.

"I'm right here."

She peers down from the landing in the pajamas I packed for her. "Where are we?" she asks, her voice as diminished as her demeanor.

"Santa Barbara." I repeat my answer from yesterday.

"Room service doesn't answer."

"There is no room service," I say again.

"Just me. What do you want? We have peach pie."

"That's my favorite."

"You want to come down? Get some fresh air?"

"In this?" She tugs at her top.

"Sure. We're the only ones here."

"Oh, okay." She ducks back into her room. In the kitchen Michelle is sitting at the table with her Nora Roberts. "We've had a request for pie," I say brightly.

"Help yourselves." Michelle drops the book flat on the placement and walks right out the screen door. O-kay.

Kelsey shuffles in, her hair in a knot, her glasses on. She roots through the plastic bag from the hospital that I'd left on her dresser, shoving the red dress aside to dig out her K necklace.

"Can you?" She sits down and lifts her hair.

"Of course." I hold up the chain to ensure that the K faces out. Then, unexpectedly, a tiny hinge opens, revealing a photo of Delia. "I never knew this was a locket."

"No one does." Her eyes land on the book. "Wait — is my *mom* here?" Kelsey drops her hair.

"We're all here."

"But I fired them." She twists to snatch

the locket. "They're fired."

"You did. But then you were in the hospital. Do you remember that?"

She nods.

"So now they're taking care of you — just for a little while."

"The judge," she says, remembering.

"Yes."

"I have to get out of here." She pushes her chair back so quickly it topples, and she grabs the rim of the table to steady herself.

"Kelsey, you're not —"

"I have to explain to the judge that I fired them."

The crash brings Tom and Andy running from the yard. "Everything okay?" Andy calls.

"What are you doing here?" she yells.

"Kelsey, you remember what we talked about?" Tom says in a dulcet tone.

"I fired you," she repeats to Andy. "It's over. Logan, get my clothes, we're leaving."

"Kelsey, you can't leave," the doctor says gently.

"I am leaving. Oh, and Logan knows everything, Daddy, now. She knows why you went to jail, so don't think she thinks you're a good person." She strides to the stairs, leaving me frozen.

"Kelsey, I made them a deal. It's this place

or you have to go back to the hospital," he calls apologetically after her. "Kel, I freed you."

"I'd rather go back."

He puts his hand on the banister. "You'd rather go back to the psych ward than stay with me?" he asks as if she'd said it in another language.

She slams her door.

"As I live and breathe." Travis sits on the edge of the pool table, wearing only his board shorts and chewing on a toothbrush as if it's a cigar.

"Hey." I greet him, inching around a pile of boxes that have my name scrawled on them. "Is Finn here?"

"He is." Finn climbs out from between the wall and the arcade game he's installing. It has a big Jeep seat, a steering wheel, and Travis's face garishly airbrushed all over it. Finn wipes his brow with his T-shirt, and as it drops I see that his expression is uncertain.

"Sorry to just — it's been . . . we've been out in Santa Barbara, kind of off the grid."

"The only way." Travis's bare feet slap the floor as he switches his toothbrush to the other side and climbs into the driver's seat. "Love off the grid. Love. It." He hits a button, and the sound of revving engines and electric guitars blasts out. "Yee-haa!"

"Do you think we could talk?" I ask, nodding at the stairs. Finn extends his hand that way, indicating I should go first. I climb to the loft, the sound of screeching brakes and explosions underscoring that the relocation was pointless. I check my phone. Finn leans against another stack of boxes. "I — she's taking a nap," I explain. "It's the only time she's okay not having me right there."

"How long do I get you for?"

"With the drive, um, about fifteen minutes. I should have called first." I bite my lip and sit on the edge of the bed, the fact of the cartons catching up with me. "How's your movie project? How was New York?"

"Fine."

"Guys love me!" Travis yells. "I don't need to be air — just gotta be me."

"Oh, good." I lob my voice over the half-wall and look questioningly at Finn.

"Yeah," he answers. "Turns out the texturizing campaign was unnecessary. It was just a matter of the getting tabloids to run the pickup-truck-brushing-teeth-in-traffic thing."

"That's great. I'm really happy for you."

"Logan."

"Yeah?"

His voice drops. "It's been *two* weeks."

"Have you turned on the news while you were packing me up?" I ask. "I haven't exactly been on a cruise."

"That girl's in trouble," Travis yells up.

I extend my finger toward the bathroom, and Finn goes in. I pull the door shut tight behind us and hit the ceiling fan for extra measure. "I'm sorry I was out of touch. This has been disorienting, to say the very least."

"Everybody's talking about this conservator thing like Andy's daddy of the year," he says, studying me.

"It's just until she can show the judge she's okay."

"And she's cool with it?"

"It's only for two months — six more weeks, really."

"And then?"

I shrug, wanting to pull his arms around me, to admit that I don't know.

"So you're sticking with this. With them." He clenches his jaw.

"Look we're *both* making our living as crutches to the weird and wounded. You had no right to forbid me —"

"She's fucked up."

"And who's that freak?" I point at the toilet paper with his boss's likeness. "Maybe this isn't even a relationship, Finn. Maybe

410

it's just a really hot hookup we tried to turn into normal life, but the problem is, neither of us has one."

He grabs my face and kisses me so hard I taste blood. His hands spread into my hair, pull me into him. I feel my body press lengthwise against his, and all I can think is yesyesyes, and then, just as fast, he rips me off. We stare at each other as we catch our breath. *Say you love me. Say it's okay. Say we'll figure out how to make this come clean.* "What kills me is that you'll give that fucking family enough rope to hang you. But you don't give me even an inch to figure this out with you." He puts his hand on the knob and pushes it open.

"Dude!" Travis yells with exasperation "I was calling — let's go find those Kangaroo Jumps up at the house." Then I realize that all of the boxes up here have Fs scrawled on them.

"You're moving out?" I ask.

"I got an apartment."

"You did? When?"

"Before you disappeared. A friend of mine needs to give up his lease, and I hoped — look, it's not a mansion, but it has a real kitchen. An actual ceiling over the bed. One-ten Normal Street." He smiles weakly before peering at me, his blue eyes searching mine. "I want you to come so badly. But, Logan, they're so far beyond weird and wounded. If you can't see that, then . . . I can't do it."

"Finn —"

"Christ, you were right, I was so jealous when you first told me."

"Of what?"

"Being part of that family." He runs his hands through his hair. "I move first of the month, so let me know where to ship your stuff by then, I guess. You know where to find me."

"One-ten Normal Street."

"And just, take care of yourself." He jogs down the stairs, and I hear the door slam behind them, the guitar starting up again as the game plays its electronic siren to an emptied room.

A few days later, I help Andy pack up a rental minivan to drive us all back to L.A. Kelsey has gained some color and much-needed weight. As she and I talk about what we're going to get on our In-N-Out burgers, we watch the landscape whiz by unencumbered by motorcycles. "I've got a surprise," Andy says when we turn left toward Wilshire. "There's somebody who's very excited you're back in town."

"Jessie?"

Andy pulls into the label's basement garage.

"You know what else I love that you do?" Terrance asks the sixth such question in the last hour. "The way you connect with your audience — the sexuality, the animal — it's so powerful."

"Yes," someone agrees. More clapping.

"So, what we want to do with this album is a three-sixty comeback." Terrance shakes his large gold watch back down his arm, and I dart my eyes to Kelsey's inscrutable face. "But we gotta acknowledge the car accident — I don't mean the actual car accident, I mean you — but hey." He points across the table. "Make a note. A video that does some twist on the accident — maybe we set it at Disney. You could run over Mickey." He cracks himself up. "Nah, that'll cost — but damn . . . damn! That's it!" He slaps the marble. "*Car Accident.* That's the album. Slow down and have a look."

Kelsey's semblance of a smile dies.

"I want these to be the best fucking songs ever." He tents both hands on the table. "The best fucking songs this label has ever recorded. This is gonna be huge. Huge!"

■ ■ ■ ■

We don't make the turnoff for the Canyon. Instead, we proceed through the looming palms of Beverly Hills, and I wonder who we're picking up now. A vocal coach? A live-in trainer? We arrive at a gated community, and the guard waves us through. Farther down the road, we drive into the courtyard of a hulking mansion suggesting a French chateau by Donald Trump. Andy pulls the car around three stone dolphins rising from the central fountain.

"Uch, I told them no roses in the urns. The sun will burn those petals right off." Michelle hops down.

"Come on out, Kel."

"I thought we were going home. I really want to go home, Daddy," she says, her voice faint as I unclick my seatbelt.

"The comeback starts now." I follow them into the grand entryway, which looks as if Norma Desmond is about to swoop down the staircase in a caftan. The living room beyond is filled with their oversized peach furniture, every surface clustered with Michelle's objets as if they'd been living here forever.

"This is your house," I confirm.

"All of ours," Andy corrects me. "And, Logan, you're welcome as long as you care to stay."

"But I want to go to *my* house," Kelsey says, backing up, her hands feeling for the doorknob.

"Baby, that place had bad vibes. We thought you needed a change of scenery. Something more homey to ground you."

"I don't care what you think — I want to go there."

"Hon," he says gently, "we sold it." He looks at me. "In about a minute flat, which shocked the hell out of me. Never could see the appeal. Kel's bedroom is up the stairs and to the left. Logan, why don't you see her up, and y'all can just take a load off."

We follow a long hall past a series of bedrooms until we get to one that is unmistakably hers. A replica of her room in Malibu, complete with mantel and canopy bed, only instead of pink, every surface is the same butter yellow of her wedding roses. Kelsey sinks to the floor. I close the door and, seeing that the lock has been removed, slide down against it.

I pull up my knees and lift my fingers to my mouth. She curls into a fetal position. "Can he really do this?" I ask. "Who should I call? I don't know who to call."

"Going to . . . throw up." Kelsey pushes herself to stand. Swerving, she spots the bathroom and darts in. I hear the toilet flush a few moments later. "Logan?"

I find her slumped beneath another display case of her childhood glory.

"I have to live here for how long exactly?"

I go back to her room to get her laptop. But it's not on the dressing table or the desk or anywhere. I slip my phone from my pocket, pull up Wikipedia, and type in *conservatorship.* "Conservatorships are put in place for severely mentally ill individuals, the gravely disabled, or elderly patients with dementia or Alzheimer's. The conservator must prove to the court that the patient is unable to make legal, medical, or financial decisions on behalf of themselves and are unable meet their basic needs of food, clothing, and shelter." I look up. "I mean, obviously, you don't fit any of the criteria."

She shakes her head.

I keep reading. "It says the conservatee is subjected to the legal control of the conservator."

"He has control over me? What does that mean?"

I read down, the implications sinking in. "You've legally ceased to exist."

"Girls? Got your dinner right here."

We don't answer.

Andy comes in, tray in hand. He chooses to ignore my wet face. "You don't want to eat in here. Come on into the bedroom, and we'll fire up the TV for you. What do you think? Your momma thought the trophy wall would inspire you."

"She wants her laptop."

"What, now?" he asks distracted by soda sloshing over the cup rim.

"Kelsey wants her laptop and a cigarette," I repeat, battling the impulse to upend the tray in his face, gauging if she's up to making a run for it.

His smile falters, and he looks down. "I'd love to be able to give you that. Laptop, that is. But I can't."

"I can't have a laptop?"

"Not with Sage and Pedro and the like out there waging legal wars. We can't risk you doing things you might regret. And baby, we have to admit there's been plenty of that. I'm sorry, but you can't be trusted right now. Y'all want to eat in here." He slides the tray onto the sink console. "Be my guest."

"How about the cigarette?" Kelsey repeats. "In prison, they get cigarettes," she says as his foot crosses the threshold.

He flinches. "Get a good night's rest,

because tomorrow morning we're having a little visitor."

"Here?" Kelsey stands. "Jessie's coming to see me?"

"I told you I'm making things right." The door closes behind him.

"The judge said sixty days, Kelsey. There's a review. We'll figure out how to challenge this. They can't —"

"I have to lie down." She walks carefully to her bed.

Neither Dan nor Bob ever returned my messages, leaving me no choice but to start cold-calling law firms. All of whom have staunchly told me that since Kelsey no longer exists, only Andy, as her conservator, can retain them on her behalf, at which point I hang up. With one day to go until the final hearing, I'm desperate to find someone to see past the impossible.

Andy's had Kelsey scheduled from the moment he brings her morning coffee till she pops her sleeping pill at night. The label's team has been working around the clock as well, this endeavor on its way to being as huge as Terrance predicted. That being said, if it's possible to sing a pop song with the enthusiasm of a late-shift drive-through operator, Kelsey does. I sit on the edge of a folding chair waiting for a lawyer to call as Duane works Kelsey on the studio floor.

"Awesome!" he shouts, and I wonder if he has his contacts in. Every vertebra used to be expressive, every movement sinuous. Now she looks locked from shoulders to hips. Her hands don't flex. Her face, once powerfully engaged, remains passive well after the music blares on.

"And two and three and spin and done. Yea!" Duane claps. "Okay, from the top!" As he turns away ostensibly to check his BlackBerry, I see tears in his eyes. Maybe the judge could just watch her dance. Or listen to her sing. How could anyone witness this and not understand how much she does not want it?

"She's killing it, huh." I look up to see Andy dropping off some sandwiches.

"Not really," I say quietly.

He steps closer, ducking his head and opening the bag so it looks to those nearby as if we're discussing the lunch. "Come again? I need to speak to someone?"

"Maybe just stay and watch."

"Oh, I gotta keep moving," he says as he does every time I try to talk to him. "The meds are what's making her slow."

"The meds are what's making it possible

for her to tolerate this."

He pushes out the door like I didn't say it.

That evening, Andy says he's as fired up as the grill to have a "family meal while the sun sets." On the last night before he's indefinitely named her conservator. That kind of family.

I pace on the end of the patio, gripping my phone and whispering to yet another administrative assistant. "But he said he would call back. I have got to talk to him tonight. *Tonight.*"

"Logan," Andy summons from the table.

"I'll give him your message," she says without conviction.

"Doesn't he have a cell?"

Andy pushes back his chair and strides over. I turn away, hunching my shoulders protectively.

"I can't give that number out if you're not a client."

"But I want to be. I'm trying to be. I have money —"

The phone is tugged from my hands.

"Andy, I wasn't done! Andy!" I follow after him — he drops it into the pitcher of iced tea.

"Now you are." He sits. "We're eating."

Speechless, I watch my phone sink into the crushed ice.

Michelle comes out in her tennis skirt, taking in the spread. "I have drinks tonight. I told you."

"You can sit with your family for five minutes." Andy passes the coleslaw to Kelsey as Michelle tugs out her chair. She turns her Rolex to check the time, deciding not to comment on my hovering presence. "You girls going to watch something fun tonight?" Andy asks as he bites into his chicken.

"Nothing left," I say. Fuck it, I'll use the house phone.

"What's that?"

"We've been watching fun things for fifty-nine days. There's nothing left." Kelsey flinches. I'll go up to my room. There must be somebody still in that lawyer's office; otherwise, I'm Googling a directory and going door to door.

"Sit down, Logan," Andy instructs, as if he's done with my funny business. "You're making Kelsey upset. She's —"

"*She's* right here. Ask her what *she* wants," I challenge, my heart thudding.

"Logan." Andy wipes off his fingers. "I'm gonna have to insist that you ease up with those scumbag lawyers."

"Excuse me?"

"I don't think I will." He lifts a chastising finger. "You've called over thirty firms. You don't think those people have secretaries who'd go to the press? You realize the risk you're putting Kelsey in, spouting off about private family matters?"

"Is there something in the news?" I'm confused.

"I'm just saying."

"How did you — are you checking my call log?"

"You're acting out."

"You know you don't own *me,* right? You know I can call whoever the hell I want?"

"Enough, Logan."

"You threw me into a wall, Andy." And suddenly I realize that this is what I can do. What I have. "Which is on police record. You assaulted a minor. And I'm going to tell them tomorrow at that hearing what you're capable of."

To my surprise, he gets up, strides to the French door to his study, and reemerges a second later with a paper and pen. He puts them in my hand. "I made my amends when you got here. That was the disease. It was not me." I scan the document, dated a few days after Kelsey was taken from the Magic Kingdom. A letter to the judge attesting to my confidence in my uncle Andrew, the very fact that I've been voluntarily working so closely with him for the past two years proving that he's a changed man.

I drop it onto the table as if it's ignited.

"There's no way I'm signing this."

"Have you seen me so much as touch a beer since you came?"

"No, but —"

"Have I once raised a hand to you, to anyone?"

"Has he even made a threat?" Michelle asks me.

"You busted Delia's bookcase, you smashed that remote in Nebraska, you drowned my phone two minutes ago! I — I don't know how to describe what you are now. Sober?" I battle with the certainty of my indictment, emboldened by the fact that he needs me. Has to have my endorsement to pull this off tomorrow. "You still scared the childhood right out of me. Still screamed for hours that you were going to kill me and the other women at this table. That still happened, Andy."

"It's not fair to rub it in my face. I told you I accept it."

"I don't give a shit what you accept. You haven't once asked me how it felt. What it cost. Least of all the years, Andy, *years* of friendship! Fuck, it cost me my parents!"

"I get it!" he roars.

"I don't believe you."

We stare at each other.

"You could never do this if you got it," I say.

"I'm doing this because I get it." He takes a steadying breath as he stands, backing away from me. "I am making things right."

"This is the twenty-first century. In a civilized society. You don't get to kidnap your twenty-five-year-old daughter and force her into a second childhood at the threat of taking her own baby away. That is the opposite of right."

Kelsey jerks her chair back and walks into the house, but I can't stop.

"She's damaged because you damaged her. And now you're turning that into an opportunity. No matter what you tell yourselves, nothing will change the fact this is the single most selfish thing you could do." I walk away on shaking legs.

That evening, Kelsey holes up in the bathtub, watching old episodes of *Will and Grace*. I lie in her bed, rehearsing my speech for the judge, until at some point I wake to her sliding in next to me.

And then, in the early dawn, I roll over,

and she's gone. There's no light from the bathroom. At the opposite end of the hall, I spot the glow of Jessie's dresser lamp spilling onto the runner.

Pushing the door open, I see signs of Kelsey's recent presence, the dent in the toile day bed's pillows, the mohair throw in a heap on the floor. I go to fold it and spot a slim hardback of *The Velveteen Rabbit* splayed on the carpet. Flipping through the pictures of the stuffed bunny on his journey through the seasons of a child's favor, I arrive where the book's spine naturally opens from repetitive reads. " *'Real isn't how you are made,' said the Skin Horse. 'It's a thing that happens to you. When a child loves you for a long, long time, not just to play with, but REALLY loves you, then you become Real.'* "

Letting out a long breath, I slide the book back into its thin slot and click off the lamp.

There's a door ajar at the end of the other wing. In the third-floor gym, I find her silhouetted against the wall of blue glass, her legs spinning fast on the bike.

Seeing me, she sits up, pulling out her earphones. She touches the resistance knob, slowing her pace. "Can't sleep?" I ask.

"Needed to move." She takes a sip of water.

"I'll let you be." I walk around the pyramid of weights for the door.

"You can't do that, Logan."

"Check on you?" I turn back.

"Go at them."

"Sorry."

"It's not helping. You're not helping."

"I'm trying to."

"I don't need another person *trying* to do anything."

I push my hands into my cardigan pockets. "Kelsey, I didn't handle that perfectly. I can't be perfect for you all the time."

Her feet pause in their treads as she works her way up to continue. "You need to sign it."

"What?"

She lets out a breath. "I'm asking you to."

"Kelsey."

"This is his way of making things right, and I'm just too tired to fight it."

"But I'm not!"

"Lo."

"What?"

"This is what it's going to take to get Jessie back. And I can get through it. But not with you watching."

"Okay," I say, my mouth drying. "I won't watch. Is this because of what I just said?"

"No, I'm glad you — I respect you, all of you, especially the not-doing-it-perfectly parts. So fucking much. I respect you more than anybody I've ever met. Which is exactly why I need you to go —"

"No."

"I should never have sucked you back in."

"Yes, you should have," I say fervently. "You should have. I would have come for anything."

"Logan, I was fine without you. I'll be fine."

"This isn't fine."

"And neither was fucking some random in a stairwell." Her voice hardens as she starts to pedal. "You were a mess when you came out here."

"Oh, my God, Kelsey, are we really fighting about this?"

She grabs the towel to wipe her eyes.

"You're crying."

She doesn't answer or look at me. "I'm firing you."

I am standing in her yard, and I don't know where she's gone. "If I leave." My voice breaks. "I won't have any way of reaching you. They won't let me."

She nods, pedaling harder.

"But how will I know you're okay?" I ask. "This time, how will I know?"

"Because," she manages, reaching forward for her headphones and fumbling to put them back in, "I'll know you are." She turns up the volume, and I hear the tinny thud of Pat Benatar. I take a step toward her, but she lifts herself to crouch over the bars, barreling into the night and willing me to be the one to leave.

I drive out of Los Angeles, my car filled to the roof light with everything I've acquired since I arrived, my boxes making it impossible to look back. I just get on the highway and drive all night and late into the next day, until my head's heavy and the wheel's starting to swerve onto the cement grate meant to wake truckers. At dusk, I pull off in search of a motel, but as soon as I lie on the bed, I'm wide awake, restless, wretched.

The outdoor hallway looks over four lanes of speeding traffic to a mall. Taking my wallet, I make my way through the tall grass lining the road, then dodge honking rush-hour drivers. As I near the entrance, I pass a father and his teenage son with a game disk already torn from its packaging. A woman holds the doors for me, and I stand in the wandering flow of shoppers across from an island of dusty fake plants. A fountain littered in pennies. I don't know what day it is.

Two giggling teens lean their doughy faces

into each other as they stroll. I find myself pulled into their wake. They are simultaneously the only two beings in each other's orbit and completely self-conscious in front of everyone they pass. I drift under brightly lit signs, into the mix of salty/sweet smells at a food court busy with what must be dinner.

One of the teenagers I followed gets in line at the Wok'N'Roll. She starts to sway her hips and mouth a song. I realize it's "Chemistry Lesson." And I am just one of the hundreds here at this mall listening to it. The ache breaks across my body, and I realize I am crying, really crying. I look for an exit and push out under the darkened sky. A salesgirl on a smoke break lets me borrow her phone. Then I dig through my wallet to find a scrap of paper, Fergie's Stockholm departure time printed on the back.

"Hello?"

"Delia?" I whisper.

"Logan, hi."

But all I can do is cry.

"Where are you? Your momma's been lookin' for you."

"She wears your picture around her neck, every day."

Delia is quiet.

"I fucked up everything," I say, wiping my face. "It was my idea to invite Aaron on tour, my idea that he get a job. And now I'm a character witness. If I had just stayed away —"

"You can't blame yourself for any of that."

"I let her down."

"That girl loves you. She's always loved you." She pauses. "You know she paid your tuition."

"What?"

"Right after you hung up on her. She saw you needed help to make it happen. Told those NYU folk it had to be presented to you like some scholarship and to leave her name off it. She *wanted* you to do your thing. Live your life."

"So —"

"So live it."

EPILOGUE

Dear Logan,

Thank you so much for your birthday card. I realize now you haven't gotten my letters. Sending them to Kelsey's fan club was a long shot, I know. Just please don't think I didn't try.

We were so glad to get all your news. Finn sounds like a good guy, a "keeper." Good luck on your job search. I'm sure you'll figure out the whos and whats.

The rest of what I have to say I've written you many times now. But I have the comfort of knowing this time there's a good chance it'll reach you.

I don't know why I handled it so badly when I found out you were working for them. I don't know why I handled it so badly when you wanted to be over there all the time as a girl. I think maybe, and I'm embarrassed by this, I was jealous. That you preferred Michelle. That you had somewhere to go outside this house.

Everyone always felt so sorry for Michelle, wondering how she managed with Andy. But no one ever asked me how I coped with your father. Ours was a private sadness, wasn't it, Logan?

Which I see now wasn't fair. I should've been glad for you when you came home talking about some new dance routine of Kelsey's. But, and I know this may seem silly for a grown woman, I felt left behind.

If I'd stopped judging and sulking, you wouldn't have had to lie, maybe I'd have been over that night. Maybe I'd have taken you home at bedtime, promising to drive you to Kelsey's contest the next day. I replay so many what-ifs.

We never meant to lie to you. Saying you were in an accident was the first thing that came to your father's head, and I've never known how to contradict him. It seemed the kinder thing for you to believe. And he felt so much shame about his family.

After they were gone, I stupidly just thought things would be easier — I was relieved — I didn't understand how sad you must have been.

Then, after that summer, school started, and suddenly you had so many teenage ways to be angry with me — it feels like we just fought straight until you left for New York. This just wasn't at all how I ever wanted things to be.

I am so sorry I said God sent you to test me. Maybe he did. But if so, I failed, Logan. I failed. I did not protect you. And then, after it happened, I did not look down at the girl in the black lipstick and say, somewhere in there is my baby, and she is hurting because her best friend in the whole world is gone. I did not take you in my arms.

You're a grown woman now — and it sounds like you're building an exciting life. A life I'm glad is bigger than this house, this town, or this family. But I want you to know *I* know — despite what everyone may say about that girl — your best friend in the whole world is gone. And I take you in my arms.

The truth of it is, I've always been a little in awe of Kelsey — not just her talent but her strength. Even as an itty-bitty thing, you could just tell that girl was made of flint. She will get through this, even if she just has to outlive him to do it.

I know prayer has never brought you comfort. I wish that it could, that I could. I am praying daily that you will give me another chance, Logan. Give me a date, and I will be on the first plane. Tell me about everything — I want to know.

All my love,
Mom

ACKNOWLEDGMENTS

We are grateful to . . .

The amazing Judith Curr for giving us such a supportive home. Greer Hendricks for her superlative guidance. Sarah Cantin for making every moment at Atria such a freakin' pleasure. Suzanne Gluck for coaching this little two-person team for a decade! Eve Atterman for greeting our every request with cheer and grace. Alicia Gordon and the entire WMEE Team for taking our calls and trying to make our dreams realities. Sara Bottfeld and Mahzad Babayan for keeping the fires burning. To Marcy Engelman and Dana Fetaya for not being Cheryl. Ken Weinrib and Eric Brown for holding the chair in one hand and the whip in the other while we cower behind you. Tiffany Bartok for making us beautiful with incredible skill and humor. Ted & Honey for our daily muffin and kibbitz.

The women who are persevering and

impressing the hell out of us: Evelyn, Anne, Olivia, Joan, Sarah, and Shannon. We love you.

Our families for their unflagging support, enthusiasm, and babysitting. John for always telling Emma to "please fuck it up." Jordana for making it possible for Emma to write this while providing a humbling amount of joy to her family. Heather, for stepping up to the plate with style. Catherine Mc-Keown, Andrea Shnee, and the incredible women of Carroll Gardens All Day Pre-school for being there with heart and mind when Nicki can't. Our husbands, for sticking around long after the costumes come off. Wiki David for being our L.A. eyes and ears. And finally to our little ones, who have changed our lives in every way for the better, and who already love books — especially eating them.

ABOUT THE AUTHORS

Emma McLaughlin and **Nicola Kraus** are the *New York Times* bestselling authors of *The Nanny Diaries, Citizen Girl, Dedication, Nanny Returns,* and their first young adult novel, *The Real Real.* They work together in New York City. Please visit them at www.emmaandnicola.com.

DATE		
8/6		